THE CALDWELL GIRLS

THE CALDWELL GIRLS

Rowena Summers

severn House

This first world edition published in Great Britain 2002 by
SEVERN HOUSE PUBLISHERS LTD of
9–15 High Street, Sutton, Surrey SM1 1DF.
This first world edition published in the USA 2002 by
SEVERN HOUSE PUBLISHERS INC of
595 Madison Avenue, New York, N.Y. 10022.

British Library Cataloguing in Publication Data

Summers, Rowena 1932–
    The Caldwell girls
    1. Bristol – England – Social life and customs – 20th century – Fiction
    2. World War, 1939–1945 – England – Fiction
    3. Domestic fiction
    I. Title
    823.9'14 [F]

ISBN 0-7278-5797-5

Typeset by Palimpsest Book Production Ltd.,
Polmont, Stirlingshire, Scotland.
Printed and bound in Great Britain by
MPG Books Ltd., Bodmin, Cornwall.

One

It seemed to take a miracle of planning nowadays, for the Caldwell girls to get together. This occasion had been planned for so long, and here they were, nearly through October. But now the whole family was together in their aunt's big old house in Weston-super-Mare and, after the usual joyous greetings, they were all having very mixed feelings because today was a very special day.

Imogen had managed to get leave, smart and elegant in her Auxiliary Territorial Service uniform (which Daisy thought was really rather a grand name for what everyone else referred to as the ATS), and everyone complimented her on the two brand new stripes on her sleeves. Elsie, still plump after the arrival of the baby, sat comfortably in their aunt's old armchair, cuddling the baby, already nearly two months old. And Daisy couldn't stop admiring her little niece, still marvelling that she had actually witnessed her birth without fainting right off. It was just the way a nurse should be, of course, but you could never account for feelings at such an emotional time.

Their young brother Teddy was sprawled out on the hearthrug, clutching his dog and clearly unhappy about what this day meant. His father glanced at him and then spoke firmly. 'Now, listen to me, all of you. None of us is going to be sad and miserable today. Baz will be scoffing in heaven if we all go around with gloomy faces. It's not a wake and it's not a funeral service. It's a celebration of his life, despite the fact that it was a short one. Remember that it was a happy life, too. He lived it just as he

1

wanted to, and we must do what's right by him. Is that understood?'

His sister endorsed his words. Rose was just as determined that this family reunion, no matter what the reason, was going to be something they would remember. In the circumstances it could hardly be called a party, but when they had been to church and Mr Penfold had said the solemn words of the memorial service and given Baz his blessing, they would come back to the house and have the best tea that money and rations could supply. It was so lovely that they were finally all together again – minus one. Well, minus two, Rose amended, since the childrens' mother had also passed on.

And in these uncertain times, the two older girls would be thinking about their partners, too. Imogen's young man was heaven knows where with his tank regiment, and Elsie hadn't heard anything from Joe since he'd been allowed a brief leave home to see his baby daughter. Rose knew it was best not to dwell on such matters, especially today of all days. 'Let's all get our hats and coats on,' she said briskly. 'Your Uncle Bert will take you and Teddy in the car, Elsie, since you won't want to carry the baby all that way to the church. The rest of us will walk.'

She organised them all, the way she always did, and the three sisters managed to resist grinning at one another as they were all shepherded out of the house into the crisp October afternoon. They could almost imagine it was like days gone by, as they proceeded down the hill towards the Methodist church. Their father and aunt walked in front, with Teddy dragging his feet between them, still grumbling that he didn't see why he couldn't bring George with him, and Imogen and Daisy walked behind.

'Don't be daft, Teddy, you know very well you can't bring a dog into church,' Daisy said with a giggle.

'Why not?' Teddy sulked. 'Doesn't God like dogs?'

'Of course He does,' Aunt Rose said smartly. 'But George doesn't like Mr Penfold, does he? I'm sure he wouldn't be

2

too pleased to have George snapping at his heels all the way through the service. Baz wouldn't like it, either,' she added. 'So come *on*, Teddy, and don't dawdle.'

Hearing her aunt's sensible words, Daisy still felt a surge of disbelief that they were actually doing this. Marching down the hill in a small procession to a memorial service for her brother, who had been only seventeen years old when he was drowned jumping off a burning rescue ship off the coast of France during a German bombing raid. It was still so unbelievable . . .

'Brace up, Daisy,' she heard Imogen say quietly. 'We all have to be strong for one another today.'

She hadn't realised how her shoulders had drooped. 'I know, but it's not easy, is it?'

Imogen squeezed her arm. 'Just think of Baz the way he was. Always the joker in the family, wouldn't you say?'

Daisy began to smile. 'Well, a bit of a tease, certainly.'

'So let's remember that and don't let Daddy down. I hear Aunt Rose is thinking of taking in more evacuees. Hasn't she had enough of them yet?'

Daisy frowned, knowing her sister was neatly changing the conversation to take her mind off the real purpose of this walk. 'Well, you'll never believe it. She heard from Vanessa Brown's billeting officer the other week. You know, the girl who was evacuated here before.'

'The one you never got on with, sweetie,' Immy said with a grin.

'Only because she was so precocious and a know-all.'

'Takes one to know one, doesn't it? And before you get that huffy look on your face, I'm only *joking*.'

'Well, anyway, Uncle Bert was against having her back after the way she ran off and got a lift back to London with a lorry driver. *Anything* could have happened to her, but knowing Vanessa, of course, it didn't.'

'You sound as if you wanted something to happen to her.'

Daisy looked shocked. 'Of course I didn't. I just think she

was totally irresponsible, that's all, and she caused Aunt Rose and all of us an awful lot of trouble. I can't say I particularly want her back, but Aunt Rose has a very forgiving heart, so that's that.'

They were nearing the old Methodist Church now, bathed in autumn sunshine, the grounds a profusion of greenery and late-flowering shrubs. It looked serene and beautiful, and if there was any proper place to think about forgiveness, this was it, Daisy thought. So maybe it was time she did a little bit of forgiving, too, and try to forget that Vanessa Brown could be such a little snot-rag.

'I wonder how she ever persuaded a lorry driver to take her to London,' Immy said.

Just as quickly, Daisy forgot all her good intentions. 'I daresay she dolled herself up to look older. She took some of my lipstick and face powder, and she could flounce about like Anna May Wong at the flicks when she wanted to.'

'Good Lord, Daisy, I didn't realise you were so jealous of her!'

Daisy stopped walking, forcing Immy to do the same.

'*Jealous* of her! I was no such thing! She's just a kid.'

'But a very pretty one, and obviously one that Aunt Rose thinks enough of to take her back. So why don't we just forget about her for now?'

They quickened their steps, and Daisy spoke defensively.

'All right, but you should hear the rest of it. Apparently the street next to theirs was bombed, and some neighbours were killed, and a lot of others injured. Vanessa never could stand the sight of blood. She almost fainted here once, when she cut her finger on the bread knife. I don't think her mother wanted her back in the first place, but now the billeting officer says their own street has been wiped out, and both her parents are dead, and she's asked to come back to us,' she finished baldly, not wanting to dwell on the horror of it.

'Then perhaps you should show a little more compassion

towards the poor kid,' Immy said, as they pushed open the gate and followed their family to the open door of the church, where the vicar was waiting for them.

They had decided against asking Mr Penfold back to the house for tea after the small service. This was a family affair, and he would only inhibit them, especially Teddy. And they were all determined to do as Quentin suggested, and make it more a celebration than a wake, and the baby's gurgling presence did a great deal to relieve the tension.

'I promised Joe I'd take Faith to see his parents soon,' Elsie told them. 'I'd much prefer to wait until he could come with me, but it's only natural that the Prestons want to see their first grandchild.'

'And I keep telling her she should go as soon as possible,' her father put in. 'The blitz isn't going to go away in a hurry, and the sirens sound almost nightly now. Even when it's a false alarm, it can be pretty unnerving.'

'Well, you're a proper Job's Comforter, aren't you?' Rose said smartly, inclining her head warningly towards Teddy. The excitable George had been banished to the garden while the baby was on the mat in front of the fireplace, and Teddy was doing his best to amuse Faith with a string of cotton-reels he had made for her, and avidly listening to the grown-ups' conversation at the same time.

'There's no sense in shutting our eyes to what's happening,' Quentin said. 'I've told Elsie that if she wants to go to Yorkshire to visit Joe's parents, I'll go with her. It's a long journey to travel by train with a young baby.'

Elsie sighed. 'I know you're right, but—'

'Then that's settled,' her father pushed ahead with the advantage. 'Let's have no more dithering about it, Elsie. Once you've contacted Joe's parents, I'll arrange for someone to take over at the shop for a week. It will also give me a chance to see Owen Preston while I'm in Yorkshire.'

'I just wish I could let Joe know,' Elsie said, her head bowed so they wouldn't see the worry in her eyes. 'I wish he could be there, too.'

Rose could see the atmosphere of her family reunion deteriorating fast. The trip to Yorkshire wouldn't be so much a holiday as a duty visit for Elsie and Faith. Joe's parents were still virtual strangers to her. And a business trip too, if Quentin intended seeing Owen Preston, the owner of Preston's Emporium where Quentin was temporary manager while Joe Preston was away serving his country.

'I'm sure you'll hear from Joe soon,' she said briskly to Elsie. 'No news is good news, remember –'

'Oh, that's the daftest thing anybody ever said!' Elsie burst out, in a rare display of anger and frustration. 'No news is not good news! It's exactly *no* news, just as we had with Baz, and look what happened to him!'

'Is Joe going to get killed as well then?' Teddy said fearfully.

'Of course he isn't,' Imogen said.

'Certainly not!' Uncle Bert boomed in unison.

Elsie scooped up the baby from the mat, cuddling her into her chest and ignoring her protests at being snatched away from her new playmate. Elsie's eyes burned as she glared at them all.

'You all know that, do you? You're all clairvoyants now, I suppose. Well, I don't know it, and I won't feel safe until Joe comes home again. And if you'll all excuse me, my baby needs changing.'

She rushed from the room with Faith while they were all digesting this unusual rage from Elsie, who was normally the most placid one of the family.

'It'll be post-natal effects. That's what they call it,' Daisy said knowledgeably, having read some of the books about midwifery and childcare. 'It'll soon pass—'

'Oh, do shut up, Daisy,' Immy snapped. 'You don't know what you're talking about. I'm going to see if she's all right.'

She found Elsie in Daisy's bedroom. She had lain Faith on

the bed, and was sitting beside her, absently stroking the baby's cheek and staring into space with her hands clenched.

Immy sat beside her and put her arms around her. 'Darling, I'm sure it will be all right. I don't hear from James nearly as often as I'd like to either, but this is what happens during wartime, isn't it?'

'How can you say it will be all right? You don't know that, any more than I do. It wasn't all right for Baz, was it? Even Daisy should understand it, too. Her young airman friend from Locking was killed, wasn't he? None of us knows what is going to happen any more. And I miss Joe so much, Immy. You don't know what it's like . . .' she said, starting to crumple.

'Yes, I do.'

'No, you *don't*. You and James – it's not the same for you as it is for Joe and me. He's my husband – and there's a difference.'

Immy knew Elsie was being fiercely defensive of the fact that because they were married, she and Joe were the most intimate of lovers, and therefore no one else's feelings or longings could ever touch theirs. But Immy's did.

'Elsie, darling,' she said hesitantly, 'I do know. James and I spent a weekend together in London, and I *do* know what you mean. I don't need to spell it out for you more any graphically, do I?'

Elsie's eyes widened. 'You mean you and James?'

Immy felt her face grow hot. She was the elder sister, but she was still unmarried, and therefore supposedly chaste. 'That's exactly what I mean, and I miss him so terribly, too. I wouldn't normally confide such things to anyone.'

'And I would never tell, but oh, Immy, how daring, and how brave of you.'

Immy gave a rueful smile. 'I wouldn't call it brave or daring, really. It was just that we needed so desperately to be together, to feel that we really belonged, no matter what happened in the future.'

'Yes. That's just how it was when Joe and I decided to get

married without letting any of the family know. When you love someone that much, it's important to know that you truly belong.'

'And whatever happens – not that I think anything bad will happen – you've always got Faith, haven't you?' Immy went on, determined to lighten the charged atmosphere that neither of them quite knew how to break.

Right on cue, Faith began kicking her legs in the air, gurgling and smiling, and the sisters both laughed, leaning over her and tickling her toes.

Although Teddy Caldwell was eight years old now, he was still a very young and naive eight-year-old, not in a vacant way, but in a particularly loving way. There was still an innocence about him, and a wonder about life that was lacking in the young East End boys who had been evacuated to Weston-super-Mare a year ago.

It was not their fault, of course, and neither were all the wartime evacuees full of aggression; some were frankly terrified at being wrenched away from everything they knew and loved, especially the very young and vulnerable ones, who were little more than babies being sent away for safety from the bombing. Some had come from privileged homes, and considered themselves far superior to their country hosts, and expected everyone in the south-west to have hayseeds sticking out of their mouths.

But those who had been sent to Rose Painter's home in Weston-super-Mare had come from poor homes and been brought up in a less than savoury atmosphere, and had never quite been able to decide whether they cared for the other boy who was living there. Even though he was only Rose's nephew, it still made Teddy part of the family, and not one of them.

Teddy had been cosseted by his family ever since his mother died when he was only five. Sometimes Rose wondered whether it had been right or sensible to make such a pet of him, but because he was so much younger than the rest of his siblings, and so lost, it was one of the reasons she had opened her home to him in the first place, and later to the evacuees. That, and the more self-indulgent reason of not having children of her own, and being able to fill the house with laughter and squabbles and whatever else came with them, she admitted honestly. Even though Bert constantly told her the children were only on loan, and would have to go back one day, she still did it. And she hadn't hesitated for a moment when she was asked to take Vanessa Brown back, even though the girl had caused them so much trouble in the past.

Despite her sometimes caustic manner, Rose had a big heart, and fortunately a big, rambling old house for them all. In the days when it had been built, overlooking the town of Weston-super-Mare, it had been part of a grand area of elegant houses where the elite of the town lived, waited on by many servants.

Such hierarchy was long gone now, and in any case, Rose and Bert weren't that kind of people. They were just comfortably middle-class, willing to share that largesse wherever it was needed. And Daisy and Teddy were their own. They were family.

Teddy had been bewildered and distraught after his mother died, and needed care to recover from the trauma. Weston-super-Mare had seemed the perfect answer, and when Daisy had decided to come, too, and eventually to apply for a nursing career at Weston General, it seemed as if fate had been kind to Rose and Bert after all. There were more than enough children in the world to go around, and they had finally been blessed with a houseful. The evacuees were an added bonus, and if there was one thing in this world anyone could thank Hitler for, it was the chance to make a decent home for those who needed it most.

Rose was angry with herself the moment the thought entered her head. There was nothing to thank Hitler for, least of all the fact that there were so many children far away from their parents, and those who would have no one to go home to, and they could only pray that the invasion would never happen.

'I'm hungry! When are we having tea?' Teddy complained, bored now, and breaking into her thoughts. 'I want to show Daddy my chickens before they go home, and it will be getting dark soon.'

Rose shook herself. It was barely mid-afternoon and a long way before sunset, but the last thing Quentin needed would be to drive his girls and the baby back to Bristol after dark. She was tempted to ask them to stay, but she knew they wouldn't. Stubborn, the whole lot of them, she thought, hiding a smile, and knowing that they were all tarred with the same brush.

'We'll have tea right now,' she announced. 'It's all ready, and you and Daisy can help me carry it all to the table.'

'Is Vanessa coming back here to live with us, then?' Teddy persisted, unsure what he felt about this.

'She is, and we must all be nice to her, because she wants to be with us.'

Rose could have added that it was also because Vanessa's friends and now her parents had been killed, but that would been a disastrous thing to tell him.

'She never wanted to be with us before,' Teddy grumbled, never knowing when to leave things alone.

'Well, she does now, apparently,' Daisy said. She caught her aunt's small frown and smiled at her brother instead. 'Anyway, Teddy, you can show her how well your plants are doing in the garden since she's been away, can't you? The ones George hasn't dug up, that is.'

Teddy hooted at that. 'Vanessa said the garden was a nasty messy place ever since Norman chased her with a worm.'

'Yes, well, not many little girls would like that,' Daisy said with a shudder. 'And I don't want to think about it, either, thank you very much.' She might be eighteen years old, and had seen plenty of gruesome things now, far more than would be expected in normal times, but she still didn't relish being chased by a horrid little boy with a worm draped over his fingers! And these were far from normal times, she thought, realising that the discussion between her father and her uncle had become more serious. She wanted to listen, but so did Teddy, and she knew that if he heard too much about bombing raids and the voluntary fire-watching that their father did, he would start having nightmares.

He pretended to be so brash and brave, but he was still a little boy, and his world was a completely different one to the serene and comfortable one in which the older Caldwell children had been born. It had changed with his difficult birth and the traumatic after-effects it had had on their mother. It had worsened as Frances grew progressively weaker, and it had culminated when Teddy, and all of them, had seen their mother fall to her death into the Avon gorge.

Daisy shivered, knowing that the memory of that day would never leave her. It was still there, still vivid, ready to take her unawares whenever she was least expecting it. It was probably the same with all of them.

'Are you cold, Daisy?' her aunt said in surprise.

She shook her head quickly. 'Just hungry,' she invented. 'And I've got my eye on a special piece of cake before Teddy can get to it.'

It was enough to start him clamouring over which piece it was, so that he could get his greedy little mitts on it first.

Quentin, Immy, Elsie and the baby left Weston-super-Mare while it was still daylight, assuring Teddy that he would be seeing them all again soon, even while the boy was trying hard to pretend that he didn't mind too much, anyway.

Daisy helped Aunt Rose clear away the tea things, agreeing with her and Uncle Bert that it had been a good day, and that they had all done Baz proud. And then she went to her room for a few blessed solitary moments alone. She loved all her family dearly, but these private moments were precious and necessary.

It was only a few months since she had had the first

letter from Glenn Fraser, right out of the blue, as they said. *Appropriately* so, she thought with a smile, since he was one of the dashing RAF Brylcreem boys. And since then, after her hastily written reply, more letters had passed between them, and she was finding it hard not to tell someone other than her friend, Alice Godfrey.

It was all right to tell Alice, because it was when she and Alice had been to the dance-hall in Folkstone right after Dunkirk that she had first met Glenn and been more than intrigued by his Canadian manners. Alice knew of her confusion over whether she should even feel remotely attracted to another young man, when she was in love with Callum Monks. But it hadn't meant anything more than a brief flirtation on a dance-floor – then. It hadn't affected her feelings for Cal.

It was only when she had heard the news that Cal had been killed that shock and guilt rushed in. She had needed time to grieve for Cal, to finally accept that it had happened, but that life had to go on. And in particular that it was foolish to feel guilt over something that had been harmless.

Just a casual few dances – and the realisation that someone other than Cal was attracted to her, too, admiring her for her bravery in working on the hospital ships that had plied to and fro between here and the French coast. It had done her self-esteem so much good after the horrors of Dunkirk that they had all come through so recently. But she had never expected to see him or hear from him again, until the letter had arrived at the hospital a few months ago, and now he filled her thoughts.

She shivered again. The family had always thought her a bit frivolous, flitting from one idea to the next, and she had rather believed it herself for a while, wondering if she would ever settle to anything, let alone anything as serious as falling in love. She had proved them all wrong; by her dedication to nursing, and by the way she had loved Cal.

Even so, it had been a sweet, innocent love. He was hardly any older than herself, and they had had so little time to get to know one another before he was killed. Daisy already knew that her feelings for Glenn were different. He was different, too. He was older, more mature and in her dreams he swept her off her feet and carried her off on a white charger like Sir Galahad.

'Daisy, what on earth are you doing up there, girl?' she heard her aunt call out, and she realised she had been dawdling and dreaming for some time without even noticing it. But that was the way it happened when you were eighteen years old and on the brink of falling in love. Really in love.

Two

Neither of Daisy's sisters was having such ethereal thoughts that evening. Elsie had made a promise to Joe, and now to her father, and he wasn't going to let her forget it. The visit to Yorkshire was going to happen as soon as Quentin could organise his staff at the shop, but with so many of them away at the war, she wasn't sure how long that would take. As well as the frequent air raids over the city, there was the added earth-shaking noise of the retaliating ack-ack guns from the Downs. And now that she had Faith to think about, there was little choice but to take her to the garden shelter as soon as the sirens began.

Now that she had made up her mind, Elsie was just as anxious to take her on the visit to Yorkshire as she had always been never to leave Bristol. It wouldn't be for ever, but it would be a brief respite, and she refused to feel guilty about it. There had been a time when she thought she would be abandoning the city to the German bombers, but it was silly to think that way, because what earthly difference to the fate of the city was her presence going to make! It wasn't as if she did anything useful, like her father. She just cared for Faith, and made a comfortable home for them all.

Elsie had always been content with her life, never as strong-willed as Immy, and nothing like as daft as Daisy with her butterfly mind. But things had changed with Faith's birth. Now she had someone who was totally dependent on her, and she had become fiercely protective, and vowed that Hitler wasn't to make a victim out of her. Joe was going to have a family to come home to, which was why she knew the time had come to make no more objection about going to stay with his parents for a while.

She telephoned his mother as soon as they reached home that evening. They had spoken on the telephone before, although they had never met, but her comfortable voice did much to ease them both over the awkwardness of the discussion, and also the difficulty Elsie had in deciphering the more pronounced dialect of the countrywoman.

'You and the babby will be as welcome as a Dales summer, lass,' Hetty Preston said. 'And your father, too, and you mun all stay as long as you like.'

'It's very good of you, Mrs Preston,' Elsie said, her throat catching.

'Now don't go piping your eyes, Elsie. You're family now, and we mun all care for each and t'other, and get you away from them dreadful bombs. Our Joe would want that.'

'I know. Have you heard from him lately, by the way?' Half of her wanted his mother to say yes, and the other half knew she would resent it shamefully if the Prestons had heard from him while she hadn't.

'Not a word, but they say no news is good news, don't they?'

Elsie held her tongue as the usual platitude tripped out. 'I'll be in touch again as soon as our plans are made then, Mrs Preston,' she said quickly.

'Aye, and whenever 'tis, we'll be ready to welcome you all, love. We've been fair fretting to see our grandchild.'

Elsie hung up, hoping this wasn't a bit of censure because she hadn't been in any hurry to go north. But it was such a very long way, and she was still getting over the trauma of childbirth and getting to know Faith herself. Selfishly, she didn't want to share her with anyone else, but Joe. Already the baby was changing so quickly, and he was missing the first part of her life, because of bloody Hitler.

She gave a rueful smile as the swear word slid into her

mind. It was unlike her, or at least, unlike the Elsie she used to be, more serene than her sisters, more relaxed. But Elsie had discovered that when you married someone, you moved imperceptibly away from your birth family. You didn't love them any less, but now you had new obligations, new feelings, new intimacies that belonged to just you and one other very special person. And now she had Joe and Faith, and they were a complete family unit of their own, and she would do anything to defend that unit and keep it safe.

'Are you going to stand here for ever without telling me what Joe's parents said, Elsie?' she heard her father say in some amusement.

As she realised she had been standing transfixed, gazing into space and lost in her own world, she laughed self-consciously. 'Joe's mother will be happy to see us whenever we can get there,' she said, then added: 'I'm looking forward to meeting them and introducing them to their granddaughter.'

'And not before time,' Quentin said, as they heard the mournful wail of the air-raid siren, the almost immediate drone of airplanes and the answering thunder of the big guns. It grew into a crescendo of noise that almost split the ear-drums, and started Faith crying at once as Immy tried to soothe her.

'You girls get down to the shelter with her,' Quentin said urgently.

'Aren't you coming, too? You're not on fire duty tonight, are you, Father?' Immy said at once.

'Being a volunteer means you're on duty whenever you're required,' he said. 'I'll see you all safely inside the shelter first, though.'

Elsie had taken Faith from her sister now and was trying to calm her. She hated it in the Anderson shelter at the bottom of the garden. They had made it as comfortable as possible, with camp beds and plenty of blankets, a primus stove for making tea, packets of biscuits, tea and dried milk to keep up spirits during the night. They had remembered books and magazines, playing cards and draughts and snakes and ladders, and a gramophone to play their favourite records of Vera Lynn and Frank Sinatra to try and drown out the noise outside.

It was as cosy as it could be, considering, but it smelled damp, even though it was insulated against the air outside. Like most families, they had covered the metal exterior with earth and grass and planted flowers on the top, and it was inevitable that the earthy smell permeated inside. But they all knew it was safer than staying indoors while the bombs rained down on the city.

Already, they could hear deafening explosions from the docks area. Red and orange flashes lit the sky as the beams of searchlights picked out the silvery shapes of the lethal planes and the huge barrage balloons over Avonmouth. Elsie shivered, hurrying down to the shelter with Faith in her arms, wrapped warmly in a shawl and blanket. The planes were so beautiful in flight, and so deadly in their destructive powers.

Once inside, their father left them to it, saying in a jocular voice that he'd see them when he saw them, and Immy took charge. 'Let's play cards once we get Faith settled with her bottle,' she said, determined to make the best of it.

'I shan't be any good. I can never concentrate while all that racket's going on,' Elsie said, flinching as a sudden explosion nearby shook the shelter and knocked some of the provisions to the floor. She picked them up mechanically, her hands shaking, and then cuddled Faith to her again, as if the baby's very presence was giving her comfort.

'Elsie, don't jump down my throat, but have you ever thought that once you get to Yorkshire you might consider staying there until the war is over, or at least for a while?' Immy said carefully.

'Why would I jump down your throat?' Elsie said, ignoring the rest.

Immy gave a small smile in the gloom of the shelter, lit only by a paraffin lamp kept well away from the door with its heavy curtain to keep any light from shining outside. The result was that it was practically airless, and they could only stay inside for short periods of time without opening the door to breathe properly. Even the underground tube stations were better than this, Immy thought, refusing to admit to feeling claustrophobic, but already wishing she was back in London.

'Well, darling, you have to admit you've become far more jumpy than you used to be, and I'm not blaming you for that. You've got responsibilities now that you never had before –'

'I hope you're not implying that I can't cope with them!'

'Of course not, but that's just what I mean. You jump in and criticise before you've had a chance to think. More like Daisy, in fact!'

'Aren't you criticising me now, then?'

'Good Lord, of course I'm not. I think you and Joe were very brave to go off and get married the way you did without telling anyone, if you must know. And even braver to have a baby in the middle of wartime.'

'That wasn't brave. That just happened.'

Immy laughed. 'Yes, well, I know all about the birds and the bees, thanks very much, but you still had her, didn't you? And she's so gorgeous that I know you want to do what's best for her. So I just wondered, that's all, if you thought it might be safer for you and Faith to be with her grandparents in Yorkshire.'

When Elsie didn't answer immediately, Immy wondered if she had gone too far. The baby was sleeping peacefully now, oblivious to the raging air battle outside. Lying in her mother's arms, her long eyelashes were twin crescents on her downy cheeks, the rich crown of red hair a perfect foil for her creamy skin.

Immy had no maternal instincts as yet, but she could easily

imagine how fiercely protective her sister was of her baby. She was part of herself and Joe, living proof of their love for each other, and some day she and James might be feeling exactly the same way. Though not in the middle of a war, Immy vowed.

'I know you're right, and I'm sure Joe's parents would have us to stay, because they've said so many times, but they're not my family, are they? I would miss you all so much.'

'Oh, come on, Elsie,' Immy said briskly, before she got too maudlin. 'We've all moved on, haven't we? We've had to because of the war, but also because of Mother. It all changed when she died. We had already begun to drift apart then. It's part of growing up, I suppose. In fact, even before Mother died, Baz had already gone his own way, hadn't he? He would never have been a shopkeeper like Father wanted him to be. The sea was his life – and his death too, and before you think I'm being insensitive, remember it was his choice, Elsie.'

'I know,' Elsie said in a muffled voice. 'And then Daisy and Teddy went to Weston, and you joined up. There was only me left to be with Father.'

Immy gave an impatient sigh. 'Good God, Elsie, you're not starting to think of yourself as a martyr, are you? The days when the last remaining sister had to stay at home and care for an ageing parent are long gone. Besides, I can't see Father seeing himself in that light, can you? He wouldn't thank you for suggesting he's in need of care and attention.'

'And if he was –' Elsie began, and then stopped abruptly.

'Yes? And if he was?' Immy prompted her.

'Well, he's not exactly old, is he? He's still handsome, and it's not unreasonable that he might think of marrying again some day, is it?'

'Has he ever suggested as much?'

'No, but I know he's been seeing someone recently. Just friendly meetings, I'm sure, but he does look much brighter these days, don't you think?'

'And it would ease your conscience about going to Yorkshire if you thought he wasn't going to be lonely,' Immy supplied.

'I didn't mean any such thing!'

'It would though, wouldn't it? So, who's the lady?' Immy said.

And why did she feel slightly put out that she hadn't heard anything of this? She was the oldest, after all. She dismissed the silly feeling at once, knowing she was retreating ten years or so, when the rivalry between three sisters was at its height, and each one tried to outdo the other in gaining bits of information.

'Mary Yard.'

'Ah.'

'You don't sound surprised!'

Immy shrugged. 'I know she and Father had a special rapport with one another at one time. Is she back in Bristol then?'

'I'm not sure where she's living now, but she was here for the funeral of an old friend, and she made a point of calling on Father at the shop. I know they've seen a bit of one another since then.'

She flinched again as another loud explosion shook the shelter, but she kept on talking determinedly.

'Does it bother you, Elsie? Because it shouldn't, especially now, when life's too short and unpredictable to waste it on being lonely if companionship is there for the taking.'

Elsie bit her lip. Immy was the unmarried one of the two, but she had always been older and wiser than Elsie in so many ways. And Elsie just had to ask.

'Yes, but do you think it would just be for companionship? A sort of looking after one another in their old age?'

Immy burst out laughing. 'What you're trying to say is, if they got married, would they sleep together and make love!'

'I wasn't going to put it as bluntly as that, but I suppose I do.'

20

And somehow it was easier to discuss such things in the confines of the dimly lit shelter, where Immy couldn't see her fiery face.

'Well, darling, you can hardly call Daddy a geriatric, can you?' Immy said gently. 'He wouldn't be out there at all hours taking his turn with the fire-watchers if he was. He's still young and active – and yes, of course they would – if it happened. Do you and Joe plan on living separate lives once you turn fifty?'

'Good Lord, I hope not.'

'Then there's your answer,' Immy said airily. 'It's his business anyway, and he's not going to ask our permission! So let's stop worrying about things we can't change and play cards. We're not likely to get any sleep while this bombardment goes on.'

Privately, she thought it would be a very good thing if her father did marry again. He was a vibrant, virile man who needed to be married, and they had all liked Mary Yard when she and her friend had moved into the self-contained flat that was now Elsie and Joe's. Everyone needed someone special, and Immy knew it wouldn't change a thing as far as cherishing her mother's memory was concerned. It would simply be a new phase in her father's life.

Quentin Caldwell wasn't thinking about anything as frivolous as getting married again as he joined the hose gangs that night. The fires from the incendiary bombs were in danger of raging out of control in the north of the city, and the whole sky was lit up with an unearthly red glow as the hours passed. The bombardment was relentless, whole streets were being wiped out, and the centre of the city was taking a battering as never before.

The ARP and ambulance people were doing a magnificent job of rescuing people, scrabbling about in muck and rubble, often with the tottering buildings in danger of crashing down on them at any moment. And more than once he heard the terrified cries of infants as one after another was brought out in a rescuer's arms. Sometimes there were no cries at all from the bombed-out houses, just a scattering of broken toys and shoes, and the remnants of what had once been a home, and they all knew what the grisly search through the debris and shattered glass would reveal. It made him all the more grimly determined to get his daughter and granddaughter away from here as soon as possible.

'Over here, quick!' he heard someone shout urgently.

Then there was no time to think of anything but forcing the water hoses on to the new fire that had suddenly erupted, with the noxious smell of gas insidiously filling their noses as gas mains were hit. Gas was always an added hazard, but this time the flames were rapidly contained before the licking fingers of fire reached the outlet, and experienced hands were able to seal it off.

The air raid continued through the night, until at last the raiders had finally finished with the city, and the reedy, welcome sound of the all-clear filled the thick, smoke-clogged air. The ARP and other rescue services would work on into daylight, until they were certain they had done all they could. The injured would be transported to various hospitals, and the dead to the mortuaries.

Once it was decided that all other volunteers could disperse, being more of a hindrance now than a help, Quentin wiped the grime from his eyes and made his way exhaustedly back to Vicarage Street. A thin, streaky dawn was already starting to lighten the sky a little by then. He had always thought Bristol was incredibly beautiful in the freshness of dawn. But it was no longer that way, and conversely, Quentin wished fiercely that the darkness of night would stay forever. If it did, then the ashes of a once-beautiful and historic city would remain hidden.

But such things couldn't happen, and dawn revealed even more of the smouldering destruction from the brutal attack that would make tomorrow's newspaper headlines, and the topic of a wireless announcer's sombre speech. The local newspapers would make much of the city's valiant efforts to resist, with the big guns on Durdham Downs and the heroic RAF retaliation vigorously counter-attacking, but nothing seemed to stem the onslaught of German bombers.

The smell of death and destruction enveloped him. It was in his mouth and in his lungs. He could smell it, breathe it, taste it. It hit him with a feeling of utter hopelessness such as he hadn't felt in a long while. Not since Frances had fallen to her death. Not since Baz had drowned.

Such negative feelings were unlike him. He had weathered many storms in his lifetime, but this unreasoning sense of failure, not only in himself, but in all mankind, was so much harder to bear.

He was gripped by a sense of total unreality as he walked up the path to his front door, feeling as though his feet were dragging him there as if he was a very old man. The logical part of him knew it was all due to utter fatigue, and that food and sleep would restore him, but he wasn't thinking logically right then. Which made him register the bizarre sound of laughter inside his house with an incredulity bordering on unmanly hysteria.

'What the devil's going on in here?' he almost snarled as he let himself inside the house and saw his daughters drinking tea and dunking biscuits just as if they were at an informal party.

Elsie leapt up at once and threw her arms around him, disregarding for a moment the weariness in his eyes and the dirt and grime on his face and clothes. There was a streak of blood on his cheek that he hadn't even noticed, and for the moment his daughter hardly noticed it either. He could sense the bubbling excitement in her, so different from the ghastly scenes he had so recently witnessed. In those few seconds of disorientation it seemed almost obscene that one person could be brimming with such life, when others had had life extinguished so brutally.

'I've just had some wonderful news,' Elsie told him joyfully. 'As we came back indoors from the shelter the telephone was ringing, and you'll never guess who it was!'

Without waiting for an answer, she rushed on. 'It was Joe! He's coming home on leave in two days' time, and he was overjoyed to know that I've agreed to go and visit his parents. In fact, he said . . . he said . . .' she stopped, disengaging herself from her father, and he saw the uncertainty that passed over her face. But he didn't need to hear the rest and he finished it for her.

'He said he would take you and the baby to Yorkshire himself,' he stated. By now his mouth was so dry he almost croaked the words, and Immy recognised the state of him. She had seen it before in London, emerging from the underground after an air raid to find the rescuers in that same state of hoarseness. She had seen that mixture of exhilaration and despair, depending on the success or failure of their mission after hours of expending furious energy in digging out people from the wreckage of their homes. She knew it took time to allow the rescuers to return to some kind of normality again, and Elsie must know it, too, but right now, her mind was totally focused on the fact that she would be seeing Joe again very soon.

'Daddy, sit down and take your shoes off,' she ordered at once, reverting to her childhood name for him. 'I'm sure you've had a busy night, and what you need right now is a large cup of tea and some breakfast. Aunt Rose gave us some eggs and I'm going to fry one for you with some bread while you and Elsie talk.'

She left them to it, hoping her words might have slowed Elsie down a little. Her father would still be caught up in whatever traumas he had seen during the night. But she also understood Elsie's need to blab everything out at once.

After the telephone call from Joe, Elsie had already danced around the room with her sister, crying and singing in turn, admitting how badly she had dreaded that she was never going to see Joe again, and then vowing that she had always known he would be safe because he had her and Faith to come home to. They were his talisman. And Immy knew this was the way people reacted in war.

She left Elsie pouring her father a large cup of tea with hands that still shook with simmering excitement, and liberally lacing it with sugar. There were times when you forgot about rationing, and catered to the needs of the body.

'You needn't worry about offending me, Elsie,' Quentin said gruffly, when he had taken several great gulps of welcoming tea. 'It's only natural that Joe would want to see his parents, and I was yet to arrange things at the shop anyway.'

'But I know you intended seeing his uncle on business, Daddy,' Elsie said. 'So there's no reason why we can't all go to Yorkshire together, is there?'

Quentin sighed. 'As a matter of fact, there's every reason. My visit was mainly on your account, since I would never have let you travel all that way by train with a small baby. Besides, there's no earthly reason why any business that Owen Preston has with me can't be conducted over the phone and by post. Things have run perfectly smoothly all this time, and after what happened tonight, I would feel guilty at going away right now. I'm of far more use here, my dear, so you don't need to have any qualms on that score.'

'Well, if you put it like that, of course . . .'

He gave the ghost of a smile for the first time in hours. 'And don't tell me you and Joe wouldn't far rather spend the travelling time alone than having your old father around!'

Elsie laughed, unable to pretend to be gloomy for long with the joyous prospect ahead of her. 'We'll hardly be alone, what with the baby and a few hundred other passengers crammed into the train!'

But nothing was going to dampen her spirits now. And before the train journey, there would be the reunion here at home, and then the days spent in the Yorkshire farmhouse where Joe was born, hearing about his childhood, and most important of all, learning to love each other all over again.

Her cheeks glowed with anticipation, and she turned away, not wanting her father to guess at the turbulent feelings churning inside her.

But she needn't have bothered, because his eyes were closed, and he was almost dropping off with tiredness. Once he had had his tea and breakfast, she knew he would go straight to bed for a few hours. Immy intended going back to London on the first train today, and Elsie could spend the rest of the time to herself, planning the blissful reunion that she and Joe were going to have.

Three

Daisy was ecstatic to receive another letter from Glenn. Why she didn't give him her home address and have the letters sent home, she didn't quite know. The correspondence had begun with a letter sent to her via the hospital, and it had just continued that way. She was sure her aunt and uncle wouldn't have objected to her writing to an airman. Even the Advice Columns in the weekly magazines suggested that no harm could come of writing to servicemen, providing the letters were kept friendly, and cheered up their brave fighting boys.

Except . . . well, Glenn *was* Canadian, and if he ever asked her to marry him, she would be whisked to the other side of the world, and never see any of her family again, and none of them would be very pleased about that! And who was letting her imagination go mad now?

But there was no doubt that the letters between them had become a little more than friendly of late. For a start, Glenn always began with 'My dear Daisy' now, and ended 'with fond affection', or sometimes even 'with fond love'.

She didn't particularly like that word 'fond'. It sounded a bit feeble, but she guessed he was just being gentlemanly and not too forward. It was what her friend Alice Godfrey said, being her one confidante about Glenn. 'These chaps have got a bit of a reputation for being fast, Daisy,' Alice said. 'I'm sure they're not all like that, but you know what some of the Yanks are like at the dances. I think they have to be careful not to go upsetting people.'

'But Glenn's not a Yank, and anyway, it's just their way. They're different from us, that's all.'

'He talks nearly the same, and most people can't tell the difference.'

'Well, I don't think Glenn's fast at all. He's very nice.'

'Oh, Daisy, I didn't say he wasn't. I did meet him at that dance in Folkstone, remember? I'm just saying that if you expect him to write to you with undying love, you've been reading too many novelettes lately.'

'I don't expect that,' Daisy said. 'But we have been writing to one another for a few months now, and I still don't know how he feels about me. Or how I really feel about him.'

Alice laughed. 'What you mean is, you don't know if it's worth spending your time and energy falling in love with him, if he doesn't feel the same way!'

'Good Lord, do I seem that shallow to you?' she said indignantly.

'No, darling, just young!'

'And twenty-two makes you so matronly, I suppose,' Daisy said with a grin. For one thing, she didn't want to stay mad with her, and for another, the image of a stiff and starchy matron came to mind, and Alice was nothing like that.

'So what does the gorgeous Glenn have to say to you today?' Alice asked her later, when they had finished their shift at the hospital for the day and were walking home together.

By now, Daisy was hopping from foot to foot, and hardly able to suppress her mixture of excitement and apprehension. 'He's been invited to spend a week's leave in Cheddar with one of his colleagues and his family, so he wants to come to Weston to see me,' she finished with a gulp. 'I'm thrilled, of course, but it's a bit of a muddle, isn't it? I mean, Aunt Rose doesn't even know about him. Do I invite him home, or suggest seeing him at the pictures or at the beach? We only met once, after all. What if we actually hate one another when we meet? Tell me what I should do, Alice!'

'Well, if you go on as you are now, you'll be wetting your knickers with excitement long before he gets here,' Alice said dryly. 'But I'd say the first thing you have to do is tell your auntie about him. She's not going to think too kindly of you if you suddenly produce a handsome chap out of the blue, who talks like a Hollywood movie star and calls you his dear Daisy, is she?'

'He's hardly a Hollywood movie star.'

'He looks like one though, as far as I can remember. And hadn't you better explain that you've been writing to him all this time as well? Or are you in the habit of receiving letters from strangers asking to call on you?'

'I've messed things up a bit, haven't I?' Daisy said, feeling her excitement draining away. She dearly wanted to see Glenn again, but it was suddenly producing all kinds of complications.

'Not really, but I'd say you have to put it right pretty quickly. When's he coming on leave, anyway?'

'In two weeks' time,' Daisy said, her heart jumping again. 'Just after Vanessa arrives back here.'

'Lucky you!' Alice laughed. 'From what I heard, you'd better keep your eye on Glenn, or she'll be sneaking him from under your nose.'

'Hardly. She's only twelve, maybe thirteen, now.'

But remembering the way that little madam had flounced about, using make-up and generally looking a lot older than she was, Daisy couldn't help thinking Alice was probably right. Vanessa was trouble. But then common sense took over. She would hardly be the sort of trouble Alice was anticipating, for heaven's sake. And since hearing that she was coming back here, with the shocking news from the billeting officer that Vanessa's parents had been killed in another air raid, they were also advised that the girl had totally refused to talk about it to anyone. Knowing what it was like to lose some of your family, it was just too awful to think about, and Daisy resolved to be more tolerant of her than before.

29

But that evening, she knew she had to broach the subject of Glenn with her aunt, and predictably, she got what the movie cops called the third degree.

'Do you mean to say you've been corresponding with this young man all this time and you never said anything?' Rose said indignantly. 'When did you meet him, Daisy?'

'When Alice and I were working on the hospital ships. We went to a dance in Folkstone, and there were a lot of other nurses and servicemen there. It was perfectly respectable, Aunt Rose, and Alice and I stayed together the whole time.'

'So why haven't you mentioned this young man before? Is there something wrong with him? Is he engaged to someone else? Daisy, he's not married, is he?'

She said the word as if it was something outrageous. Which it would be if he was married, of course. And Daisy didn't know that he wasn't. Except in her heart – if her heart was to be trusted. Oh *Lord*!

'Of course not,' Daisy said crossly. 'He's a Canadian.'

As if that explained everything.

'Oh. I see.'

'There's nothing wrong with Canadians, Rose,' Bert put in lazily, seeing that the conversation was about to get heated. 'I knew quite a few of them in the last lot, and very nice fellows they were. Always polite and well-mannered.'

'But you weren't a girl, and you didn't get invitations from them, did you?'

Bert's eyes twinkled. 'I should hope I did not. I'm not that particular way inclined, thank you, old girl.'

Rose glared at him as Daisy went a distinct pink at the implied topic that nobody ever spoke about in decent circles, and Teddy looked up with renewed interest, aware that there was something here that he didn't understand, and that probably nobody was likely to tell him about, either.

'Glenn really is very nice, Aunt Rose,' Daisy went on, more humbly than usual. 'Could I invite him to tea while he's here? I'd like you to meet him, and then you'd see that there's nothing to worry about.'

'I certainly hope there isn't—'

'And it must be strange to be so far from home. Imagine how grateful Baz must have felt when those French farmers took him in and got him to the coast. He was a stranger to them, wasn't he?'

She forced herself to say her brother's name as naturally as possible, despite the fact that getting him to the coast had resulted in his being put on a rescue ship with its own tragic events.

'Why not let the girl invite her Canadian to tea, Rose? We can all give him a good looking-over then,' Bert said. 'There's no harm in that, is there?'

'I still think we should have known that she was writing to this young man,' Rose said severely, not prepared to let her off the hook quite so easily.

'Would you like to see one or two of his letters?' Daisy said. 'I'm quite happy to show them to you.'

But only the early ones, she amended, not the later ones, where the tone had definitely changed. And when Rose said, yes she would like to see them, Daisy knew she had won. Glenn was nothing if not impeccably mannered, and Rose would soon see that. There was never anything in the slightest bit salacious or objectionable in the letters. Nothing even remotely passionate.

And Daisy Caldwell, eighteen years old, and an out-and-out romantic, yearned for a bit of passion in her life. Not the intimate, married kind of passion her sister Elsie had with Joe, of course, she thought hastily . . . more like the nearly-engaged kind of passion her sister Immy had with James Church.

But half an hour later, when Rose had perused the first letters Glenn had written to her niece, she gave her approval, and told Daisy to invite him for tea while he was in the vicinity. And then suggested that he might send his letters to her home in future. It was a suggestion, but Daisy also knew it was an order.

It didn't matter. She wrote back to Glenn that night, inviting him to her home in Weston for tea, and giving him her home address. Somehow it made the whole thing more official. It made *them* more official, and as yet, she didn't have the faintest idea whether or not Glenn even wanted it that way.

Vanessa Brown arrived at Weston on the crowded train from London, and took a deep breath of relief as she stepped on to the platform and gave up her ticket. Not that she particularly wanted to be back with the little brats from Kent who lodged with the ones they called Aunt Rose and Uncle Bert. But anything was better than being back in the smoke, with all them bombs whizzing down, and people rushing around with scared faces and bleeding hearts. Literally.

She shivered, blotting out the memories of that terrible night when she had been so lost and alone in the muck and rubble of her house. Unable to find anyone . . . blinded by dust . . . deafened by people screaming, and the sound of guns and the bombs exploding, hurting her chest with the noise.

Everywhere she looked there had been blood, and she had never been able to stand the sight of blood. It was her one weakness, and one that nobody knew about except herself – and Daisy Caldwell, she remembered. She just hoped Daisy wasn't the sort to tell, and even more, that she wouldn't even remember.

'So, here you are,' she heard Bert Painter's hearty voice say.

She tilted her chin in the air. 'Yep. Turned up again just like a bad penny. I bet you're sorry to see me, ain't yer?'

'Of course not,' Bert lied gallantly. 'If we thought that, we wouldn't have said we'd have you back, would we?'

He could have added, Especially after the disgraceful way you ran off, hitching a ride back to London with a lorry driver, when anything might have happened to you! But now your folks are dead, it makes us think differently, even if you don't look in the least bit concerned!

They went out of the station to Bert's battered old Morris car. Privately, he was startled at how changed she was in just a few months. It was more than the defensive air he remembered, as if daring anyone to feel sorry for her. She could be no more than thirteen years old now, but she had the self-assurance of a girl much older. She had long dark hair, high cheek-bones and wide brown eyes. Bert hoped they weren't in for another kind of trouble, having her back.

But Rose, of course, welcomed her with, well, not exactly open arms, because Vanessa wasn't a cuddly sort of girl, but with real affection, ignoring the suspiciously bright lips and cheeks for the moment. Teddy looked dumbfounded by her newly-sprouting bosoms, and tried not to look too obviously at the small twin peaks, reminiscent of the Hollywood movie stars.

'You've grown since you were last here,' Rose said, ignoring them, too.

Vanessa tossed her hair like a horse's mane. 'I know. I'm twice as big as that little squirt now, aren't I?' she grinned with a snide look at Teddy.

'I'm not a little squirt!' he howled at once.

'Now then, don't start the minute Vanessa gets here,' Rose said, knowing the girl had provoked him, but not wanting any upsets before they had even got to know one another again. Teddy responded by hauling his dog out to the garden before George yapped himself senseless in his joy at seeing a familiar face.

But they all needed to get to know one another again, Rose realised. It was Vanessa who had caused the minor upset, but she was the least perturbed of them all. And they all had to go carefully, considering her bereavement. She thanked God they had got through the memorial service for Baz before she came here. Despite her seemingly uncaring air, it would surely have been too much to bear.

'Am I still in my old room?' she said airily. 'And where are the brats?'

Rose counted to ten, reminding herself that the girl had undoubtedly seen more traumas and troubles in her short life than she and Bert had seen together. If you disregarded the last war, of course.

'If you mean Norman and Ronnie Turvey, they're no longer with us,' she said calmly.

'Blimey, you don't mean they've snuffed it? I know their old lady was keen to get 'em back home, but that's a proper turn-up. Bombed out, were they?'

Rose should have known that counting to ten was never going to be enough where Vanessa was concerned. She was brittle to the point of crudity.

'I do not mean they've snuffed it as you so charmingly put it, Vanessa,' she said, as evenly as she could. 'Their mother's taken them to live with her and an uncle in Wales. Now, take your things upstairs and then we'll have some tea.'

But she didn't miss the knowing look in the girl's eyes. The goings-on in some families were part of a different world as far as Rose Painter was concerned. She knew what was what, as they said, and the Turvey boys' mother was definitely a fast one, but that didn't mean she had to approve of it, nor the way times were changing so fast nowadays, with servicemen dancing with young girls they had only just met, and writing letters to them care of their work places.

She was thinking of Daisy at that moment, but her thoughts followed Bert's, knowing that if this war went on much longer they would probably have Vanessa to think about in that department, too. It would have been far easier on the nerves to have been allocated a couple of docile little girl evacuees instead of this precocious little actress in the making!

'I've got a letter for you, Aunt Rose,' Vanessa announced when she had unpacked her belongings, scattering them about in her usual haphazard way.

'A letter?' Rose said in surprise. Her heart sank, wondering what misdemeanours the girl had been up to with the neighbours who had taken her in, and what new problems they had to watch out for now.

Vanessa's laugh was triumphant. 'It's all right. It ain't bad news—'

'It isn't bad news,' Rose corrected automatically.

'That's what I said. So are you going to read it, or what?'

Rose took the official-looking letter and opened it cautiously. And then she sat up straighter, her eyes widening.

'Good heavens. Bert, what do you think of this? Vanessa's passed her thirteen-plus exam, and subject to an interview with the headmistress, she's been offered a place at the County School, right here in Weston!'

'I always told you I had something in the old brainbox, didn't I?' Vanessa said cheekily. 'So what's this County School like, then? I'm not so sure I like the sound of it. I bet it's posh, ain't – isn't it?'

Rose began to laugh. Whatever it was like, she had the certain feeling that Vanessa Brown was going to cut them all down to size.

'It's a very nice school,' Bert put in. 'All girls, of course—'

'*What*!' Vanessa yelled, her smile fading at once. 'I ain't going to no all *girls* school! They'll be a bleedin' lot of toffee-nosed twerps!'

'Oh, I think you are going there, my dear,' Rose said determinedly, ignoring the colourful language for the moment. 'It's quite an honour, and as you say, you've obviously got the brains for it.'

Daisy came home from work to find the lot of them still arguing over the merits or otherwise of Vanessa attending the County School for Girls. The autumn term had already begun, so she would be thrown in at the deep end, as she called it, but as far as Rose was concerned, at least it was one point in the girl's favour that she had been brainy enough to pass the second exam they offered to thirteen-year-olds now, as well as the usual eleven-plus. It gave Rose herself a bit of status, which she wasn't exactly averse to.

'Cripes, I never thought you had it in you, Nessa,' Daisy said with a grin.

Vanessa glared at her. 'Don't call me Nessa.'

'Well, I think it's quite a feather in your cap, isn't it? None of us Caldwell girls went to anything as fancy as an all girls school, nor one where you had to wear a uniform.'

This stopped Vanessa in her tracks. 'I ain't wearing no uniform. I'll think I'm in bleedin' prison or something.'

Bert wasn't standing for any of this, bereaved or not.

'Now you look here, my girl. I don't want to hear any more talk like that, and you can just cut out that bad language. You're living with us now, and I won't have it. And just you remember that there are thousands of young men and women wearing uniforms for their King and country right now, and proud to be doing so.'

'And gettin' blown to bits, too,' Vanessa muttered.

Nobody seemed to know how to continue the conversation for a few minutes, and then Daisy spoke coolly.

'Well, this is a jolly homecoming, isn't it? I'll tell you what, Vanessa, I've got a free afternoon tomorrow, and if you like we can cycle along the beach and you can take a look at the school. If you've already seen the outside of it, it won't be so scary when you go for the interview.'

'I'm not scared!' Vanessa said predictably.

'There, now that we've got that settled, let's have some tea,' Rose said. 'And don't forget to let me have your ration book, Vanessa.'

Daisy mentally dared her to make any more comments about the school uniform, and had the satisfaction of seeing her shrug and fold her arms mutinously. Little madam, she thought, as she always did. But there was something engaging about her – apart from those startlingly large bosoms appearing in that small frame. Her bodice would be stuffed with cotton wool, if Daisy knew anything about it – or old socks.

She didn't feel quite so magnanimous when Teddy came out with the news that Daisy's young man was coming to tea on Sunday.

'Blimey, what's he like? I should think the smell of all that hospital stuff would put him off,' Vanessa sniggered.

Daisy glared at her. 'All that hospital stuff, as you put it, is very necessary when you're tending to people who are sick, and especially when they're war casualties with open wounds. It's to ward off germs.'

'All right, I don't want to know any more,' Vanessa said tightly. 'So what's this bloke of yours like?'

'He's not a *bloke*. He's a very nice young Canadian airman—'

'Blimey! Where'd you meet him then?'

'At a dance in Folkstone when my friend Alice and me had been working on the hospital ships after Dunkirk. You have heard about Dunkirk, I suppose?'

'Course I have. It's in France. A bloke down our road got killed there.'

And so did my brother, Daisy thought with a pang. The unbelievable knowledge could still make her heart miss a beat for a moment. But right now she wasn't prepared to share any of her family's heartache with Vanessa.

'So do you want to take a ride with me tomorrow to see your new school?' she said instead, diverting her attention from Glenn.

'Oh, all right.' She gave Daisy a rather peculiar look. 'Will I have to be called Vanessa Caldwell, then? I don't fancy being Vanessa Painter.'

'Why on earth would you think that?'

Vanessa shrugged. 'Dunno. I thought p'raps Aunt Rose might like it, seeing as she'll be taking me for this interview. It sounds a bit posher than Vanessa Brown, don't it?'

'Maybe it does, but that's your name, and you can't just change it because you think you will. Knowing you, I daresay you'd want to change it to something else next week.'

Vanessa flounced off to her room, leaving Daisy wondering why she had thought of such a thing. Unless it was her way of saying she wanted to belong to them. To shut out the past completely, since she had no one of her own now.

They had heard from the billeting officer that all the houses in Hollis Mews where she lived had been flattened in a bombing raid several months ago. She had been staying since with neighbours who were glad to be rid of her. But she never referred to it in any way. And Daisy knew very well that bottling things up inside was no good at all. The longer it remained there festering, the bigger the explosion when it eventually happened.

But maybe there was something in her comment about being known as Vanessa Caldwell, after all. It could have been just a spur of the moment idea, of course, or more likely said to annoy Daisy with her cheek . . . or it could have been a genuine need to feel part of a family once more.

She talked it over with Alice Godfrey at work the next day.

'Well, I think it's a damn cheek!' Alice said. 'From what you've told me about her, would you want her to be part of your family? What would your sisters say, and your father, come to that? And what does your Aunt Rose say?'

'As far as I know, Vanessa hasn't said anything to her about it. I'm not sure what to think. I suppose I should tell her, and anyway, can you just call yourself by some other name, just because you want to?'

Alice frowned. 'Well, the movie stars do it all the time, don't they? So I suppose you can *call* yourself anything you like, even if it's not strictly legal. I mean, it wouldn't be on her birth certificate, would it? She'd still be Vanessa Brown on that, wouldn't she?'

'If she's still got one. It probably got lost in the bombing raid, along with everything else.'

'Well, I'd let your Aunt Rose sort it out, Daisy. In any case, I expect the girl's forgotten all about it by now.'

But she hadn't. It was a fine afternoon when Daisy and Vanessa cycled along the beach road to the far end of the town, where the splendid edifice of the County School took up an entire road's length of space. They happened to get there as school was ending for the day, with the blazer-clad girls pouring out, satchels on one shoulder, gas masks on the other. And Vanessa's eyes suddenly brightened as she saw a crowd of boys in their red and yellow caps, coming out of another entrance.

'You said it was a girls only school,' she accused Daisy.

'So it is. It just so happens that the County School for Boys adjoins it. Did I forget to mention that?' Daisy said innocently.

'Well, that makes it a bit better.'

'Forget it, Nessa. Girls and boys are kept strictly apart. Let's ride around the grounds to the playing fields and you'll see what I mean.'

They got back on their bicycles and rode around the perimeter fence to where the twin playing fields were separated by a wide dividing pathway. At the far end, there was an imposing clocktower. They paused to take a good look.

'One field is for the girls' sports activities, and the other one's for the boys, and heaven help those who cross the dividing line,' Daisy said with a grin. 'It's the same with the school buildings, so don't think you're going to get away with anything here!'

Vanessa tossed her head, the way she usually did. But not for the world was she going to tell Daisy that just for a minute – just for one bleeding minute – she had fancied seeing herself like one of them girls flocking out of the front of the building with their satchels and their uniforms.

And even more than that. She had really fancied sticking

her nose in the air and announcing herself as Vanessa Caldwell. It sounded real flash. A bit different from Hollis Mews and the snot-nosed kids around the back alleys there.

It would be like pretending she was somebody else, and then maybe she could forget all that other stuff; that terrible air raid when her mum and her dad, swaying about with the drink as usual, had been blown to smithereens, and when she'd gone back from the shelter to find them there was no house to go back to no more, and she'd had to go and live with them neighbours who hadn't wanted her. If she was somebody else, maybe she could forget all the blood and the screaming and the awful smells. And people peeing themselves in the street as their guts turned to water, waiting for the next bomb to fall.

And kids dying in front of you, with arms and legs and bits of bodies flying about in the air like bleeding rag dolls. They didn't know anything about it down here. They didn't know what it was like.

'Are you all right, Vanessa?' Daisy said sharply, seeing how she had suddenly gripped the handlebars on her bicycle until her knuckles went white.

'Yeah,' she said thickly. 'I just want to go home.'

Four

Joe Preston arrived back in Bristol, feeling considerably more alarmed than when he left. Everywhere he looked now, there were bombed-out buildings, whole streets razed to the ground in some places, and the air seemed constantly thick with dust and smoke. Rubble was still smouldering in places, and the smell of burning was everywhere.

As a soldier Joe had seen and smelt his fair share of death, but this burning of a once-beautiful city was bringing the obscenity of war into the daily lives of the people he loved, and he knew more than ever that he had to get his wife and baby out of there.

Everyone had predicted that the city would be a prime target for air raids, and it hadn't taken long for the supposition to become a grim fact. And once he had got Elsie and Faith safely to Yorkshire, he intended to move heaven and earth to persuade his wife to stay there with his family for the duration.

She greeted him at the door of number 17 Vicarage Street with cries of excitement as she fell into his open arms, her heartbeats erratic at knowing that at last he was here. He was warm and he was solid, and in Elsie's mind as long as they were together, nothing could hurt them now.

'Oh, Joe, darling, I've missed you so much!' she whispered into his cheek.

'No more than I've missed you, my love,' Joe said huskily.

She felt so small in his arms, so fragile after the birth of the baby, even though she had protested to him in her letters that

41

she was still hideously plump, at least in her eyes. Joe saw none of it. He only saw his lovely wife, and felt the primitive need to protect her at all costs.

'Come inside, for heaven's sake, Joe,' Elsie said with a nervous giggle, after those heady first moments. 'The neighbours will think I'm a fast woman, embracing a soldier on the doorstep!'

'Just as long as the only soldier you're embracing is your husband, I don't mind giving them something to gossip about!' he said breezily, the brief awkwardness of the reunion passing swiftly. 'Is your father at home?'

They were inside the house by now, still held tight in one another's arms, and Joe kicked the door shut behind him.

'No – he's at the shop.' Elsie's voice was suddenly breathless, seeing the darkening of her husband's eyes. It was the middle of the afternoon, and respectable people didn't normally think of making love in the afternoon . . . not unless they were young and in love, and had been apart for far too long.

And then, right on cue, they heard the fretful wail from somewhere in the flat above, and they broke apart with a rueful laugh. 'Your daughter's anxious to see you, Joe,' Elsie said softly.

'I want to see her, too, but once we've settled her down, I want you all to myself, just for an hour,' he said, more urgently. 'If the Jerries come over tonight and we have to go down to the shelter, it won't be the most romantic of places for a reunion, will it?'

She hugged his arm as they went upstairs to the flat. 'Any place will be romantic as long as we're together.'

But her heart was thudding with excitement, knowing how much he wanted her. And she wanted him, too, so much . . . and she didn't want to wait.

But Faith demanded attention first, a bottle and a clean nappy, and to be hugged in her father's arms as he noted and admired the changes in her since he had last seen her.

42

Then Joe laid her tenderly in her cot, and as he watched her sleeping for a few more minutes, Elsie felt as if her heart would burst with love for them both.

She had never thought she would feel this way about anyone, but she would have died for Joe . . . except that she didn't want to think about anything so sombre, or anything but the fact that they were here together at last. Dying was the very last thing on her mind.

Moments later he was straightening up from the cot, smiling into her eyes and holding out his arms to her. And then they were leaving Faith to sleep and dream, while they went to their bedroom and made their own dreams come true.

Quentin came home from the shop a couple of hours later, smiling faintly as he saw Joe's kitbag slung carelessly on the mat inside the front door. Not for the world would he intrude on them until they were ready to be sociable. He hadn't forgotten the way it was, those wonderful, euphoric moments of reunion after a long parting, and he felt a deep pang of regret that it would never come again for him and Frances. The final parting between them had been for ever.

But now there was Mary, who was becoming dearer to him than he had expected her to be. She was filling his heart in a way he had never thought to have it filled again. As yet it was no more than a dear friendship, but he knew it could very well become more.

Neither of them was in any hurry to push their relationship a stage further, and he liked that. Mary had been a widow for many years, and from the moment they had met, he had realised that she wasn't one of those women who was desperate to marry again.

As for himself, there were others to consider. His family. But even as he thought it, he knew that in the end, there were only two people to consider. A marriage needed no more than that, providing they were the right two people.

He heard movement from the flat above, and with it the

sound of his granddaughter demanding attention. He knew Elsie wouldn't leave Faith crying for many minutes, and he called up the stairs to ask if anyone wanted a cup of tea. For the first time, he knew how much he was going to miss his daughter when she took Faith to Yorkshire, but just like Joe, he was determined that she would remain there as long as Bristol was unsafe. In his mind, he was sure that this was going to be a long parting, even if Elsie was still stalwartly saying it was only going to be a visit.

'Come on up, Daddy,' Elsie called down to him. 'We're just having some tea ourselves.'

'I'll bring Joe's stuff,' he said, 'I guess he was in too much of a hurry to bring it up himself.'

His daughter's flushed face told its own story. Her eyes were almost luminous now, and she looked so beautiful and so like her mother that for a moment it tore at his heart. He turned to his son-in-law, almost afraid of the raw emotion such a moment could evoke.

'It's good to see you, Joe,' he said, shaking his hand before he could get maudlin. 'You're looking well, all things considered.'

'I'm well enough, and will be all the better when I can get my family safely away from the bombing.'

He didn't mean anything untoward by the words, but it seemed to emphasise in Quentin's mind the fact that these three, Elsie, Joe and the baby, were a complete unit now. A family. And it would be quite wrong to try to hold them here. If Elsie had any thoughts about staying here just to keep him company, he had to squash it at once.

Over tea and cakes, he spoke casually. 'I've been telling Elsie for months now that I think she and Faith should stay with your folks for the duration, if they'll have them, Joe. Do you think they will?'

'I know they will. They've told me so a dozen times.'

'Excuse me,' Elsie put in mildly. 'Remember me, when

44

you're making all these plans? I do have a say in this, I suppose?'

Her father laughed. 'Of course you do, darling, and before you think I shall pine away and fret over the loss of all my children, let me assure you that I'm quite capable of filling my days and my nights. The Jerries will see to that,' he added, before either of them might think he was implying anything else.

'You're not going to miss us one tiny bit, then?' Elsie teased him.

'Well, perhaps a tiny bit,' he teased back, and as Faith began gurgling up at him, he knew he would miss this little one a great deal more than that. But war had always separated people, and the one great joy about parting was that it made every reunion the sweeter. There was enough evidence of that here in this room.

He cleared his throat. 'I'm thinking of offering part of the house for billeting purposes,' he stated. 'Not this flat, of course. That belongs to all of you for as long as you need it. But since there are so many empty rooms now, I thought it could be better used by some of the military who need housing accommodation.'

'I think that's a good idea, Daddy,' Elsie said, trying not to show her relief. And what about Mary Yard? Where did she fit into his plans, she wondered. But now wasn't the time to ask.

'So have you two made any plans about leaving?' he said next.

Elsie and Joe looked at one another. It was Joe who spoke, seeing the sudden tug of loyalties in Elsie's eyes.

'We thought the day after tomorrow. There's no sense in prolonging it now we've made the decision, and naturally I'll want to see my parents, too.'

'Of course,' Quentin said evenly.

His daughter suddenly jumped up and put her arms around his neck. He could smell the delicate perfume of her skin, and sense the emotions in her heart.

'You know I would never leave you unless I felt it was the right thing to do, don't you, Daddy? I have to do this for Faith.'

'My darling,' he said, extricating himself from her embrace, 'I've told you a hundred times I think you should leave Bristol, so don't start wavering now. This little one has a lifetime ahead of her, and it won't break my heart not to see her for a few weeks, or a few months – or however long Adolf is pulling our strings. I'll expect you to send me photos of her quite frequently though.'

'Of course I will.'

Two days later they left on the morning train out of Bristol, after two nights of heavy bombing raids that shook the house and the shelter, and during which time they hardly saw Quentin at all. Elsie still felt as if she was deserting a sinking ship, but since she always hated the expression every time it came into her head, because of Baz, she simply wouldn't allow herself to feel guilty any longer.

By now, most of her clothes, and the baby's, were in the suitcases Joe bundled into the luggage racks along with Joe's kitbag, and she was resigned to the fact that it might be a long while before she saw Bristol again.

As the train snorted and steamed out of Temple Meads station, she felt her mouth tremble, and her arms closed more tightly around the sleeping baby in her arms. She was going north for safety, but she was still going into the unknown, and the nagging anxiety that she and Joe's family might not even like one another was never very far from her mind. She had never said as much in words, but it would be simply terrible if they couldn't get along.

She felt Joe's hand close over hers. 'Getting cold feet?'

'Is it that obvious?'

'Elsie, they're going to love you,' he said quietly.

She kept her eyes lowered as she nodded. He couldn't guarantee any such thing, of course, any more than he could guarantee that she was going to love his parents. It was the thing that almost scared her the most, because now they had finally made the decision, how could she turn around in a couple of weeks – or months – and say it had all been a ghastly mistake, and she wanted to go home?

Joe's fingers squeezed hers, and she took a deep breath, knowing how foolish she was being, when all around here in this stifling train, overcrowded with servicemen and women, were people who had been separated from those they loved best, and were likely to be for a very long time yet. It was time she stopped being so spineless.

'It's just that I want everything to be right,' she said hesitantly. 'I'm going into their home, and I'll be the stranger—'

'But not for long. Not for longer than a heartbeat,' Joe said. 'They'll take one look at you and love you as much as I do, sweetheart.'

They were suddenly aware that several young soldiers and airmen in the compartment were grinning.

'You tell 'em, mate,' one of the soldiers said. 'Got to keep the little ladies in their place these days, 'aven't yer?'

Elsie averted her eyes as she met the boldly admiring gaze of the men, reminding her of Joe's cousin Robert Preston, whom she was bound to run into during her time in Yorkshire. She had never cared for Robert very much. He was too charming, too brash, too irritatingly self-assured, and obviously thinking himself every girl's dream man. After intending to take over the Bristol branch of Preston's Emporium where Joe, and now her father, was manager, Robert had been ordered back to Yorkshire in some haste.

There had been something hush-hush about the whole thing, and Elsie had finally got it out of Immy. When she learned the truth, it had shocked her to the core to learn that he had tried to assault Immy's friend Helen Church under the pretext of teaching her to drive. She wished, now, that she had never egged Immy on to tell her about it, since she was sure she would find it difficult not to let her derision for the man show. But remembering again how brash and irritatingly self-assured Robert had always seemed in comparison with Joe, he probably wouldn't even notice it.

Faith stirred in her arms, and she eased her into a more comfortable position, smiling into Joe's eyes as their travelling companions settled into their own easy chatter.

With their own little enclosed world, it wasn't difficult to shut them out after all, and she was perfectly sure she could do the same with Robert Preston if the need arose. In fact, thought Elsie, with more deviousness than was usual in her nature, she imagined that one innocent mention of Helen Church's name would soon bring him to heel.

'I'd like to know what's going on inside that head of yours,' Joe's voice said softly, as her mouth curved into a secret smile.

'Oh, it was just something Immy said. You wouldn't be interested, honestly.' And she was perfectly sure Joe had no idea of what had occurred, nor that Immy had gone storming to the hotel where Robert Preston had been staying, and told him exactly what she thought of him. Immy had behaved like a proper Emily Pankhurst in Elsie's opinion, strong and fearless and a champion of good causes, and she had never admired her more.

'Let me have Faith for a while, if you want to close your eyes and have a sleep, Elsie, we've got a very long journey ahead of us.'

She handed over the baby half-reluctantly, but knowing that Joe needed to do this. He had already spent so little time with his own child, and the two of them needed to experience the bond that existed between them. And she was feeling extraordinarily tired all of a sudden. It had been a hectic couple of days, apart from the weariness of dodging the air raids that interrupted their packing.

They had managed a brief few hours in Weston to say goodbye to the rest of the family, and learned the incredible fact that Vanessa Brown, the impossibly precocious evacuee who had now come back to live with them, wanted to be known as one of the Caldwell girls when she went to the County School. It was almost insulting, as far as Elsie was concerned, but to her surprise, Daisy didn't seem to mind, and Aunt Rose was surprisingly touched. Teddy wasn't sure if this meant Vanessa was to be his sister or not, and had decided to ignore it all.

But they didn't linger in Weston very long, because there was a danger of it all becoming far too emotional, and besides, Elsie needed to spend the time in Bristol with her father, and for him to see as much of his grandchild as possible.

The train rattled northwards, and she slept for much of the journey, interspersed with taking Faith from Joe's arms, eating the sandwiches she had packed, drinking tea from the flasks she had prepared, and making up Faith's bottles from the separate flask of boiled water. Other passengers came and went from the compartment, and after many hours the journey eventually came to an end as the train began to slow down as it neared York station.

Her heart was thudding as they got ready to leave the train. As she held Faith tightly in her arms, Joe was already craning his neck to see familiar faces among the crowds.

'There they are,' he said as they stepped on to the platform.

Elsie saw the two portly people hurrying towards them, and Joe's mother immediately enveloped him in her arms and then turned to her.

'Now then, Elsie lass, let's take a good look at you,' she said, beaming broadly. 'You're every bit as bonny as our Joe always said you were, isn't she, Dad?' she said to her husband.

'She is that,' Joe's father said solemnly.

And then Faith had to be inspected and gushed over, and Elsie was embraced as well, until Joe's father told her to give the lass room to breathe, and they finally began moving out of the station towards the big old car that was reminiscent

of Uncle Bert's battered old Morris. But once they were all
settled inside it, he turned back to Joe before they set off for
the farmhouse in the Dales.

'You've done well for yourself, lad, I'll say that for you.
Mother's hair was on the red side when she were young too,
afore it turned pepper and salt like.'

'There you are, Elsie,' Joe said with a laugh. 'You're
accepted on account of your hair, if nowt else!'

'Get on wi' you, our Joe,' his mother said, and still
talking about Elsie as if she wasn't there. 'She's a lovely
lass, even if she does want a bit of filling out. But we'll
soon take care of that once she gets some good Yorkshire
food inside her. But for now, let's get home with that
babby, and then you can tell me all about yourself, Elsie
love.'

And if anything was guaranteed to make a person more
tongue-tied than usual, that was it. But somehow, not with
these two. They were so open-hearted, such quaintly, friendly
people, who were just as eager to make her welcome, to tell
her how Joe used to scrape his knees climbing up to the
tree-house in the big oak tree in the yard, and how Joe's
favourite place in all the world was scrambling up to the
wild, rocky outcrop above the farm and imagining that he
owned the world.

'For pity's sake, Mother, you'll have Elsie thinking I'm a
crackpot,' he said at last, laughing at the memory.

By then, his mother had been softly crooning to the baby,
who was gazing up at this new person in her life with sleepy,
Caldwell brown eyes, her small, perfect mouth making soft,
kittenish little noises of pure contentment.

'No, I won't,' Elsie said, her hands round one of the huge
cups of tea his father had made for them all. 'I was just
thinking what a marvellously happy and loving childhood
you must have had here.'

'He had that, all right,' his mother said. 'He were the apple
of his daddy's eye, and mine too. 'Course, we clung to him a

bit more after we lost t'other un. Probably more'n we should, but he didn't turn out too badly, for all that.'

Her voice was faraway for a moment, as if seeing something other than the bright farmhouse kitchen, steamy with the delicious smells of baking, and their supper of shepherd's pie slowly cooking on the big old range, and with it all, a sense of continuity that had gone on for generations. For the first time, Elsie realised how very far away the war seemed from here.

Before they ate their supper, Faith was going to be put to bed in the cot that had once been Joe's, in the bedroom the three of them were to share. This had been Joe's, too, an old-fashioned room with a door that creaked, and pencil marks on the walls, and scuffed skirting-boards from childish boots.

'What did your mother mean by losing t'other un?' she asked him as soon as they were out of earshot, falling easily into the unfamiliar language.

'I had an older brother,' Joe told her. 'He drowned in one of the swollen streams when he was six. I was only four at the time, but he was my hero. We never really knew how it happened, but we think he must have hit his head and become unconscious before he fell in the water. What made it even more traumatic was that my father found him, and Mother especially never really got over it. She became over-protective of me, until my father told her she was smothering me and had to let me grow up in my own way and not in Matthew's shadow.'

'Joe, how terrible! But why have you never told me any of this before?' she said, appalled, as the story came out in a flat, monotone voice that seemed to help with the telling. And how little I really know you, she couldn't help thinking.

'There never seemed time or necessity for such confidences, Elsie. And then, of course, after what happened –'

'And then? After what happened?' she said, as he hesitated.

'Then Baz happened. It was almost a coincidence too far. My brother was a child who died in tragic circumstances many years ago. Yours happened more recently, in even more terrible circumstances. I can't pretend that it didn't bring it all back to me. The feelings, the suffering I felt in my family, even though I was too young to fully understand. All I knew was that Matthew wasn't there any more, and it was as if I had lost my right arm. We never talk about it now, but I know the scars are still there, especially as far as my mother's concerned.'

And for you, too, thought Elsie.

He caught sight of the troubled look on her face, and wished he hadn't mentioned Baz at all. He hugged her close for a moment, his voice lighter.

'Don't let it dampen your visit here, Elsie. It all happened a long time ago, and we don't dwell on it any more. When Mother gets to know you better, I'm sure she'll bring out my baby photos, and you're bound to see the ones of Matthew then as well. So it's as well that you know about him in advance.'

He kissed her cheek. 'Mother always wanted a daughter, and now she's got one, hasn't she? And a granddaughter, too, so she'll be feeling twice blessed. And I think we'd better start unpacking now, or the folks will start thinking the worst of us, up here all this time.'

But Elsie knew they wouldn't. Joe was an honourable man, and she loved him for it. And he might have been a small child when his brother was drowned, but he still had feelings for him, the same as she still did for Baz. You didn't need to mention them constantly, but they were always in their hearts. Which endeared Joe to her even more.

If the farm was rural enough to make Elsie feel instantly at home, the obligatory visit to Joe's relatives in York was not. Like most other towns and cities, it was bursting with folk in military uniforms, and it was apparently a matter of discussion within the family whether or not the reason for Robert Preston not going to war was genuine or not. Elsie couldn't see how anyone could fake the repercussions of a childhood illness that prevented him passing his medical, as she had been told, but when they were all invited to dinner in Owen Preston's impressive mansion, there was a definite prickle between the farming Prestons and the businesslike city ones who had forged the Preston Emporium dynasty.

'It's the uniform,' Joe murmured to her. 'For all Robert's disinclination to go to war, he'd dearly have loved putting on a uniform to attract the girls.'

'So I would imagine,' Elsie said dryly, unable to forget Immy's disclosure about Robert's abortive seduction of Helen Church.

Even now, knowing she was married to Joe, he found it hard to keep his bold, roving eyes away from her, and she disliked him even more, although Owen was as jovial as she remembered, and his wife was a suitable consort. Elsie could hardly think of her as anything less, and since they all made such a fuss of Faith, she could forgive them anything. It was only for one evening, anyway, and they could soon go back to being themselves.As the words slid into her mind, her composure slipped for a moment. Soon, all this would be changed again. Being with Joe, being a family. It was an interlude, no more. War wasn't here in York the way it was in Bristol, tearing into peoples' lives and ripping them apart with death and destruction. It was why she had fled, to keep her baby safe.

But of all of them sitting sociably around the dinner table while she tried not to be suspicious about the amount of food Owen Preston seemed able to obtain, Joe was the one in uniform. The only one who had to leave this idyllic place, wearing a uniform for King and country, and risking his life for them all.

'Your lass looks a bit peaky, Joe,' Owen was saying genially. 'But I daresay she'll do right nicely once she gets some of Hetty's good solid pies inside her.'

'Not so much of the solid, lad,' Hetty Preston told him smartly, at which they all laughed, and got on with the important business of piling their plates obscenely high, in the circumstances.

And Elsie told herself she had better stop being so critical and keep reminding herself that she had to fit in – if she was going to stay.

Five

The weather was turning cold by the end of November. It was bad enough keeping track of what was happening in faraway war zones, as well as the more immediate effects of the sporadic raids that had begun as far back as June, let alone trying desperately to keep warm and to keep cheerful as much as possible.

Due to a shortage of nurses doing routine jobs, Daisy Caldwell had been transferred to the burns unit in Frenchay Hospital for a couple of months. She hated it there. The constant seeping wounds and blackened, blistering skin of the poor wounded soldiers and airmen who were sent there for specialist attention, were hard to bear.

But almost harder on the emotions were the everyday victims of bombing raids. Wives and mothers and children, just going about their daily business, could be caught up in a shower of incendiary bombs falling indiscriminately. The staff dealt with the wounds with analgesics and morphine, but it didn't stifle the pain, nor the fear, nor the smell . . .

Nurses weren't supposed to show their emotions, but this was nursing at its most raw, among patients at their most vulnerable, some with half their faces burned away who would be disfigured for life, no matter now gentle and patient the treatment given.

'Sometimes I don't know how to bear it,' Daisy wrote to Elsie, since the two sisters had vowed to write to one another weekly. 'You daren't let the patients guess at your reaction when you see them being brought in on stretchers, but sometimes it takes an almost superhuman effort to hide your disgust at the sight of that livid red flesh with all the skin and bone ripped away and virtually nothing left to repair. I shouldn't be telling you all this, Elsie, because I'm sure it will upset you, but I have to tell someone, and it's not fair to burden Daddy with it all, since he looks so weary these days, looking after the shop and fire-watching every single night now. It's too much for him, but he won't listen to me – nor even to Mary Yard, who he's seeing more often now, by the way.

'Oh – and Glenn's been posted overseas, which makes me all the more depressed! I don't know where, of course, they never tell you anything these days. But after Aunt Rose had taken such a shine to him, it's such a shame that she couldn't have got to know him a little better.'

She paused in her letter-writing. The afternoon tea with Glenn had been a spectacular success, even though she had been all fingers and thumbs waiting for him to arrive on the afternoon train on the strawberry line.

'What the bleedin' 'ell's the strawberry line?' Vanessa had said predictably, and was told it was the local name for the branch railway line from the fertile Cheddar valleys, where the strawberries grew in such abundance.

Vanessa had hooted, but she hadn't been so scoffing when she had caught sight of the tall, handsome Canadian carrying a huge basketful of the juicy red berries, endearing him to Aunt Rose even more.

As for Daisy . . . in the intervening months, she had forgotten just how very handsome he was, how film-starry, how attracted to her . . .

And now he was God knew where, fighting Jerries overseas, while she was stuck here, in this awful burns unit at Frenchay Hospital, and trying to snatch a few minutes' break to write to her sister. She brushed away a self-indulgent tear, telling herself not to be so feeble. Even Elsie was bearing up well, settling into Yorkshire farmhouse life with her in-laws now that Joe had gone back to his unit.

'Mother Hetty is a really wise woman, Daisy,' Elsie had written recently. 'That's how she likes me to refer to her, though I still find it a bit odd. She never interferes with the way I'm bringing up Faith, but she's always there to give advice if I ask for it. I must admit I feel more at home here than I ever expected to. To give you an example: Faith was really fretful the other night, and I couldn't settle her no matter how hard I tried. The poor little love is suffering with wind quite badly now and can't seem to get rid of it.

'Anyway, I had to bring her downstairs one evening and felt really embarrassed that she kept on crying all the time, and Mother Hetty said Joe used to be the same until she gave him the cinder tea. Well, naturally, I didn't know what she was talking about, so I asked her what she meant. I know you're not in the least interested in all this baby stuff, Daisy, but I'm so thrilled to have found a remedy, and since you're a nurse, perhaps you can pass it on to anyone who might need it.'

Daisy grinned as she read on, sensing just how enthusiastic Elsie was becoming, and knowing she was about to learn the rest of it. Modern medicine had nothing on country cures, apparently.

'Cinder tea is well used in the North of England for helping babies bring up their wind. First of all, you drop red hot coals into cold water, then let it cool and settle. Then you strain it, add sugar, and put the liquid into the baby's bottle, and it works like magic. Isn't that amazing?'

Amazing, Daisy thought. And it was obvious that Elsie was becoming firmly indoctrinated into country ways now, old folklore remedies and stuff like that. It was a pity that not all the world's ills could be cured by something so simple and so readily obtainable.

Christmas was only a month away, and more families were separated by necessity than ever before. Those who could be sent home from hospital were being despatched as soon as reasonably possible, if only to make room for the new intake of war casualties and normal patients. Everyone wanted to be home for Christmas, but although Elsie had never been away from home at such a time before, she had accepted that she would stay in Yorkshire with Joe's family. Bringing Faith back to Bristol would be madness, since it was doubtful that Adolf would stop his onslaught for the sake of Christmas.

It was a first time for Daisy, too, since she was detailed to work over the whole period. It upset her when she realised it, but then she decided to make the best of it, knowing she would be helping those far less fortunate than herself.

'I sound so blessed noble, don't I?' she wrote passionately to Glenn, 'and I honestly don't feel that way at all. Some of the sights I'm seeing in this hospital are really getting me down, and I'm starting to feel as if I'm out of my depth here. That's a fine thing to admit, isn't it? But all these poor wretched people – what hope do some of them have of ever living a normal life again? And I'm not cheering you up too much either, am I? Sorry, sorry, sorry!'

She re-read the letter and immediately tore it up. What kind of an idiot would send such a missive to a serving airman with their appalling statistics of survivors and devastating injuries? There was nothing so demeaning as a pecking order of injuries among the services, but Daisy knew full well that being shot down in a burning airplane produced some of the most horrific burns.

There had been two terrible air raids on the BAC at Filton, and then, in subsequent ones, the German bombers tried to target the goods yard at Temple Meads station. The railway horses were stabled at the end of nearby Redcliffe Street, and in the carnage many of the horses were killed and their carcasses left to rot, because nobody could get near them to remove them. The stench became unbelievably putrid, until it got so bad that a near riot occurred when people protested at the risk to public health, and order was finally restored when the carcasses were able to be transported away for disposal.

It was just one more thing in a city already crumbling, and yet the end of November proved a turning point in how resilient the people of a city could be. Everyone knew it had to be their turn soon. Coventry had already been devastated, and the only question was when?

Soon after six o'clock on the Sunday evening of the twenty-fourth of the month the sirens began wailing, and immediately afterwards, waves of enemy aircraft could be heard droning overhead. Incendiaries started dropping almost at once, whizzing through the streets and peppering the city with dozens of fires, the bomb blasts shattering the ear-drums and terrifying young and old. Retaliating ack-ack guns added to the bedlam of noise, going off like fire-crackers.

Daisy was at work in the hospital, but she knew very well that her father would be out in the thick of it. It had become almost a vocation for Quentin now, almost as if he was realising some childhood dream of being a fireman. But never in these circumstances, she thought grimly.

Right then her father was thinking very much the same thing. There had been many intermittent raids on the city, but none with so much savagery as on that particular night. On and on it raged, as if those in command were intent on wiping out Bristol completely, and as the hours of slaughter went on, the whole of the city was ablaze. Streets of houses were demolished, wiped out in a single bomb blast, bringing death and terrible injuries.

Time and again, the names of the famous old streets became known to the rescue teams, detailing where the bombs had struck. Names that had their significance in Bristol's long history: Corn Street, Wine Street, College Green, Castle Street; all were ablaze as was the entire city centre that night. The water mains had fractured, so water to fight the fires was in short supply, and the river was well down, so there was little to draw on from there. The north of the city had gone, up towards Park Street; the museum was demolished; the Princess Cinema destroyed . . . On and on the list of names and places filtered through as the firefighters tried vainly to quench the fires. Churches were destroyed: St Peter's and St-Mary-Le-Port, the Bethesda Chapel in Great George Street; the Holy Nativity in Knowle. The historic Temple Church near Temple Meads railway station was gutted, with only the famous leaning tower remaining.

Newspaper hacks were trying to get first-hand reports from anyone who would talk, hampering the efforts of the ARP and other rescue services and only adding to the chaos.

'Bugger off, you vultures,' Quentin bellowed at one of the bastards tugging at his arm.

'We're only trying to do our job, same as you, man,' the man yelled back. 'Give us a quote, can't you?'

Quentin vaguely recognised the whining Welsh voice. It was Morgan something or other. Young enough to be in uniform, or at least to be reporting at the Front, not hovering around like some ghoul at a funeral pyre, ready to pick over the pieces. Without thinking, he lashed out at the man and struck him on the cheek with the back of his hand.

'It's Caldwell, isn't it?' Morgan Raine shrieked out above the noise of splintering glass and crashing buildings. It was nearing midnight, but the entire area was as light as day with the sky a deep red now from all the burning buildings. 'Caldwell from Preston's Emporium?'

'Get out of here, you bugger, I'm giving you no quotes at a time like this,' Quentin roared again, but the man wouldn't be deterred.

'Did you know that entire row of shops has been flattened?' Morgan Raine yelled, in a kind of desperate triumph, his little Welsh eyes gleaming in the light from the fires raging all around.

Quentin wouldn't listen. If it was true he didn't want to know right now. If it wasn't, it was just the sort of thing these people said in order to make you give them a reaction. Liars, the lot of them. Anything for a story.

Without another thought, he whisked his fire hose around

as if to quench the licking tongues of flame creeping towards them, and sent the man flying with a sudden blast of icy water. The last thing he heard was Morgan Raine yelping furiously as he dashed off to get dry, and no doubt there would be a vicious attack on himself in the newspaper tomorrow, but he didn't care. It was the last thing he was worried about. There were more important things to do here than to worry about some ferret-faced Welshman.

The all-clear finally sounded at a quarter past midnight, and it was as if an entire underground city gradually emerged from shelters and cellars and hide-outs to take stock at the nightmare scenes all around them. It was as if an earthquake had struck without warning, and even though the heart of the city had been the predominant target, reports were coming in of other districts that had been hit, too; Clifton, Bedminster and other suburbs of the city.

But if the raids had ended, the rescue services toiled on into the early hours of the morning, aided now by civilians helping to clear away rubble, working hand over hand, and trying to make sense out of what had happened to their city. Women openly wept at the sight of the ancient and famous Old Dutch House on the corner of High Street and Wine Street, now tottering on its foundations, and clearly set for demolition. What the Germans had so cruelly begun, the city itself would have to finish.

It was nearing four in the morning before Quentin's hose gang was finally told to go home. He was nearly dropping with sleep, but in the way that incongruous thoughts entered the mind, something told him he must first go and check that all was well at Preston's Emporium. If any damage had been done to the row of shops of which Preston's was the largest, then looters could easily get inside. And it was his duty, as manager, to see that all was made secure.

He walked through streets that were no longer streets, but simply masses of rubble. He walked on broken glass that cut his feet through his boots, but he hardly noticed it. The air was thick with dust and destruction, the sky still as red as blood, and when he came to the row of shops that no longer existed, his knees simply buckled beneath him, and he fell to the ground and wept.

The influx of casualties at all the hospitals was enormous that day, and Daisy had stayed on for longer than she was required to do, until she was finally sent home around six o'clock in the morning. A bus took her the first part of the way to Vicarage Street, until it terminated because there was simply no more street for it to drive through. She walked the rest of the way, her heart pounding, terrified at what she might find when she got there. If she found anything at all.

All through that night they had heard reports of what was happening in the city. The hospital buildings had shaken on their foundations, and the already vulnerable patients were terrified they were going to be burned to death in their beds, some of them blaspheming and screaming to be let out of there and needing to be heavily sedated.

But the night had been too hectic to know exactly what was going on outside, except for the brief glimpses they had seen from the hospital windows of the city burning in front of them, and the garbled reports from patients and ambulance drivers. But now, her heart in her mouth, Daisy turned the corner into Vicarage Street, and heaved a huge sigh of relief as she saw that their house was still standing, along with all the others in the street. Vicarage Street had survived, this time at least. But had her father?

For the first time she let the thought enter her head. She wouldn't even consider such a possibility before, but she knew he would have been out all night in the heart of it all along with his other fire-watchers. He wouldn't have given up until there was nothing more he could do.

She let herself in, closing the door behind her quietly, and leaning against it for a moment, thankful that she still had this place to come home to. This precious haven. With the wild rush of relief, scattered thoughts flashed through her head. The folks in Weston would have seen the glow in the sky all night. They would have heard the bombing and the sound of planes overhead, since there was little more than twenty miles between Weston and Bristol. They wouldn't have known the full horror of it all, but they would be frantic with worry, and needing to be reassured as soon as possible. She should phone Aunt Rose, if there were any telephone lines still working.

A sudden sound in the house made her heart freeze for a second. After the hellish noise all night and the frantic work at the hospital, it had been blessedly silent to shut her own front door on everything. But now she realised she wasn't alone. She wasn't afraid, but her mouth and throat were gritty from the dust in the air and she felt as if she was breathing sand as she croaked out a question.

'Daddy, is that you?'

She moved forward to the sitting room just as he rose from the armchair in which he had been slumped, and she gasped at the sight of him. His face was gaunt and dazed, almost black with the effects of fire and weariness, and she guessed that it was smarting painfully too. He had taken off his boots and socks, uncaring about putting on slippers, and she could see the cuts on his feet. He looked in a state of shock, and she said the first inane thing that came into her head.

'Goodness, a fine state you'll look when you open the shop tomorrow—'

She never got to the end of the sentence because he began laughing, a wild, high-pitched laugh that she recognised only too well. She had heard it often enough, from young men and old, from women and children and babies. She took his hands in hers, and made him sit down on the sofa, while she sat beside him, still holding him tightly. She had also gone through a night she would never forget, but it was obvious that his had been so much worse.

'Has the shop gone, Daddy?' she said quietly, because that had to be the reason for this hysteria. He was a strong man, and nothing else had affected him like this, except losing Frances and Baz.

She dreaded his reply, knowing that all his life, all his love – except the love for his wife and family – had gone into that shop. It had been Caldwell's shop, long before it had been taken over by Preston's Emporium. His pride. His joy.

'The whole row is gone,' he said raggedly. 'Wiped out in a single night. Nothing left at all, as if it had never been. My heart and soul was bound up there, Daisy, even when it was no longer mine, and now there's nothing. My heart is dead.'

She was frightened by such rhetoric. He wasn't a poetic man, and she had never expected him to speak so baldly. She spoke quietly but urgently, knowing how deeply she might be offending him and hurting him, but it had to be said.

'Daddy, it was only a shop. In the end, it was only a shop. Sticks and stones. It wasn't your heart. It's still beating, feel it.'

She moved his hand over his heart, her own still covering it. 'You're still here, Daddy, and so am I. We're still alive, and the heart of our family is still here. Mother's still here, because she left us to remind you. It was her legacy to you. You told me that once, do you remember?'

So he had, in a rare, intimate moment. When he said nothing, she went on, knowing she had to keep talking, the way you did to people in shock.

'So you've lost the shop. But it was no longer yours, was it? It belonged to Preston's Emporium, and didn't you always say it was a mistake for them to open a Bristol branch when the city was likely to be vulnerable if war came? Well, now it has, and you were proved right. You were wiser than Owen Preston after all, weren't you? And now I'm going to make us some strong sweet tea, and then I think you should go to bed for a few hours. There'll be time enough to think about what to do when you've had a rest.'

And in one way, this awful disaster might not be so much

of a disaster after all, she was thinking. He couldn't have gone on for ever doing two jobs, and the firefighting was getting a real hold on him now. Daisy knew it was a dangerous job, and at times it must be like entering hell to pull people out of burning buildings, even in normal times, but she knew that in her father's eyes it was far more worthwhile than standing behind a shop counter. It may have taken a war for him to see it, but when he had had a proper sleep and got over the initial shock, she knew it was the way she should make him think. There were times when the child could be wiser than the parent, and perhaps this was one of them.

But she wilted as she turned on the tap for the trickle of water that came out of it and put the kettle on to boil. She, too, had seen sights that night that made her more determined than ever that she had had enough. If it also made her feel guilty at knowing what she planned to do, she was reassured by the thought that she didn't mean to leave nursing for ever. Just that she would adapt the way she would use her skills. In the new year, she promised herself again.

When she had made the tea and taken two cups back to the sitting room, her father had already fallen asleep. He suddenly looked old, she thought with a pang. Old and lonely. A ship without a rudder, as they said. A man without a wife.

The sound of the telephone ringing startled her. She had never thought it would still be working, but she ran to the hall to answer it with shaking hands, sure it would be Aunt Rose checking to see that they were all right.

'Is that you, Daisy?' she heard the voice say. It seemed vaguely familiar. 'It's Mary Yard here. I've been so worried about your father. Is he all right?'

'Yes,' Daisy said mechanically. 'Yes, he's exhausted, but quite all right. He's been firefighting all night, and he's just fallen asleep now—'

'Oh, please don't wake him. I was just anxious, that's all, but if you would just tell him I called – and I trust you're all right too? We could hear the bombardment from here, and we were all so worried.'

Daisy had no idea where 'from here' was, and didn't feel like asking. But she was galvanised into action by the thought that there was still a telephone lifeline, though heaven knew how long it would last, and she had to contact as many people as she could.

'Mrs Yard – Mary – I'll pass on your message as soon as Daddy wakes up, and I'm sure he'll be in touch with you.'

'Take care of him, Daisy,' Mary said softly, 'and take care of yourself, too,' she added, as if it was an afterthought.

Daisy didn't take offence. And if that wasn't a clear indication of how far this relationship had gone, Daisy didn't know what was! It was one small spark of optimism in a day when everything around them was in a state of upheaval and chaos. But she had no time to think of that now. She had to try to call Aunt Rose. But even before she picked up the receiver to ask for the number, the phone rang again and she heard her aunt's voice at the other end.

'We're both all right,' she said in answer to the frantic question. 'I've been at the hospital all night, and Daddy's been firefighting. He looks exhausted, and he's fallen asleep on the sofa, so I'm not going to disturb him.'

'So the house is intact?' Aunt Rose said anxiously. 'We could see the glow in the sky from here, and we've been praying all night that you were both all right, since we weren't sure which areas were hit.'

'The centre, mostly,' Daisy said in an understatement. 'Many streets were demolished, and churches were hit, and we've had a pretty horrible night of it. And I'd better tell you, Aunt Rose – the shop has gone.'

Rose would know how much the shop had always meant to her brother, and how the news would be affecting him. But then she spoke briskly.

'I'm sorry to hear that, Daisy, and I daresay your father will be heartbroken. But in the end, a shop is only a building and buildings can be replaced. It's people that matter, and you be sure to remind him of that when he wakes up.'

'I will,' Daisy said humbly. 'Oh, and by the way, Aunt Rose, do you happen to know where Mary Yard is living now?'

Six

As Quentin slept on, Daisy couldn't resist going outside to view more of the city in daylight. The night had been full of noise and ferocious colour, a mixture of red and orange and white-heat, the buildings vividly lit as they were struck; almost obscenely beautiful at times as showers of incendiaries rained down and illuminated them, and then exploded violently as shards of splintering glass and silvery slivers of deadly shrapnel added to the bombardment.

Everything was different now. Away from the toilers still struggling to free the streets of debris and search for missing relatives and possessions, it was silent and eerie. The city was covered in a pall of smoke, and grey ash drifted over everything. The smell of burning was still paramount. Burning buildings, burning rubber, burning flesh. After a few moments wondering if this was what hell looked like, this greyness everywhere with no sight or sound of life, Daisy shuddered, and went quickly back indoors again.

Her father was sitting up now, his eyes more normal that they had been last night, no longer so haunted, though he still looked unutterably weary. The angry darkening skin of his face looked sore and was almost certainly about to peel.

'You're awake,' Daisy said abruptly. 'Before you do anything else, Daddy, I want to put some salve on your face before the skin cracks completely.'

'I'm all right, girl.'

'No, you're not. For pity's sake, let me be the nurse I'm supposed to be and tend to you!' she burst out without

68

meaning to. She bit her lip, furious to find it was trembling. His night had been so much worse than hers, and here she was, almost having a tantrum worthy of Teddy at his worst.

'You are a nurse, Daisy, and a very good one, darling,' he said gently. 'So find your salve and do your worst, and I'll try to be a brave soldier.'

She gave him the ghost of a smile, knowing he was reminding her of the words the parents had always used when they were small. Be a brave little soldier and keep a stiff upper lip and it will soon be better.

'Mary Yard telephoned,' she said, when she brought back the pot of soothing ointment and began gently touching it to the angry flesh. 'She wanted to be sure you were all right, and I told her you were. And then Aunt Rose called, and she said she was sorry about the shop, but that buildings could be replaced, and it was people who mattered. She said I had to be sure to tell you that.'

She was avoiding his eyes as she spoke, wondering if it was far too soon to be saying this, but he caught her hand, and she knew he had somehow come through whatever demons had been haunting him.

'Your aunt is perfectly right, Daisy, so if you think I'm about to do anything stupid because of it, you can think again.'

'I never knew you to do anything stupid in your life,' Daisy said. And she realised he was carefully avoiding mentioning the fact that Mary Yard had called.

'But now that I'm rested, perhaps we can have some breakfast, and then I'm going to see if anything at all can be salvaged of the place, though I doubt it very much. But Owen Preston will need to know the full extent of the damage.'

And now that they were both thinking laterally again, Daisy realised there would be others who would be worried about them. There was Immy and Elsie and Glenn, though of course, the news that one city in England had been bombed wouldn't have reached the ends of the empire wherever he was stationed now. And even if it was announced, the name of the city would be suppressed. It was the way the War Office handled things. But there were sources. Some people outside the city would know what had happened. Immy would know.

Immy managed to get through on the phone that afternoon. She was so casual after the first few minutes that it was almost unbelievable, until Daisy recognised the professional manner that was almost detached, and designed to keep feelings and emotions under control.

'And you're both really all right?' she said for the third time. 'No damage to the house either?'

'None at all, honestly. Daddy's gone to take a look at what's left of the shop now before he reports to Owen Preston, but I doubt that there's much left to look at. The city looks as if it's been hit by an earthquake, Immy, and it's so awful –' she felt the breath catch in her throat and swallowed quickly.

'I know, darling,' Immy said sympathetically. 'I know what it's like.'

'Yes, but this is Bristol. This is *home*, and it doesn't look like it any more.'

'Chin up, Daisy. The main thing is that you and Daddy are safe. Everything else can be put right, no matter how long it takes.'

'Aunt Rose said the same sort of thing.'

'Oh well then, it must be right!' Immy said, with a smile in her voice. 'Now then, have you managed to get through to Elsie? She probably doesn't know anything about it yet, but it might be as well to warn her before she gets to hear the news officially.'

'Not yet –'

'Well, leave it to me. Communications are probably better from this end than down there, and I'll do it, all right?'

'All right,' Daisy mumbled, feeling oddly deflated at having the initiative taken away from her – and relieved at the same time.

'And Daisy,' Immy said, 'there's something you can do for me, if you will.'

'Of course.'

'Will you go up to Clifton and check on James's parents? Helen called me an hour ago, having got the gist of the raid somehow and she can't get through to them, so she's pretty frantic. Call me back on this number, will you?'

As she rattled it off, Daisy wrote it down quickly, realising it was an official number. Priority. And although she was nearly dropping with sleep now, she knew she had to do this first. She would never be able to rest until she had found out for herself that James's parents were safe, and reported back to Immy.

In a way, it made her feel better that she had such a task to do. There was nothing she could have done to save Cal from being blows to bits in his airplane all those months ago, and there was no means of getting a message through instantly to Glenn to tell him she was safe. But she could reassure Immy that her young man's family had survived. If they had. But she wasn't going to let herself even think of the alternative.

It wasn't too far to Clifton from Vicarage Street, or at least, it never used to be. Now, Daisy had to pick her way more carefully than usual, because boulders and debris covered the streets that had once been part of Bristol's civic pride. She had thought it blessedly silent earlier on, but people were everywhere now, digging away at collapsed buildings, listening intently for any human cries that might come from the demolished houses, scraping away at the litter-strewn streets in order to make a passageway for buses and ambulances and rescue vehicles.

She could have gone through the street where her father's shop used to be, where Baz had so rebelled against being a shop boy, and where the Caldwell girls had all gone willingly into the family business, until it had been taken away from them by a bigger concern.

But if it hadn't been, then Elsie wouldn't have met Joe, and been the happiest woman alive, by all accounts. And there would have been no Faith. Daisy determinedly kept the thoughts running around in her mind to stop feeling guilty for not going to see how her father was getting on. But she just couldn't bear to see him there, almost certainly helping to clear away the remains of what had once been his own pride and joy and seeing it all reduced to dust. That was too much.

But to her wild relief, the elegant Clifton mansion where the Church family lived was still intact, as were all the others in the area. It was almost bizarre to see parts of the city virtually untouched, when down in the centre there was so much devastation. Not that any of them could escape the rising pall of dust, however high above the city they were.

Now that she had done what Immy had requested, Daisy didn't want to loiter about, and in fact, she had never been inside this house. Helen Church was Immy's friend, and James was now her lover. She wasn't sure how true that was in the biblical sense, but she knew they were very much in love, and it gave her romantic heart a thrill just to think the word.

She became aware that a tall, well-dressed woman had opened the front door of the house, and was looking at her curiously. Daisy blushed, hoping she didn't look too much like a snooper, hovering there, and then the woman smiled.

'From the look of that glorious colour hair, I think you must be one of the Caldwell girls – Imogen's sister, perhaps? Let me guess. Would it be Daisy?'

'Yes, Ma'am,' Daisy practically stuttered, feeling all kinds of an idiot for gawking like this.

But Mrs Church was so beautifully turned out on a Monday morning when so many people were homeless and in rags – it was almost obscene, even though she couldn't help being the way she was. Daisy knew it was totally illogical to be suddenly so full of rage, but she wished she dare say something really cutting, but you didn't, did you? Her father would have been furious with her if she had been so rude as to show her feelings.

'Would you like some tea on this cold morning?' she heard Mrs Church say as she approached her. 'Though I doubt the poor folk in town will be feeling the cold with so many buildings on fire.'

'It's pretty warm down there,' Daisy muttered, wishing she could feel generous to this woman whom she doubted ever went short of coal or anything else. But she was feeling the cold and the reaction to the night's events herself by now, and she gave a sudden shiver, pulling her coat around her more tightly.

Mrs Church continued. 'You only just caught me, in fact. My volunteer helpers and myself are gathering soon to go down to the city to see what help we can give, dispensing tea and distributing warm clothing to those who need it – that kind of thing. But do come inside and warm yourself by the fire for a few minutes, Daisy, and give me news of Imogen.'

Horrified at her earlier thoughts, Daisy felt instant shame, remembering now how Immy had always said in amusement that Mrs Church was very much into 'good works', but for all her money and position as a solicitor's wife, she was a stalwartly good-hearted woman, and Immy was obviously fond of her.

'It's very kind of you,' she croaked.

'Nonsense,' Mrs Church said briskly. 'You look frozen, and I daresay you've been on duty throughout the night too, haven't you? Imogen always says what a brave little soul you are.'

'Good Lord, does she?' She didn't feel like a brave little soul. She felt totally out of her depth as she went inside the house where Immy apparently felt so at ease. She didn't really want to be here, especially when several other ladies turned up, bearing bags of what was presumably second-hand clothing, all determined to do their bit to help those less fortunate than themselves.

'It was a bit of an eye-opener,' she wrote to Glenn that evening. 'There I was, practically bristling with indignation that she was looking so smart when there was so much misery and heartache going on, when all the time she was preparing to do something about it in the only way she could. People are wonderful, aren't they?'

She paused in her letter-writing, chewing the end of her pencil. People *were* wonderful, and maybe it took a war to prove just how resilient and resourceful people could be. Bristol would rise from the ashes like a phoenix and, good Lord, if she wasn't careful she'd be turning into a flipping philosopher next.

Anyway there was only one wonderful person she wanted to think about right now, and that was the one she was writing to. But she didn't just want to be writing to him, Daisy thought with a sudden rush of blood to the head. She wanted him *here*, right now, talking to him, hearing his lovely Canadian accent that thrilled her so much, looking into his dark eyes and seeing the way the little laughter creases at the sides of them made his face light up.

She caught her breath, knowing she was falling headlong in love with him. She had seen him so few times, shared a few dances, invited him into her home, and got Aunt Rose's definite approval. Even so, she had told herself she must go cautiously. Her friend Alice had told her the same, not wanting her to be dazzled by the uniform and the accent and the fact that she knew very well Glenn Fraser was falling for her, too. Anyway, how long did it take to fall in love? A minute or a year made no difference . . . when you met the right one, it took no more than a heartbeat.

Glenn's last letter had been more amorous than previous ones. It thrilled her – and it scared her. Elsie had been the daring one of the family, marrying Joe and not caring what anyone thought, because it was so right for them to be together.

Imogen and James were apparently just as determined not to make things official between them until the war was over, which to Daisy's mind was both noble and crazy. And she was the youngest and scattiest of the Caldwell girls, and not supposed to fall in love until the older sisters had done it first, keeping things in their right order.

'Oh phooey,' she said out loud. 'Who ever decided when it was the right time to fall in love, anyway?'

As Quentin came back to the house in Vicarage Street from his grim and sorrowful perusal of what was once his shop premises, he felt his mouth quirk into a small smile at his youngest daughter's words. He walked into the sitting room where she was sitting at the table, poised over a pad of writing paper, her pencil still stuck between her teeth, dreams in her eyes despite the prosaic words he had overheard.

'So, who's falling in love at the wrong time, Daisy?' he said casually, ridiculously thankful to be saying something so banal, so blissfully ordinary, after the extraordinary and tragic events of the night.

He saw her blush. She was so beautiful, his Daisy. A beautiful fragile butterfly child. He cleared his throat, seeing how discomfited she had become.

'You weren't meant to hear that,' she said, trying to smile.

'I thought perhaps you were referring to me!'

Her heart leapt. 'You?'

He lost his moment of jocularity and his voice became awkward. But now that he'd started, he knew he couldn't leave it there.

'Daisy, you do know I've been seeing rather a lot of Mary, don't you? Mary Yard, I mean. And, well, we've become quite fond of one another.'

God, how did you say these things to a wide-eyed daughter who looked more than the image of her mother at this moment? If she showed disgust or disapproval, it would be as though Frances was chastising him, besides which, Quentin wasn't in the habit of opening his heart to his children. But perhaps it was time.

'Are you going to marry Mary Yard, Daddy?' Daisy said, forestalling him.

'What would be your reaction if I did? Or if I said I was even considering the possibility of marrying someone else – not necessarily Mary.' Unable to look at Daisy, he heard himself floundering like a schoolboy, and the next minute he felt his daughter's arms around him.

'Oh Daddy, did you think any of us would begrudge you a second chance of happiness? None of us would, and neither would Mother, I'm sure. But there's one thing you'd better remember.'

'Oh yes? And what's that?' he said, as she paused, and then he heard the laughter in her voice and saw it in her dancing brown eyes.

'I think you should marry Mary and make an honest woman of her, or I'll have to warn her you're seriously thinking of marrying this "someone else" you just mentioned.'

He visibly relaxed. 'There's no one else, darling. Just Mary.'

'And that just about said it all,' Daisy continued in her letter to Glenn, when her father had gone to try to call Owen Preston. 'He's obviously in love with Mary Yard. And far from feeling affronted that he wants to marry again, I know it's the right thing for him to do. He needs to be married, Glenn, and Mary is a lovely, comfortable kind of woman. A real home-maker.'

She paused again, sure that this was not the only reason that her father would want to marry Mary. But she didn't really want to think about the physical side of it, just that she knew it would *happen*, or else why would anybody get married at all? She didn't yet know the feelings of being intimate with someone herself, but she knew well enough that it was all part and parcel of loving that special person. She had listened often enough to the sad, whispered words of the lonely wounded soldiers who needed to talk, and to open up their hearts to a sympathetic nurse in the darkest hours of the night.

But she wasn't going to write all that to Glenn! She had to tell him about last night's terrible raid, of course, even though she knew much of it would be censored, and she might as well make reasonably light of it all. He would know, anyway. He would read between the lines, just as she did. Which meant that she knew how he felt about her, just as he would know how she felt about him. Some things didn't need to be said.

But she signed off daringly with a row of kisses instead of her usual three, and added 'with my love', which sounded more special than just 'with love'.

The raids continued throughout December and the newspaper headlines screamed that Hitler was evidently trying to wipe Bristol off the map, but it would take more than that to erase their spirits. Easy words, some said grimly, and when even the Bishop's Palace and a children's hospital were destroyed, it was clear that the city would take many months, if not years, of rebuilding.

Even so, people were resilient, salvaging and rebuilding what they could, digging themselves into temporary accommodation and refusing to be moved, although more and more children were being sent away to the country now in a new and urgent wave of evacuation.

Daisy was sent back to Weston General after a few more weeks at Frenchay, and she was more than thankful to be there. Nursing was still her vocation, but there were also the spiritually restoring concerts to be organised before Christmas, and she told her little band of helpers and entertainers that there was no way Adolf was going to spoil the Christmas celebrations completely.

Imogen was getting some leave, and although she was sad that James wasn't due for any, he would be home for a few days in the new year. Helen had to be on duty all over the Christmas period, catering for a new influx of Australian and New Zealand soldiers in her area.

'Not that she'll be worried about that,' Immy told Rose over the telephone. 'Helen will be in her element with all those lovely tanned young men. We've seen quite a number of them in London now, and if I wasn't spoken for, I'd be quite tempted myself,' she added teasingly, knowing this would get her aunt bridling.

'Now then, my girl, that's quite enough of that kind of talk. You're not too old for me to scold you –'

'Oh, Aunt Rose, don't tell me you never felt your heart skip a beat or two when the Americans came to town in the last war!' she went on, laughing.

She heard her aunt give a throaty chuckle. 'Perhaps I did, but that's not for you to know, nor your Uncle Bert neither!'

'Anyway, with luck we can all be together for Christmas Day,' Imogen went on. 'At least, those of us who are still around.' She bit her lip, not meaning to say anything so blatant, and quickly covered it by hurrying on. 'I mean, without Elsie, of course, since I suppose she'll be having Christmas with Joe's family. By the time we see Faith again, she'll probably be walking.'

'You can blame Hitler for that, my love,' Rose said dryly. 'If it hadn't been for the danger of bombing, Elsie would never have left Bristol, but now that the raids have begun in earnest we should all thank heaven that she did.'

'I know,' Immy said, more serious now. 'So do we all come to you for Christmas dinner, Aunt Rose? If you'll have us, that is!'

'Of course. When did I ever turn any of you away? And your father will want as many of his family around him as possible, especially in the circumstances.'

'What circumstances?' Immy said, just as Rose had known she would.

'Oh, well,' her aunt said with all the mock innocence of imparting some secret information, 'he's asked if he can bring a friend here for Christmas Day.'

'A *friend*? What friend?' Immy said at once, just as if her father never had any friends. But he didn't, not really, she thought, he had always been content enough with his large family. Until that family began to dwindle.

'One of the ladies who used to have the upstairs rooms in the house. Mary someone, I believe.'

Immy started to laugh again. 'Oh come on, Aunt Rose, stop being so arch. You know very well her name is Mary Yard. So! It's gone as far as Daddy inviting her for Christmas Day, has it? It must be serious, then.'

'Do you mind?'

'Of course not. As long as he's happy. And he hasn't been really happy for a very long time, has he?'

As she said the words, she recognised the truth of them, and that was something she didn't want to dwell on. She made her goodbyes quickly, before the conversation became too intimate. You didn't discuss your father's personal business with his sister. But how *intriguing*, she thought. Her father and Mary Yard. But remembering the empathy those two had always seemed to share, it was not before time, she supposed. And of course she wanted him to be happy again. They all would. As happy as she and James were going to be one day.

She and James had a whole lifetime of happiness ahead of them. Once this war was over they would be married and start a new life together. A family life, that would be as blissfully contented as her parents' life had been, and as James's parents' lives continued to be. As long as there was always something to look forward to, it wasn't all bad news . . .

*   *   *

Daisy was thinking very much the same thing when the telephone rang that evening, and Glenn's deep Canadian voice came on the line, sending her spirits soaring and her pulses racing.

'How are you, honey?' he said. 'I've been thinking about you a lot lately, and hoping that things have settled down in your part of the country now.'

He meant the air raids, of course, and she tried to speak as nonchalantly as possible, considering the state of her emotions and the jumping of her heart, to say nothing of her damp palms as she clutched the receiver.

'Pretty much,' she said as coolly as she could. 'Or perhaps it's just that we're getting used to it now. Weston's not doing so badly, of course, but we're probably not big business as far as Jerry's concerned!'

She chewed her lip, knowing she shouldn't have mentioned the name of the town at all, even though she'd managed not to say Bristol. Just as if some German spy was listening in on the line, and noting down where she was calling from to report back to Hitler. Just as if the telephone operator who had put the call through to her didn't know it anyway, and might even be a German spy in woman's clothing. Did they have women spies? But why not? Why the dickens not?

Daisy realised her thoughts were leaping about irrationally, because Glenn was on the line. It was awful to let herself act this way. He'd think she was a madwoman at the very least, and a stupid child at worst.

'Daisy, I've got some news,' she heard his delicious voice penetrate her scattered thoughts. 'I've got Christmas leave, and I'd very much like to spend some of it with you.'

She gulped. She positively gulped. Just as all the romantic novelettes told you girls did when someone they loved to distraction said something wonderful.

'That's marvellous,' she squeaked.

She was eighteen years old, and she had just bloody *squeaked*!

'I'll try to book into a hotel for the four days, and hopefully we can spend some time together. I wouldn't want to intrude on your family gatherings, and I know you'll have your family around you at that time.'

But he wouldn't. He would be thousands of miles from home, away from his family and the friends he knew, and spending Christmas in a soulless hotel wasn't on. It just wasn't on.

'Glenn, you'll do no such thing. Please come here and stay with us. My aunt liked you so much, and I know she'll want me to ask you. We have a big house here as you know, and my father's coming to stay with his friend, too, and I'd love you to meet him. Please say you will.'

She paused for breath, knowing she was gabbling, and inviting him without even asking Aunt Rose first. But somehow she knew there would be no objection. There mustn't be – and if Glenn declined, she would just want to die.

'I was so hoping you'd say that, Daisy, and of course I accept gladly, subject to your aunt's approval, of course. I think I should call again tomorrow evening, just to make sure, and perhaps to speak with her.'

'All right, but I know she'll welcome you, Glenn,' Daisy said, her heart singing, just because he would be calling again, and she would be talking to him again, and falling in love with him again.

She heard his low, soft laugh.

'You know what I love about you, Daisy-belle?' he said. 'You bubble over with enthusiasm. You fizz like champagne, and I'm very partial to champagne.'

Daisy, who had never tasted champagne in her life, laughed back, but all she could think about when the call had ended was that he had said those words. Those magic words. The love words.

He hadn't actually said he loved *her*, but it would do for now. It would more than do for now.

Seven

V anessa Brown, now calling herself Vanessa Caldwell, and sometimes even Vanessa Caldwell-Brown for added effect, had absorbed the life of a County School girl far more easily than anyone had expected. She had a quick ear for mimicry, and almost to her own amazement, she decided she wanted to fit in as she had never wanted to before.

So, trying hard to leave behind her old East End habits of sloppy vowels and non-existent consonants, of 'bleedin' this' and 'bleedin' that', she had practised losing her careless speech and was trying to sound a bit more like the Somerset girls she mixed with now. Not that she thought they were any better than she was, Vanessa thought defiantly, but once she had thought up the idea of being one of the Caldwell girls, even if she could never be a real one, she had wanted to be more like them. More like Daisy, really, whom she admired to blazes. Not that she would ever tell her so, of course. And it still didn't stop her arguing with her.

The fearsome old dragon of a headmistress – Miss Farthing, for Gawd's sake – had fixed her with a beady-eyed glare, and been a bit touchy when Aunt Rose had said she wanted to be known as Vanessa Caldwell, despite the name she was born with. But in the end she had agreed to it, because Aunt Rose could be just as uppity as the old trout, she reported gleefully to Daisy. Anyway, knowing her Ma's inclinations, she went on, Gawd alone knew who her real father was. He might just as easily have been called Caldwell as anything else.

Vanessa, at thirteen, looking and acting much older, had

an easy knack of shutting out the things in her life that were no longer necessary. And after only a few weeks at the new school, she had gathered her own little clique around her.

'So your bloke's coming to stay for Christmas, is he?' she asked Daisy, when the news had been circulated. 'P'raps he'll bring one for me as well.'

'One what?' Daisy said, not really paying attention.

'Bloke. A Brylcreem boy. Canadian for preference. You *know.*'

'Good Lord, Vanessa, you're only thirteen years old. You shouldn't be thinking of boyfriends yet.'

'Well, *pardon* me for breathing! And don't lecture me,' she said rudely. 'I know what's what wiv boys. A lot of it went on around Hollis Mews.'

She clamped her lips shut as the words slipped out, wishing she hadn't mentioned the bleeding place. It didn't exist any more. Not since that night when it was all flattened, and her Ma and everybody else in the Mews had gone to Kingdom Come. And so would she have done if she hadn't been squabbling and fighting with some of the kids who hung around the Dog and Drake. She shivered, willing the images away. What she'd been expecting was for her Ma to give her a clip round the ear for staying out late, and instead she'd gone back to a street of stinking rubble and not much else.

'Well, Glenn won't be bringing any of his mates with him,' she heard Daisy saying firmly. 'We'll have a houseful all the same, and we're all going to have a nice Christmas, *aren't* we?'

'Yeah, yeah,' Vanessa muttered. It would be the first one without her Ma, and she remembered that these folk would be having the first one without Baz as well. She had never known him, but he was Daisy's brother, so she supposed they'd all be missing him, too. Anyway, she didn't want to talk about it any longer, nor think about it.

She flounced up to her room and Daisy watched her go with relief. She wasn't at all sure whether she preferred the old stroppy, bad-mouthing Vanessa, to this new one who tried to be something she wasn't. All credit to her for trying, of course, and Aunt Rose certainly welcomed the fact that there were less swear words floating around for Teddy to copy. But all the same, it wasn't entirely natural.

Then she gave up worrying about Vanessa altogether and concentrated on the programme her small band of entertainers was arranging for the Christmas hospital inmates. No matter how many visitors they had at home Daisy would be in the wards each day to help entertain the patients staying in over Christmas. As chief organiser, it was her duty to do so.

Besides, she couldn't be with Glenn every hour of the day and night, much as she wanted to. Well, not every hour of the night, of course, but every waking hour, anyway.

Just for a moment, she imagined what it must be like to wake up in someone's arms. Breathing the air that he breathed, being warmed by his skin, and learning the intimate ways of love.

'Daisy, stop dreaming, and help me get these bedrooms ready,' she heard Aunt Rose order. 'Teddy will have to move in with you while they're all here, so we'll set up the little camp bed for him in your room.'

And if that wasn't certain to put a damper on any vague thoughts of clandestine night-time shenanigans, Daisy didn't know what was!

But apart from having to sleep in Daisy's room, which he felt he was too old to do, Teddy was feeling cheerful, because they were getting a new evacuee right after Christmas, a small boy whose Bedminster home had been bombed out. His name was Harry Laver. He was five years old and had hardly opened his mouth since his family had been killed, according to the overworked billeting officer.

Rose had immediately offered to take him in, while Teddy had begun bragging that this Harry was going to be somebody he could boss about at last, at which he had received a severe telling-off, even from Vanessa, who knew all about being bombed out. But no matter how much he nagged at her to tell him all the gory details, she remained tight-lipped and wouldn't tell the bloodthirsty little rat a single thing.

'Joe's not getting Christmas leave,' Elsie wrote complainingly to Daisy. 'Our first Christmas with Faith, and he won't be able to see her. She's growing so fast now, Daisy, and she's so bright and bonny, and trying to sit up all the time, though Mother Hetty says I shouldn't let her do so without a support behind her back.'

It was obvious to all of them, as Daisy read out Elsie's letter, that Faith was the brightest and cleverest baby in the world, and that Mother Hetty was the original wise woman. She continued reading the letter aloud.

'I do wish I could be at home with you all, but we've all been invited to Owen Preston's house for Christmas dinner, so I'm sure it will be a feast. I'd like to know how he comes by it all, but it's probably best not to enquire. I still don't care for Joe's cousin Robert, and I don't think he cares for me too much, either. But I'm sure I can live with that! Anyway, Daisy darling, kiss everyone for me, give them my love, and save a huge chunk of love for yourself.

'Your loving sister, Elsie. And lots of kisses from Faith.'

'She sounds happy enough, doesn't she?' Daisy remarked. 'It's my guess that she and Joe will settle in Yorkshire when the war's ended.'

'That may well be,' Rose agreed.

'And if the war goes on much longer, Elsie will be well and truly northernised. Did you notice how she called Faith bonny? And I don't suppose Joe will have any reason to come back to Bristol now that the shop's been demolished, will he?'

Bert put in: 'Oh, I don't imagine Owen Preston will be slow in rebuilding another southern branch of his Emporium once things get back to normal.'

'And when he does, Daddy will be manager again,' Daisy

said. 'Unless he decides to stay with the Fire Brigade now that he's joined on a regular basis.'

Everything's changed, she thought, as they all agreed. Nothing ever stayed the same. None of them was the same as they had been before this war began. Especially Aunt Rose, who had become more fulfilled than before with the brood of children in her house that had always been denied her.

Everyone knew that war was a terrible thing, and already there were few families who hadn't lost someone, but you had to be as positive as possible or go under. It might be a trite thing to say, but there was always a glimmer of light at the end of the darkest tunnel. In her case, there was Glenn, because if there hadn't been a war, they would never have met. And now that they had, she couldn't imagine a world without him.

Her heart soared, counting the days until they would be together again. She also realised how little she actually knew him. They had shared one magical evening at a Folkstone dance, when she had warmed to his voice and the feel of his arms around her and known that he was attracted to her, and one afternoon here in Weston when he had come to tea and Aunt Rose had taken to him as instantly as if he had been her long-lost son.

But now there would be four days for them to get to know one another. Four blissful days before the war separated them again and while he was here she was going to tell him what she was planning to do, and hope for his approval. But even if she didn't get it, Daisy thought, with her usual burst of spirit, she was going to do it anyway.

The first of the special Christmas concerts began on Christmas Eve, and the hospital patients responded to the Christmas carols just as the little concert group expected, joining in where there were voices to sing, nodding and smiling where there weren't; some with tears in their eyes, or lumps in their throats, and one or two diehards with the predictable scowling 'humbug' reaction to it all.

The songsters ignored them. It wouldn't be Christmas without the traditional carols, and Bill Watts with his magic and juggling act always restored the air of wonder and laughter to the wards, while Nurse Sims rounded off the evening, banging away on the piano with some rousing choruses for everyone to join in: 'Roll out the barrel' and 'It's a long way to Tipperary', and a final 'Daisy, Daisy', especially for her, their lovely organiser.

By the time Daisy went off duty that evening, she was in high spirits. Not least because when she got back to the house, she knew Glenn would have already arrived. In fact, she didn't have to wait that long. She went out of the warmth of the hospital, shivering in the cold night air, and pulling her cloak more firmly around her. The night was dark, with no moon and only a glimmer of stars in the sky, and she jumped when she felt a hand on her shoulder, wondering if she was going to be accosted.

'Would you be wanting an escort to take you home on this dark night, Ma'am?' she heard a voice say in an accent she recognised at once, and with a little cry of joy she twisted into Glenn's arms, and felt his mouth on hers.

It was a surreal moment, at once wonderful and poignant, because Cal had also waited for her outside the hospital on those first tentative meetings. But Cal was no longer here, and Glenn was; so alive, so dynamic, so *everything* she had ever wanted.

'Oh *Glenn*,' she gasped, feeling as though her heart would burst, and because she simply couldn't think of anything else to say.

He was still holding her tight, and she felt the low rumble of his laughter against her chest.

'Did I startle you, honey? I'm sorry – I didn't mean to. It was just that I couldn't wait another minute to see you, and your aunt assured me it would be all right for me to come and meet you—'

'Oh, of course it's all right! It's more than all right! It's – it's wonderful!'

'Come on then, let's go home, it's freezing out here and I'm looking forward to tasting some more of your aunt's home cooking.'

It wasn't all he was looking forward to, but he didn't want to frighten this delightful girl away. He was crazy for her, but she was so young, so fragile, and like a properly brought-up English girl, he knew she would be chaste, and he loved her for that, too.

'What's that?' Daisy said stupidly, as he led her towards a battered-looking vehicle, nearly as old as her uncle's old Morris.

'I hired it for the four days, Daisy. It took a heck of a lot of persuasion and petrol coupons and it was way over-priced, but I thought it would give us a chance to have a little time on our own – when you're not healing the sick, of course.'

'Good Lord,' was all Daisy could say, because no one she knew had ever gone to all this trouble before, but Canadians were different. Like the Americans, they had *style*. 'What on earth did Aunt Rose say?' she went on, as she slid inside the car and closed the door behind her.

'She thinks I'm a hell of a fellow, don't-you-know?' Glenn teased, with a mock British accent.

And Daisy was instantly aware of how intimate it could be when you closed the car doors and enclosed the two of you inside. The rest of the world didn't exist, and it was at once an exciting and scary feeling. Especially when Glenn reached over and put his arms around her, pulling her close again. Her head automatically rested on his shoulder for a sweet moment.

'You have no idea how much I've longed to be with you like this, Daisy,' he said, his voice husky. 'And I pray that it's the same for you. Is it, sweetheart, or have I been fooling myself all this time?'

'You haven't been fooling yourself,' Daisy whispered, with the dizzy thought that if this was a Hollywood movie, bells would be ringing, music would be soaring, and there would be the sound of angel voices singing.

And then it dawned on her that the sounds she was hearing were nothing so ethereal, but the sound of ambulance bells as the vehicles screamed through the night towards the hospital, and it wouldn't do for a nurse to be seen sitting here in a darkened car, locked in a young man's arms.

'I think we'd better get back to Aunt Rose's,' she said shakily, reluctantly moving out of Glenn's embrace. But not before he had pressed another kiss on her lips, and she had responded just as hungrily.

As they did as she suggested, he gave a mock groan.

'You're right, honey. I was just hoping to prolong these moments with you before I have to face the delights of Anna May Wong again.'

'*What*?' Daisy said with a laugh.

But she didn't have to ask twice. It would be Vanessa, of course, playing the part of the vamp for all she was worth, flashing her eyelashes at Glenn and practising her feminine wiles. At thirteen, for pity's sake!

'Don't worry, Daisy, you're all the woman I want, and she's just a kid, pretending to be grown up.'

'But a very pretty one,' Daisy acknowledged, glad that the night was too dark for him to see her fiery face.

In fact, they could hardly see the street ahead through the obligatory hooded slits of the car headlights, but her heart was singing all the same, just to know that Glenn considered her a woman. And that he wanted her . . .

'My kid sister's the same. They all want to be movie stars at that age,' Glenn went on, and Daisy responded in astonishment.

'Cripes, Glenn, I didn't even know you had a sister, and

I'm forever going on about all of mine! But I don't know much about you at all, do I?'

'Well, that's just why I'm here, so we can get to know one another better. It's a pretty poor state of affairs when my best girl doesn't know about my family, isn't it? And if you don't give me some directions, I swear I shall get lost in this town and we'll end up in the Bristol Channel.'

Daisy laughed, but all she could hear were those magic words 'my best girl'. She hoped she was his *only* girl, of course, but she wasn't daring enough to say so, and she directed him quickly back up the hill to Aunt Rose's house.

'OK. Well, just to put you in the picture – which your Aunt Rose has already ferreted out of me, incidentally,' he said, laughing again, 'I live at home with my parents, my sister Josie, who's going on thirteen, and my kid brother Eldon, who's nine. There was another one between me and Josie, but he died in a climbing accident,' he added briefly.

'That's something we have in common then, isn't it?' Daisy said, thinking of Baz. 'And a big family, too.'

He reached across and squeezed her hand. 'So if you had any doubts that the distance between us is too great, just remember that, sweetheart. People are all the same, wherever they come from.'

The visit was a huge success. Glenn was a hit with everyone, and the house was full to bursting by the time Quentin and Mary Yard arrived early on Christmas morning in time for church. Immy had come from London the night before and Daisy hadn't wasted a moment in sitting on her sister's bed as she unpacked and demanding to know what she thought of Glenn.

'Does it matter what I think of him, darling?' Immy said in amusement. 'It's perfectly obvious you're besotted with him, and that he's the same about you. I'm sure he'll pass muster with Daddy, if that's what you're worrying about!'

'Not really. Aunt Rose thinks he's wonderful, so Daddy

will certainly fall in line,' Daisy grinned. 'Anyway, I daresay he's too busy with his own lady love to bother too much about ours. But I still want to know what *you* think.'

'I think he's charming, and if I was clairvoyant I'd say I can see you as a future lumberjack's wife after the war.'

'Oh, Immy, not all Canadians are lumberjacks!' Daisy screamed with laughter. 'His father owns a huge general store – that's what they call it over there – selling all kinds of things, just like Daddy's old shop. Isn't that odd?'

'Very odd,' Immy grinned, seeing the charm in it for Daisy and not wanting to diminish her delight in the similarity for an instant. 'So is Glenn a general store worker too when he's not flying airplanes?'

'No, and I've only just found that out! He's a lawyer.'

'My goodness!'

'That's what I said. I'm glad he never told me before, because it would probably have scared me stiff. I mean, he must be brainy, mustn't he?'

'And so are you to have hooked him,' Immy teased. 'Now let's go down and see if Nessa's tried to get her own scheming little hooks in him yet.'

They smiled at one another, both out of uniform now, looking more like they did in the old days in their jumpers and skirts, before war came, before people were obliged to do things they would never have dreamed of doing in peacetime.

It strengthened the character though, as Uncle Bert constantly said. It made men out of boys, and proved that girls could do nearly as much, which remark always got Aunt Rose's eyes gleaming as she told him smartly there weren't many things women couldn't do these days – and men still couldn't bear children, could they? This, from a woman who had never done such a thing in her life, but still had the upper hand in knowing that hers was the superior sex in that respect.

It soon became obvious to the Caldwell girls that their

father was more than fond of Mary Yard. She found instant favour with Teddy, who clearly found her less severe than his aunt. She laughed at his jokes and enjoyed playing with George, and when Quentin cleared his throat on Christmas evening and said he had something important to tell them all, no one was in any doubt of what it was going to be. There was going to be a quiet wedding in the new year.

'So, where will you live?' Rose said, once the excitement and congratulations had died down, and George had been banished to another room to stop his frenetic yapping at all the fuss among the humans.

'That's what we wanted to discuss with you girls,' Quentin said, looking somewhere past his daughters.

For a moment Daisy didn't follow, but Immy did.

'I don't see that there's any problem, is there? Vicarage Street is still standing, thankfully, and will continue to do so unless Jerry has other ideas. And providing Mary has no objections –' She paused, and as she did so, Daisy immediately knew why her father was avoiding looking at either of them. It was still her mother's house and when they were married, her father and Mary Yard would be sharing her parents' old bedroom . . . making love.

'We'd change things around a little, of course,' Quentin went on. 'Mary will want to arrange things to her liking, and the flat upstairs will still be kept available for Elsie and Joe, unless we hear otherwise.'

And her parents' old bedroom was in one of the upstairs rooms before they converted it to a flat, Daisy remembered. So, presumably this was her father's way of telling her she needn't think that Frances was going to be usurped in any way.

Her brief moment of resentment passed, and she gave her father a hug, and then did the same to Mary.

'I think it's a marvellous idea, and we'll still be able to come home whenever we want to, won't we?'

'There was never any doubt of that,' Quentin said.

*   *   *

On Boxing Day, Daisy told Glenn there was a time-honoured ritual of taking a walk along the sands or the promenade, along with all the other folk who had eaten too long and too well the previous day. Not nearly so well as in times past, of course, but there were some things that were almost sacrosanct, Hitler or not, war or no war. It was what everyone did, wrapping up in warm clothing and saying hello to the folks they knew, and nodding cheerfully to those they didn't.

'I like rituals,' Glenn said, as the whole family prepared to do as Daisy said.

In the afternoon she would be on duty at the hospital again, so the morning was something special.

'We have them, too, of course,' Glenn went on, 'but it's usually far too cold to venture outdoors for very long at this time of year. But there are compensations. When the mountains and pine woods surrounding our property are all thick with snow, everything is turned into a shimmering fairyland. And then we all snuggle down in front of our wood fires while the older ones tell stories, and the scent is something out of this world.'

'It sounds truly wonderful,' Daisy said, enchanted, and even more so by the way Glenn had tucked her hand in the crook of his arm so naturally.

'It is, and it will be my greatest pleasure to show it to you one day,' he said, in a lowered voice so that the others couldn't overhear. But from the way her arm was pressed closer to his, she couldn't mistake his meaning. Then the sound of an aircraft overhead reminded her of something she'd been dying to tell him.

'Did you know there are decoy cities around this area to deflect the air raids from Bristol now? And should I actually be telling you this?' she added at once.

'Well, since it's pretty obvious that I'm on your side, I don't see why not,' Glenn said easily. 'But you don't sound too pleased about it, Daisy.'

She shrugged. 'I suppose it makes sense in a way. Bristol is an important city with the docks and the aircraft factories, but we also have BAC aircraft factories here, and I don't see why we should be put in danger. Do they think that folk in Weston are of lesser importance than Bristolians?'

'Hey, love, don't get het up about it. I'm sure that's not the case, and these decoys are well out of town, aren't they?'

Daisy conceded that they were. There was plenty of moorland area for mock developments of all kinds to be erected, and it had been a cause of some amusement when the townsfolk realised what was going on. But it wasn't quite so funny on the fourth of January, the night of Weston's first big raid.

By then, the Christmas and new year festivities were over. Glenn had gone back to his unit, and as James was due home on leave now, Immy was staying in Bristol with his family for a few more days.

When the first planes came over, the night shook with the sounds of guns and heavy bombardment. Daisy was at the hospital on night shift, and Rose ushered her small charges quickly down to the cellar. The noise was thankfully somewhat muted from there, but even so, Vanessa huddled beneath her blankets, and Teddy hugged George almost to death beneath his.

Heavy rain had been falling to add to the gloom of getting back to normality after Christmas, and Bert came home from his night watch on the morning of the fifth, full of importance, to announce to the family that orders had come to ignite the 'Starfish' decoy site at Uphill southwest fields, built to simulate a burning airfield.

'It was a real carve-up at first,' he told Rose. 'The rain meant that the switches wouldn't ignite the target, so one of our airman chaps crawled along the wet ditches with petrol, setting light to the dummy hangars. It was a pretty dangerous job, and bombs were falling all around him by then.'

'I know. We heard them,' Rose said grimly. Having spent the night with the frightened children in the cellar she had been more than glad to get out of there. 'Was he hurt?'

'Oh no, he got away with it all right, but you should see the mess the Jerries left. Dozens of craters and more than a thousand incendiary fires, they reckon. At least it proved the usefulness of the decoys.'

Rose shivered. 'Well, let's hope they continue to be effective. This always used to be a peaceful town, and God willing, it will continue to be that way.'

But they both knew it was an unlikely hope.

Eight

Quentin and Mary were married quietly at the end of January, each professing that they didn't need a honeymoon at their age, but taking a few days off to go up to Yorkshire to visit Elsie, and for Quentin to speak to Owen Preston personally about the fate of his shop.

'The war looks bad, lad,' Owen Preston said seriously, once the obligatory congratulations were over, and Mary had been left happily cooing over Faith at the farm with Elsie, and Joe's parents.

'It does that,' Quentin said, wondering if he had any idea how devastating it had been for Bristol these last few months. The newspapers showed what they dared, considering the dangers of propaganda and letting the Germans know too much about the success of their raids.

Though what good such hush-hush measures were made no sense at all to Quentin, since anyone with a camera could take photos of the devastation and smuggle them to Germany. The wireless announcers too, were solemn and cagey to the point of lunacy, in his opinion. People had a right to know what was going on, though if that young toe-rag Morgan somebody or other was a sample of their ferreting ways, snapping at their heels when they were doing a dangerous job at work, it was no wonder few people gave anything away. Vultures, the lot of them.

'Another glass of beer?' Owen was saying now, and Quentin tried to relax with the Yorkshireman's hospitality.

It was good to get away from it all, especially under the

circumstances. He was a newly-married man with a lovely wife who was totally in tune with his needs, and the fact could still take him by surprise at times. They weren't young lovers in the first flush of passion, and comfort and companionship was all a part of marriage, but passion didn't have to end when you reached middle-age, as he was discovering to his delight.

'Aye, it's a rum do and no mistake,' Owen went on heavily, having no idea where Quentin's thoughts were wandering. 'But we'll beat the bastards in the end, never fear. We've a bloody fine air-force, and they say this war will mostly be fought in the air, don't they?'

'Has to be, with all the new machines being built now, and Hitler's bomb factories at full stretch.'

'And ours, too,' Owen said vindictively.

'And ours, too,' Quentin said, with less relish than the other man.

Owen glanced at him, eyes narrowed. His cigar blew wreaths of blue smoke across the well-furnished room. There was nothing austere in the Preston household. Fancies himself as Winston Churchill, Elsie said with a giggle.

'You don't approve, lad?'

Quentin felt his shoulders tense. 'When you've stayed out all night on firefighting duties until your body's aching with fatigue but you daren't give in to in case there's one more person alive beneath the rubble, and you've seen at first hand the pain and horror that these murderous bombs bring, then no, I don't approve. And I don't know how any God-fearing man can.'

After a small pause, Owen spoke more crisply.

'Well, that's put me in my place then, hasn't it?'

'Christ, man, it's nothing personal,' Quentin said, remembering that he was a guest, and had just insulted his host. He took a long drink of beer and felt his hands tremble. Some memories were hard to forget, and this man knew none of it.

Owen laughed softly. 'It's all right, lad, don't fret yourself.

We've all got our opinions, and I'm sure yours is the more noble one. The point is, we've got to fight back, haven't we? You wouldn't have us lie down, bellies up, and let the bloody Huns walk all over us, would you? That's not being British, is it?'

'You're right, and of course we have to fight back. I just hate the thought of all this slaughter.'

'We all do. But you should forget it while you're here, Quent. Don't want your blushing bride to think she's not getting full value for money, do you?'

He gave a sly wink, and Quentin laughed agreeably, while disliking the man's innuendo. He quickly changed the subject to that of Owen's future plans now that his Bristol shop no longer existed.

'No plans at all,' he was told. 'Not much point at present, is there, lad? We'll just have to wait until this bloody war is over and then see what's to do. I'll tell you one thing, though. Hitler might be a bloody dictator in his own country, but he ain't bloody well dictating to me where I open my shops.'

Quentin related it all to his womenfolk when he got back to the farm, suitably deleting the cuss words for the ladies' benefit, and making more of a joke of it.

Mary was comfortably tolerant of the man, even though she didn't care for his brash manner, and Elsie's eyes twinkled, guessing full well that her father was leaving out more than he told.

'Oh, I'm quite sure he'll want to re-open a shop in the south in due course,' Joe's father put in, coming in from the fields with the whiff of the farmyard clinging to him, and in time to get the gist of the conversation. 'Our Owen would never let anything beat him, and especially not some goose-stepping Jerry.'

They smiled dutifully, but everyone knew that mocking Hitler was no more than a safety-valve. It didn't take away the uneasy fear that he was winning.

Mary snuggled into her husband's back in bed that night, listening to the creaking sounds of the old farmhouse, the occasional grunt from an animal outside, the settling down of a rural community.

'It's so peaceful here, Quentin. No wonder Elsie's so content to stay. Life goes on at a slower pace and you could almost forget there was a war on.'

'Except that we can never forget it can we, my love? It's always with us, especially if we've lost somebody.'

He was thinking of Baz, not Frances, and she understood at once. Her arms tightened around him.

'I know, love, but we mustn't forget that we're fighting for a safer world, too, aren't we?' She almost said a safer world for our children, and stopped herself in time. It wouldn't be what Quentin wanted to hear right now.

She had known in her heart that this meeting with Owen Preston would bring out the aggressor in him. She knew all about his suffering on account of his beloved first wife. She had been widowed long ago, and she knew the pain and the heartache. Quentin wasn't given to flowery speeches, he was a deep thinker, but basically a gentle man, and he didn't bare his feelings lightly. She also knew that some of the sights he saw when he was fighting fires and saving lives must truly turn his stomach. He had borne so much of it alone, but now they had each other, and all she could do was to be there when he needed her.

He turned around in the big old-fashioned bed so that she was in his arms, hearing his more regular breathing, feeling the rhythm of his heart against hers, and she sensed that the moments of self-doubt had passed.

'You're very good for me, Mrs Caldwell. In fact, I don't know how I managed to live without you until now.'

'Well, you don't have to manage without me ever again,' Mary said with a soft smile in the darkness as his arms reached for her more urgently.

*   *   *

Daisy had made up her mind, and this time nothing was going to change it. She was going to join up. She fully expected that with her training she would be put into a medical unit, and that was fair enough. But wherever she went, she was also very firmly going to offer herself as an entertainer.

According to Glenn, and everybody else, they didn't take much notice of personal wishes. Glenn told her she would probably end up doing something completely different – probably cleaning out the latrines in the officers' mess, or something equally soul-destroying. The army did that, having no sensitivity for what you were good at.

Daisy grinned, remembering. Knowing he was teasing, describing the worst scenario he could think of, but for all that, she knew she had his full approval. And that mattered more to her than anyone else's. In fact, she hadn't told anyone in the family of her decision. Only Alice knew it, and reluctantly approved, knowing how much she would miss her. And Sister Mackintosh, who hadn't been such a bad old stick, Daisy acknowledged, had to be told as well.

'Well, if you're sure, Nurse Caldwell, then of course we'll have no option but to release you. I'll be happy to give you a good report for anyone who may need to see it, and the patients will certainly miss you.'

Which was her way of saying the nursing staff would miss her, too. Daisy knew it, and she wasn't daft enough to know that she wouldn't miss them, too. But something deep inside her told her she had to do this. If she didn't, she would always regret it. And she knew her mother would have approved.

'Bringing sunshine to peoples' lives' was how some of the old posters had described Frances Caldwell's stage performances, and if Daisy could emulate her, creating that feeling in audiences in the tiniest way, then she would feel fulfilled.

And since those audiences would be in uniform, far from home and their loved ones, it would be a job well done. No matter what the family thought. Though she was sure her father wouldn't object. She had already had his unspoken agreement, and Aunt Rose would surely see that this was her destiny.

Such noble and ethereal thoughts vanished in a moment when she finally discussed it with Aunt Rose and Uncle Bert, ignoring Vanessa and Teddy who were currently squabbling over who had the biggest portion of peas on their plates. Daisy's mind had been on higher things than such trifles, but she was brought up short when Vanessa forgot about counting her peas and started shrieking with laughter.

'You're going to sing to the troops? Wiv a voice like yours?'

'What's wrong with my voice?' Daisy snapped.

'It ain't loud enough, that's what,' Vanessa said rudely. 'I went wiv my mum to a munitions factory concert once, and the singer had to bellow to be heard above the noise of them machines, and the cheering and cat-calling. 'Orrible, it was, until the comic came on and started telling jokes like Max Miller.'

'Good heavens, I hope your mother didn't let you listen to any of that!' Rose said severely.

Vanessa shrugged. 'Me mum always said the more you knew about fings – things – the less you'd be shocked by 'em.'

'I'm not likely to be singing in a munitions factory,' Daisy said, seething at the way this girl could always manage to belittle things.

Rose agreed. 'Of course she isn't. You do say some silly things sometimes, Vanessa, and you really don't know anything about this.'

'Anyway, Daisy's got a very sweet voice,' Bert put in loyally.

'Well, that's just what I mean! I ain't saying she don't sing nice, because she does, but she ain't powerful enough to sing to a crowd of soldiers, is she?'

'Excuse *me*,' Daisy said. 'I *am* here, and when you've all finished discussing my future and whether or not I'm capable of being heard in a roomful of soldiers, I shall still decide for myself!'

Vanessa couldn't resist a parting shot. 'It won't just be a roomful, though, will it? That's just what I'm sayin'! You'll prob'ly be sent overseas and have to sing to troops out in the open, like they show in the pictures when Vera Lynn and real stars like that go and sing to the troops. There are *thousands* of 'em there then, wiv airplanes flyin' overhead, and guns roarin', and prob'ly bombs falling all around 'em as well, and how're you going to sing above all that?'

'Haven't you ever heard of microphones?' Daisy said, getting more rattled by the minute with this irritating girl who never knew when to leave things alone.

'Is our Daisy going to get killed, then?' Teddy said.

They all looked at him, realising he had stopped eating his supper, and was looking from one to another of them with fear in his eyes.

'Now look what you've done,' Rose snapped, glaring at Vanessa. 'Of course Daisy's not going to get killed, Teddy. Whoever heard of entertainers getting killed? They don't have guns, and they don't go off fighting Germans. They stand on a stage and do their singing and acting and telling their funny stories to make people laugh, and at the end of the show people clap them because they've enjoyed hearing them so much.'

'*If* they can hear them—'

'Vanessa, that's quite enough. If you've finished your supper, go and do your homework, and Teddy can help me with the washing-up.' Anything to get the little madam away from him.

All the same, it started Daisy thinking. Maddening though it was, she knew the wretched girl had a point. She had a sharp brain all right, which was how she had passed her late scholarship exam with flying colours, and was now entrenched at the County School with an adoring little gang of her own.

But she was right in one respect. Daisy did have a sweet

102

voice, but it wasn't strong or powerful enough to cope with a huge audience like the one Vanessa had described, and which was sometimes shown so graphically on the Pathe News at the picture-house. They all knew such shows were put on to cheer up the troops and to boost their morale, and the news items were shown to boost the morale of the folks back home, but the sight of those vast audiences, made up of battle-hardened servicemen, were enough to make the most experienced artistes quail.

And Daisy wasn't experienced at all, except in a hospital ward with a couple of dozen attentive patients at most.

'Am I fooling myself?' she asked Alice Godfrey gloomily when they were taking a break from ward duties the next day. 'Is it all a pipe dream, and should I give it all up and decide to stay put?'

'Is that what you want?'

'You know it isn't! But I know I'm not star material either, and I've been thinking about that, too. Though perhaps I could join up with say, several other girl singers, and we could form a singing group. You know what they say. Togetherness means strength – or something like that.'

It hadn't actually occurred to her before, but she felt a small tug of excitement when it did. The only thing was, you first had to find the other members of a possible girls' singing group. She didn't have the faintest idea how to go about it, but what she did have was organisational skills. Sister Mackintosh had told her so.

'Sounds good to me,' Alice said.

'Well, it probably won't come off, but if it does, maybe I'll have something to thank our straight-talking Vanessa for after all, for putting the idea in my head that I don't have what it takes, as they say in the movies.'

But she damn well did, and she knew it.

The recruiting officer looked at her in amusement. It wasn't the same one she'd seen a year ago, when he'd put her off so thoroughly, looking her up and down, noting her glowing, eager face and wild red curls, and obviously thinking she had ambitions of being a Shirley Temple in uniform. This one was more impressed by her calm, clear way of expressing herself. He reminded Daisy of her father.

'With your experience, the obvious place for you would be a medical unit in the ATS, Miss Caldwell.'

'I realise that, and I'm sure my nursing skills would be an asset, but I have other skills too.' She ignored his lifted eyebrow. 'I've organised concerts at the hospital here, and I'm told I do a lot to raise the morale of the patients. I would very much like the chance to do the same in any entertainments opening.'

'Like ENSA, you mean?'

'Yes, I suppose I do.'

'So what you're really telling me is that you want to go on the stage,' the man said, and then relented as he saw her face, angry and embarrassed.

'I'm sorry, my dear, I can see you're serious about this.'

'Of course I am!' Daisy said huffily. 'And if you think I'm afraid of seeing enemy action, I've already seen plenty at Dunkirk when I worked on the hospital ships. I'm not afraid of being in the front line, sir.'

'That would hardly be likely if you were to join a troupe of forces entertainers,' he said.

Her heart leapt. 'Then such things do exist? I was beginning to think I was here on a fool's errand, though even if they didn't, I would still want to enlist. It's what I'm here for,' she added simply, 'and I have the full approval of my superior at the hospital. Perhaps you would care to see her letter of recommendation.'

He still looked slightly amused, and Daisy supposed it was hardly the normal thing for a prospective recruit to bring such a letter from a hospital Sister. It wasn't really intended for him, anyway. It was for the Commanding Officer of wherever she was sent.

When he had scanned the document, he looked up.

'I should like to take a copy of this, if you wouldn't mind, Miss Caldwell.'

'Well, I suppose that's all right,' she said dubiously.

'I assure you that it is. If you want to do the sort of entertaining you tell me you do, that is.'

He was suddenly dazzled by the brilliance of her smile. Good God, he was thinking, if she could sing as prettily as she looked, she was going to break a few hearts before she was done. He cleared his throat, resuming his official manner. He told her to wait there while he copied Sister Mackintosh's letter, then handed the original back to her. She signed the necessary enlistment forms he pushed towards her, and looked at him enquiringly.

'Now you just have to wait until the army sends for you,' he told her. 'It could be days or weeks, though it may well be sooner rather than later. And I hope you get what you want, Miss Caldwell.'

'Thank you, sir. So do I,' she said, and stumbled out into the grey January day, with a strange mixture of hope and let-down.

'Well, you didn't expect them to whisk you off into uniform the minute you announced yourself, did you?' Alice asked her.

'I thought they'd be glad of volunteers!'

'Yes, but they have to go through the correct procedure, don't they? Especially with someone who tells them exactly what she wants to do. You might easily end up in the catering corps. Have you thought of that?'

'No I won't,' Daisy said crossly. 'Anyway, my sister's friend is in that, and having a whale of time with all the Anzac troops, apparently. With my nursing background it's highly likely I'll end up in a medical unit and find myself entertaining my fellow nurses on our time off.'

'And the patients.'

'Oh yes. And the patients, of course.'

For a moment, she'd forgotten all about them. How awful!

'You'll probably be sent to France. The Jerries haven't overrun all of it yet, and our chaps are still being sent there, and they're bound to want medical staff. You might meet some dashing Froggie and have a passionate love affair with him, and all your children will be tadpoles with French accents, and you'll all eat snails for breakfast, ugh!' she finished wildly as Daisy started giggling at the ridiculousness of it all.

'I won't fall in love with anyone, because I'm already in love with Glenn. And I don't care where they send me, because when the war is over, I'm going to marry him and go to Canada and live happily ever after.'

She stopped as quickly as she had begun, looking round-eyed at Alice.

'Did I really just say that? About marrying Glenn and going to Canada to live, I mean?'

'You did. So did you mean it? And has he asked you? And would you really go halfway across the world to live?'

'Which question do you want answered first?'

'All of them.'

'Then yes, I meant it. No, he hasn't asked me. And if he did,' she paused, 'then of course I'd go, because I couldn't imagining living anywhere without him.'

'Cripes, Daisy, you've really got it bad, haven't you?' Alice said. 'Your Aunt Rose isn't going to like it.'

'Aunt Rose isn't going to marry him. Anyway, she's not my whole family, is she? Daddy's got his new wife now, Elsie's settled with Joe and Faith, and Immy will definitely marry James Church once the war's over. Teddy will be happy enough as long as he's got George and somebody to fuss over him, so what's to stop me?'

The hideous thought that Hitler could do something about that flashed into her head and out again before she would give it credence. She had already lost one young man in a terrible flying accident, and she had no intention of losing another one, thank you very much, she thought fiercely.

'You're pretty brave, aren't you, Daisy? Nothing ever scares you, does it?'

'Don't be daft. I'm not brave at all.'

'No? What about Dunkirk?'

'What about it? I didn't do any more than everyone else – you included – so if we're handing out putty medals, I reckon we both deserve one.'

And of course things scared her. It scared her to think she would be going into the unknown, even while it exhilarated her. It scared her every time she heard the monotonous wail of the air-raid siren. It scared her whenever she thought how Glenn was flying into danger every time his airplane took to the sky. It scared her every time she thought about what tomorrow might bring . . .

What tomorrow actually brought to the house, on the first day of February, to be exact, was the small shape of Harry Laver.

The billeting officer delivered him safely into Rose's care during the afternoon, while Daisy was at the hospital, and Vanessa and Teddy were at school.

George loved children. He went wild and slobbering at once, barking joyously when he espied Harry's thin frame with his gas mask case slung around his shoulders. With the result that the boy clung to Miss Phipps with a whimper, and a tell-tale dark stain gradually became evident at the front of his short grey flannel trousers.

'Oh dear,' Miss Phipps said briskly. 'I'm so sorry, Mrs Painter. Just one of our little troubles, I'm afraid, ever since his family – you know –' she mouthed above the boy's head. 'I just didn't expect it to happen so soon,' she added, with a glare at the excited dog.

'It doesn't matter,' Rose said at once, her heart going out to the wide-eyed child with the trembling mouth. 'We'll soon have him cleaned up, and George will be sent into the garden where he belongs. Shall we go and find the room where you're going to sleep, Harry?'

For a moment she thought he wasn't going to relinquish his terrified hold on the other woman's arm.

'Remember your manners and say yes to Mrs Painter, Harry,' the woman said, mouthing again to Rose that he didn't speak much, if at all, ever since.

Rose knelt down to his level and smiled into his eyes, and told him he could call her Auntie Rose if it made him feel better. After a minute he nodded slowly, and put his clammy hand in hers.

'We'll be all right now,' Rose said firmly to Miss Phipps, wondering just where they got these people. They did sterling work with the evacuee children, but compassion was certainly lacking in this one.

She took the boy and his bag of belongings, which seemed pathetically light, up to the room he was going to share with Teddy, and showed him his bed. As predicted, he said nothing, just stared.

He was so small and surely undersized for his age, and Rose longed for the days when she could have fed him up and made him as robust as Teddy. Rationing made such things far less possible nowadays, but none of them actually starved, and they still had their reliable chickens in the back garden.

'Would you like a special egg for your supper tonight?' she asked Harry, when the boy said nothing at all, but still stared at the bed that was to be his.

He shook his head dumbly, and she tried again.

'How about sausage and mash then?'

He lifted his shoulders slightly, which Rose presumed meant yes, and she knew she was going to have her work cut out with this one. It didn't defeat her. If anything, it challenged her, and she put her arm around him, feeling how the bones stuck out from his thin jacket.

'Let's get you out of those damp trousers and into some

tidy ones, shall we, love?' she said gently. 'Do you have another pair in your bag?'

He shook his head, and when she investigated Rose saw to her horror how pitifully few things he had brought. How few he probably *had*, she amended, since his home had been gutted, along with everything in it. It was a miracle they had found him crawling about in the wreckage, terrified, all his clothes blown off his little body and crying for his mother. If she hadn't instructed him to stay inside the coal cellar until the raid was over, he would never have survived. As it was, he had been the only one left of his family.

'Never mind, we'll find you a pair of Teddy's,' she told him brightly.

Harry was sitting glumly on the sofa in the sitting room when Vanessa came home from school in her usual whirlwind fashion, flinging her satchel on the floor and shouting out the news that she was going to be in the school hockey team because she could bully off faster and harder than anyone else in her class. She only stopped for breath when she caught sight of the boy, who was busily trying to make himself as invisible as possible.

'Blimey, who's this kid?' she said at once. 'Are you the latest?'

Harry flinched and tears began sliding down his cheeks. A minute later, Bert came home with Teddy, chattering excitedly about the planes he and his friends had spotted that afternoon flying out of Locking Airport and over their school on their way to bomb the Jerries. At which, Harry simply grabbed one of the fat cushions on the sofa and burrowed himself into it.

'Oh good Gawd, I suppose it's going to be waterworks all the way now,' Vanessa complained. 'I thought we'd done wiv all that when the other ones left.'

Nine

B eing a domestic peacemaker wasn't Daisy's ideal occupation, and she quickly decided to keep well out of it when it became evident that Teddy and Harry just weren't going to get on. Added to that the constant jeering of Vanessa as she tried to coax the new arrival into talking, grumbling, swearing, *anything* – which only made Harry clam up more.

'Stubborn little cuss,' Vanessa raged. 'I bet he talks enough when he goes to school. I bet his teachers don't stand for any of his nonsense!'

'He don't say much there either, and the teachers told us we have to be nice to him because of losing his house and all that,' Teddy said, scowling at the memory. 'He's teacher's pet now.'

'Well, I lost *my* house, but it don't stop me talking!' Vanessa said.

Teddy chewed over that statement for a moment and then went on grumbling. 'Well, anyway, he don't say anything 'cept when he has to, and at play times he just stands in the corner and won't join in our games.'

'You shouldn't bovver wiv him then. Let him stew in his own juice, like I'm going to from now on.'

She tossed her hair and stalked upstairs to do her homework. Having never had much of a disciplined existence before, with her wayward mother and frequently disappearing father, Vanessa was actually revelling in the strict discipline of the County School.

She *liked* having homework to do, and she *liked* being able to write neatly and being so clever at essays and getting good marks and approval from the teachers. She liked wearing the new uniform that Aunt Rose had got for her from the charitable ladies' groups who helped out with such things for the evacuee children, and she didn't care if it was second-hand or not. She had worn plenty of cast-offs in her time. And anyway, wearing a uniform meant that nobody was better than anybody else, which suited Vanessa just fine.

If the truth was told, she was still a bit scared of the mistresses (you didn't call them anything so common as teachers at the County School) as they swanned about the corridors with their black gowns flapping about like bleeding crows. Not that she would ever admit to being scared, of course. Not bleeding likely.

Daisy's orders didn't come as quickly as she had hoped. Now that she had made her decision and her family were prepared for it, she was anxious to join up. Until she did, the waiting made it all seem like an anti-climax, especially when a few of the long-term patients started asking when she was getting her marching orders.

But it wasn't until the end of July, when her nineteenth birthday had come and gone, that the long, official-looking envelope arrived, informing her that she was to join an ATS training unit near Chichester, called Flayton Camp. A rail warrant was included, which made the whole thing seem real at last. She and Vanessa pored over the map until they found the place, inland from the Sussex coast. But right in the thick of it, if the Jerries' bombardment of the south-east was anything to go by. And a long way from Weston.

Aunt Rose snorted. 'By the time you've been sent heaven knows where, my girl, you'll be thinking that Chichester's just around the corner.'

'Do you think I'll be sent abroad then? Attached to a medical unit?'

'It depends. If they wanted you to continue nursing, you might as well have stayed at Weston General. So perhaps they've taken your request into account.'

'And pigs might fly!' Vanessa put in scornfully. 'Nah, they only want girls to be skivvies. That's what my mum used to say about girls in army uniforms, anyway. Only good for the washin' and cleanin', and a coupla other things that I'd better not mention,' she added, catching Rose's freezing look.

'There's just one thing, Aunt Rose,' Daisy said with a sudden catch in her throat. 'I don't want any big send-off. No party or anything like that. I just want to leave as if it's an ordinary day. All right?'

'As if I was thinking of any such thing!'

But Daisy knew she might have been, and she didn't want that. She was doing no more than thousands of other men and women, and she didn't want any fuss. In any case, Vanessa and the boys would have gone to school by the time Uncle Bert took her to the station to catch the morning train.

It was going to be a tedious journey, with several platform changes, and she didn't exactly look forward to being crammed in among all those hot bodies. Trains were always crowded these days, and they were horrid, airless things, especially now the summer was here. But excitement overtook her nerves, and she reminded herself how much she wanted this. The hospital patients and staff had given her little gifts, and there was some special make-up from Alice.

'Nice and bright, to wow them with when you're on stage,' Alice had told her with suspiciously bright eyes.

If she was on stage . . .

That last morning was hard, as both Rose and Bert hugged her tightly as the train steamed into the station, and there were tears all round as they said goodbye. She knew they would miss her as much as she would miss them. It was a bit like going into the unknown, and although it could hardly be called an adventure, she tried to look on it that way as she waved out of the train window until the train curved around the bend, and she could no longer see them for the steam and smoke, and the smuts from the engine that were stinging her eyes.

'First time away from home, love?' a sympathetic middle-aged woman carrying a voluminous knitting bag asked her.

'Not really,' Daisy said. 'Just that I'm not sure when I'll be back.'

She felt stupid saying it, but she didn't want to confide her feelings to a stranger, nor where she was going. Even though she supposed it wasn't really hush-hush . . . and with the words that always made her feel a bit like Mata Hari herself, she felt herself start to relax.

The train swiftly gathered momentum, rattling along through the green fields on its way to Bristol where she had to change trains at Temple Meads station. For a moment of sheer childish nostalgia, Daisy longed to be going straight out of the station, running home to Vicarage Street and into her father's arms. And her mother's.

'Made an unholy mess of it here, ain't they?' the woman with the knitting bag went on conversationally as she waited on the platform beside Daisy for their connection. 'They say most of the city's been blasted out of existence. Poor devils never knew what hit 'em in some places.'

'Excuse me,' Daisy said in a strangled voice, her heart thumping. 'I think I've seen someone I know.'

She hadn't, but anything was better than hearing the woman's insensitive remarks about a city that she loved. A city that was home . . .

'Hold on there, girlie,' she heard a male voice say loudly. Someone whose kitbag was solid and heavy by his feet, and which Daisy had just crashed straight into. She gave a small yelp as she felt the stinging pain in her toes, and the thought flashed through her mind that a fine recruit she was going to look if she went limping into camp on her very first day!

'Are you all right?' the owner of the voice went on, his

arms still holding her upright. 'Blimey, you nearly went down a purler then, didn't you?'

'I'm fine, thank you very much,' Daisy gasped, trying to hold on to her dignity. Several other passengers glanced her way in amusement as she tried to grab her hat with one hand and keep hold of her suitcase and gas mask with the other, and then lost interest as the small collision passed without further incident.

'I see we're going to the same place,' the man said cheerily, noting her luggage label. 'Goin' to join the ladies, are you?'

Daisy stared at him, seeing him properly now. He wore a private's uniform, and he looked a few years her senior. His fair hair was cropped regulation short, and he had an ungainly set of teeth when he smiled. In no way could he be called handsome, in fact, if she was honest, he was downright ugly. And should she be telling him where she was going and why? He grinned again when she didn't answer.

'Sam Spencer's the name, love, and 'sall right, I'm not one of Jerry's spies.'

'Well, I don't know that, do I?' Daisy finally said. 'You might be! And I'm Daisy Caldwell,' she added reluctantly.

He chuckled. 'You tell that to my old woman then. 'Ere she is, mother-in-law and all. What a ruddy send-off. Anyone would think I wasn't coming back!'

Daisy caught sight of the two bustling women toiling down the platform with a screeching pair of small boys in tow. They hadn't been sent off to the country then. Sam Spencer's wife glared at him.

'Didn't take you long to find the prettiest girl on the platform, did it, Sam Spencer? No offence, Miss, but you want to watch out for this rogue if you're travelling with 'im!'

'Thank you for the advice, Mrs Spencer,' Daisy said faintly.

'Now then, old girl,' Sam said. 'You know I've got eyes

for no one but you. But I never say no to a bit o' company on the train.'

Right on cue, the train came chugging into the platform and the mother-in-law gave Sam a peck on the cheek and rushed the boys outside before they could start wailing any louder. It occurred to Daisy that most people had someone seeing them off. Well, so had she, in Weston, but now she felt oddly alone as people started to hug and kiss one another, unconcerned about showing their feelings in public, all enveloped in steam as if in some surreal scene from the movies. Except that this wasn't play-acting. This was real, and for the first time she realised just what she was doing.

But then there was no time for thinking as the carriage doors were opened and the crowds on the platform surged forward. Sam Spencer bundled her inside a compartment in front of him, followed by a group of khaki-clad chaps like himself. Sam sat next to her, after throwing his kitbag on to the rack above, and hauling Daisy's case up beside it. A good thing there was nothing breakable in it, she couldn't help thinking, because it would be in a thousand pieces by now.

But Private Spencer was clearly seeing himself as a kind of guardian angel now, as if she was a helpless female needing a big strong male to look after her. First time away from home and all that, and as she thought it, her small burst of nerves vanished. She'd been to Dunkirk and back a few times, hadn't she? She wasn't a twittering little female any more, if she had ever been.

The compartment filled up, and several of the other soldiers knew Sam, all home on embarkation leave, and headed for the desert. They didn't know *which* desert, of course, they joked. It might be the Sahara or it might be the Painted Desert – which they explained to Daisy was in America – or even the Australian desert, diggers! All of which were just as unlikely, and in any case they wouldn't know until they got their marching orders. All they knew was that they had been kitted out with hot weather gear, so they reckoned it was a fair guess.

'It sounds interesting, anyway,' Daisy said.

'Oh yeah. All that sand and no buckets and spades,' one of them sniggered. 'So what's your story, little lady?'

'I'm a nurse.'

'Well nursie, I've got this sudden pain in my leg,' he teased at once.

'Hard luck,' Daisy said, starting to enjoy herself, and thinking that in the old days, the days before war came, people wouldn't have dreamed of starting up such free and easy conversations with strangers. 'I'm getting away from all that, at least I hope so. It depends what the army has in store for me.'

'They always want nurses, Daisy,' Sam said. 'But you look too young to have had much nursing experience. And any other kind, come to that,' he added with one of his cheeky winks.

'I've worked at Weston General for quite a while, and I was at the burns unit at Frenchay before Christmas. I also did a spell on the hospital ships going back and forth to Dunkirk, so I guess you could call that a bit of experience,' she said casually, and heard his low whistle.

'My brother copped it on that lot,' one of the men said in a matter-of-fact voice. 'Cut us all up for a bit, but you have to get on with it, don't you?'

'My brother copped it, too,' Daisy said, using his words, and finding it easier than she thought to mention Baz in that way. If they could do it, so could she.

'Bad luck,' said one of the others. 'So what are you going to be doing in the skirt camp? We know it's a training centre for various branches of the ATS, but they don't have a medical unit there as far as I know.'

Ignoring the female reference, Daisy gave him a dazzling smile. This was news to her. But also the best of news, and she refused to feel guilty about it.

'What do they have then?' she countered, caution preventing her saying that she was going to be an entertainer. Maybe.

They were all beefy chaps, and she had no wish to be goaded into giving them a song. If she knew anything about servicemen – which wasn't much – she guessed that one of them would probably produce a mouth organ quicker than blinking, and she'd be expected to entertain them for the rest of the journey.

Sam shrugged. 'God knows, begging your pardon, love. They don't let on to us male mortals what goes on behind their barbed wire. Keeping us out of temptation, I reckon,' he grinned. 'It'll be the usual womens' stuff anyway, catering or clerical stuff, issuing pay slips, travel warrants, weekend passes, that kind of thing. Are you any good at typing and figures?'

Daisy managed to overlook the insulting inference that women were only good for doing cooking and clerical work. 'I've done some shop work. My father owned a shop in Bristol and we all worked in it – except my mother, of course.'

'Oh yeah? What shop was that then?' he said.

One or two of them were listening to the conversation now, but the others had got bored, bringing out a pack of cards and forming a small huddle of their own at the other end of the compartment.

'Caldwell's Supplies – at least it *was*,' she said, her composure slipping for the briefest moment, remembering how it had been all those years ago when her mother was alive and the shop had been a thriving concern.

'That big place up on Whiteladies?' Sam Spencer said.

Daisy nodded. 'That's right. It was taken over by Preston's Emporium a couple of years ago,' she went on deliberately, 'but my father is still the manager.'

'*Was*, you mean, don't you, love? That part of town got flattened during the big night-time raids, didn't it? I hope your old man was all right. They said no one was in the place at the time.'

She nodded, wishing he would stop talking. She wished they all would. She didn't want to give details. All the

117

newspapers told you it was unwise, since you never knew who you were talking to, or how much information would be filtered back to Germany. As if it made any bloody difference, when a beautiful city like Bristol was in ruins, and the German Intelligence system would be well aware that they had bombed it to near-destruction.

'You all right, Daisy? I daresay it was a bit of a shock to you, but as long as your dad wasn't hurt, that's the main thing, isn't it?'

'Of course it is.' She dragged her thoughts back to the present, and realised Sam was looking at her quizzically now.

'You remind me of somebody, and I'm trying to think who it is.'

'Oh yes? And which movie did that line come out of?' she said.

She wouldn't respond any further. It flashed through her mind that the old Daisy – the immature one who had ideas above her station, as they said – would have immediately bragged that of course she reminded him of someone. She was the image of that scintillating stage star who had been the darling of everyone in her day, wasn't she? But this Daisy had grown up. She was going to war – well, sort of.

'You any relation to that lady who used to be on the stage about ten years ago? I was only a kid at the time, but my old mum and dad used to go and watch her,' Sam went on. 'Her name was something like yours—'

'It was exactly like mine,' Daisy finished quickly, unable to let it go on any longer. She wasn't *that* grown up. 'Her name was Frances Caldwell, and she was my mother.'

'Blimey, are you a singer, too, then? You've certainly got the looks for it, and that's no flannel.'

It was one of those moments when the world seemed to close in on her. Only in this case, it wasn't the world, it was just a rattling compartment full of soldiers, all suddenly pausing in their conversations and their card-playing, to look straight at her for confirmation.

Daisy took a deep breath. 'I told you, I'm a nurse. That's what I'm expecting to do once I get my orders from this training centre.'

'Well, you'll be wasted,' Sam told her, as the others turned back to their game after a momentary spark of interest.

Sorry I'm no Shirley Temple then, Daisy found herself thinking. But she wasn't sorry, not really. Right now she had a job to do, and wherever the army sent her, and whatever job she was given, she was going to do it. And at last the excitement of it all began to return. Leaving home for any reason was an adventure – providing home was always there to return to. After a while she leaned against the back of the seat and drifted into a doze, lulled by the rhythm of the wheels as they rattled along the track.

Long before the train slowed down as it neared Chichester station, conversation had dried up. The card-players had got bored and had been snoring noisily for some time. Sam was reading his newspaper, and Daisy was now trying to think how best she was going to present herself to her commanding officer, one Captain Griggs. She was a nurse, but she wanted to do more than nursing. She wanted to be a star. Or at least to shine in a very small way. She had made that known to the recruiting officer, hoping he wouldn't think her a complete idiot, and she had Sister Mackintosh's recommendation in her bag.

The train snorted and belched into the station and all the soldiers made a concerted move, saying goodbye cheerily and wishing her luck. They would probably need it far more than she did, going into the desert, she thought. It wouldn't be all dashing sheiks of Araby where they were going.

'Come on then, girl, let's help you down with that suitcase,' Sam said, as if she wasn't capable of carrying it for herself. He was a sweetie, and by now she had seen the pictures of his kids as well as learning that his wife's bark was worse than her bite, and his mother-in-law wasn't the dragon she appeared. Distance had already made his heart grow fonder, Daisy thought, hiding a smile.

As the train stopped and doors were thrust open, it seemed as if a whole wave of khaki flowed out on to the platform and moved outside to the waiting lorries, apparently knowing exactly where to go and what to do. In the rush, Daisy quickly lost sight of her recent companions, and stood uncertainly for a few minutes, until she saw some other girls looking just as flummoxed as she was. Tentatively, she touched one of them on the shoulder.

'Are you going to Flayton Camp?'

The other girl nodded in relief. 'Thank God. I thought I was the only one, and I was almost ready to turn tail and go home again. I'm Molly Witherington.'

'Daisy Caldwell.'

They shook hands as formally as if they were meeting at a garden party, and they both suddenly saw the incongruity of it all and burst out laughing.

'Well, Daisy Caldwell, I suppose we'd better try to find out what we're supposed to be doing,' the other girl said. 'A bit scary, isn't it? Have you ever been involved in anything like this before?'

Well, only in the middle of an unholy bombardment on the hospital ships to Dunkirk, and careering around Bristol in an ambulance picking up patients after the bombing raids, Daisy mused, but thought the better of saying it.

'Not really. So what's your job?'

'I'm a clerk. Not bad at typing, pretty hopeless at Pitman's – shorthand,' she added, as Daisy looked mystified. 'How about you?'

'Nursing, but I'd like to do something different.'

'Wouldn't we all?' Molly said breezily. 'I'm keen to learn something about motors. My dad's forever tinkering beneath the bonnet of his car, and I always think it's a minor miracle when he makes it work.'

'Good Lord. You want to be a motor mechanic?'

Molly laughed. 'That's not so potty as it sounds. Anyway, you know what they say. Whatever you're good at, they're sure to put you somewhere else. My dad said that's what happened in the last lot, and he's sure it's no different in this one. It's how he met my mother, anyway, so I shouldn't complain.'

She went off at so many tangents, Daisy couldn't keep up with her, but she found herself laughing, and her nerves were unwinding as they waited with a gathering group of girls, all looking as if they had been abandoned outside Chichester railway station.

'This is great fun, isn't it?' a tall girl sauntered up to the two who looked as if they were having a jolly good time. 'Do you think they've forgotten us?'

Her clothes looked expensive, and she spoke as if she had a plum in her mouth, and Daisy had a swift image of this elegant girl being given the job that Molly wanted, and getting her manicured hands filthy beneath the bonnet of an army lorry. Before Daisy could think of a reply that didn't have her choking over the words, the girl spoke again.

'I'm sorry, I should have introduced myself. I'm Naomi Tyler-Smythe.'

Molly was almost choking by now as well, and as Naomi looked at them enquiringly with her china-blue eyes, Daisy took the initiative.

'I'm Daisy Caldwell and this is Molly Witherington. All bound for Flayton Camp, I presume?'

'So what do you do, Naomi?' Molly managed to say when the girl nodded.

'Do?' Naomi said vaguely. 'Well, nothing really, but we all have to do our bit, don't we, and I thought this would be a bit of a lark.'

'You remind me of my sister's best friend,' Daisy said, thinking of Helen Church, and managing not to look at Molly.

'Really? In what way?'

Oh God. In the way of being a social butterfly was what she meant, but one look at Naomi's earnest face and she knew she would never say it.

In any case Helen had turned out to be far more dedicated than any of them might have thought, and she only had to think of her own flibberty-gibberty fads to know that people could change.

'Um, blonde hair, same colour eyes,' she mumbled instead.

The arrival of an army vehicle skidding towards them stopped any further conversation and a burly driver in sergeant's uniform leapt out.

'Sorry I'm late, girls, but we'll get you there in the end. All present and correct, are we? Should be a bunch of ten, so let's do a swift head count and then we'll be on our way. All set for the holiday camp?'

'Some holiday camp,' Molly muttered. 'More like prison, if you ask me.'

'Why did you volunteer then?' Daisy asked, once they were on board the uncomfortable vehicle and chuntering through the town of Chichester, away from the direction of the coast and out into the country.

'It's like the duchess said – we have to do our bit, don't we? Besides, I got fed up at home. Too many kids and not enough room, so I thought I'd clear out and make a bit more space.'

'Pretty noble, all the same,' Daisy said. 'And who's the duchess?'

She followed Molly's small nod, to where Naomi Tyler-Smythe was holding court about horse trials to a couple of goggle-eyed girls, making her think instantly of her friend Lucy Luckwell, who'd been mad about horse-riding too, and would have joined up in a minute had she still been alive to do so. Daisy didn't think of Lucy so often now, but when she did, it still gave her an unpleasant jolt to remember how such a vivacious girl of seventeen had died from consumption.

'She's priceless, isn't she?' Molly whispered, looking in Naomi's direction.

'At least her intentions are good, and she'll probably end up in charge of the household cavalry,' Daisy whispered back, at which they convulsed again. But one of them had misty eyes that were nothing to do with laughter.

And a good three hours later, when they had arrived at the camp, dusty and dry-mouthed, and been checked in by the stern looking Captain Phyllis Griggs, been given their private's uniforms and equipment and assigned to their quarters, Daisy and Molly looked at one another.

'Well, this is a bleedin' turn-up, isn't it?' Molly said, in a fair imitation of Vanessa Brown's favourite expletive. 'Here I was, doing my folks a favour by making breathing-space at home, and I'm stuck in a rabbit-hutch with you lot.'

'What did you expect?' Daisy asked. 'The Ritz?'

'Oh, I don't think any of us expected that,' a cultured voice said from the other end of the cramped, eight-bed barracks, where Naomi Tyler-Smythe was systematically unpacking her suitcase and folding her clothes neatly into an impossibly small locker. 'We all have to muck in and make the best of things, don't we?'

'She's serious, Daisy,' Molly said in an aside. 'She thinks you really know what the inside of the Ritz is like. You *don't*, do you?'

'Of course not,' Daisy giggled. 'I think she's rather sweet, really. A bit vague and all that, but not as snobby as you might have expected.'

'She's not one of us, either.'

'Well, she'll have to be, won't she? There's one thing for sure, Molly. We can't pick and choose who our bedmates are going to be from now on.'

'More's the pity,' Molly said with a wink.

Ten

Imogen Caldwell was clearing out the letters from her desk, skimming through them as she did so, unable to bear throwing some of them away. One that had come from her aunt several weeks ago had made her smile. So Daisy had done it at last. It would be odd if they came across one another in the service, but stranger things had happened. It had happened on the hospital ship Daisy had been working on, when Joe Preston had been one of their Dunkirk wounded, needing desperate attention. Aunt Rose said that Daisy was now stationed somewhere in Sussex for training, though she had no idea what that training was going to involve. It was something else to make Immy smile.

'Oh Daisy dear, you were probably in for quite a shock,' she murmured, knowing how the army liked to put people in the most unlikely situations.

It tested them, James had once told her. Made them stronger. Which, to Immy, was just plain stupid, since if you had an aptitude for something, it made sense to put you there in the first place. She had found that out for herself when she had said how much she would like to be a driver. But she had been lucky – with two stripes and all now – and a superior officer who was a dear.

Right now, they were back at their home base in Oxford, after a stint of driving Captain Beckett to and from Norfolk. He had been currently involved in urgent consultations with some bigwigs about the next strategy now that Germany had invaded Russia.

Immy's smile faded abruptly. Italy had declared war on Britain and France a year ago, and France had virtually been swallowed up by the German invasion. Now Russia, one of Britain's mightiest allies, had been invaded. Only a fool wouldn't fear the outcome of it all. What had begun as a war between two nations was spiralling out of control, and however much the newspapers and wireless reports tried to play down the seriousness of it all, the dreaded thought that one day Germany might yet invade Britain could never be ruled out.

She shivered. It didn't do to dwell on such an eventuality for too long, but Immy had always been a practical person, believing in facing facts. The family used to call her the sensible daughter, she thought with a faint smile, when measured against Elsie's shy ways and Daisy's scatterbrained ones.

Immy hadn't particularly liked the thought of sounding so dull, and she hadn't been so sensible in falling for that rat of a Welshman, Morgan Raine. Thankfully none of them had known very much about that, and she quickly pushed him out of her mind. In any case, everything changed. Elsie had surprised them all when she had married Joe in a secret wedding ceremony, and Daisy had turned up trumps after all. And she had found the love of her life, more or less around the corner, in the shape of James Church. You just never knew what life had in store for you. Which was just as well, the sensible part of her brain added.

But now, this new German offensive on Russia, with reports that thousands of ordinary Russian people were being bombed and made homeless or worse, meant that the war was taking a far more sinister turn. It was turning into a global affair – apart from the Americans joining in – but at least they hadn't been slow in coming forward to provide arms and ammunition, Immy thought generously.

The Canadians and Anzacs were everywhere in Britain, too, and if this war was doing nothing else, it was bringing people from different parts of the Empire together. It could hardly be called holiday travel – but who ever heard of people travelling to such far corners of the earth on holiday, anyway!

She knew she was letting her thoughts wander, keeping them well away from the other thing that had come out of the recent reports. The thing that most affected her. The thing that was of gigantic importance in her life.

It was the news that tank regiments were now being sent to North Africa and the western desert. James was in charge of a tank regiment and he hadn't even told her the true facts himself. He was a professional soldier through and through, but she had winkled the information of his probable destination out of Captain Beckett's sources, and it frightened her to death. When all was said and done, she just wanted him home. She just wanted to marry the man she loved, start a family and live a peaceful life. Just like every other woman.

James hadn't been sent overseas yet, and according to his last phone call he was bored to death. If Immy was secretly relieved that at least he wasn't in the firing line, James certainly wasn't. His regiment was doing nothing but training, and all the real daredevil action was being done by the boys in blue. He was stuck on the Yorkshire moors, training on the roughest terrain the army could currently find, when he'd far rather be on active duty.

'This isn't what I joined the army for,' he had complained.

'Well, if it had still been peacetime, you wouldn't have had any battles to fight, would you?' she pointed out. 'Be thankful for small mercies, darling.'

'The only thing I'm thankful for is that at least I can contact you fairly often, even if I can't see you. And I do so want to see you, Immy. I miss you so much.'

'I know. I miss you too.'

'Actually, I did the next best thing. I had some time off at the weekend, and being at a loose end up here I collared a lift from a fellow who lives in the area and went to visit your sister.'

'Did you?' Immy exclaimed. 'That was nice of you, James! I bet she was surprised to see you, wasn't she?'

He laughed. 'She certainly was, but she and Joe's parents made me very welcome. And that little niece of yours is a cracker.'

It was strange to think he had seen Faith so recently, when none of them had seen her since Elsie left for Yorkshire months ago. Immy hadn't realised quite how long it was.

'She must have grown since the last time we saw her,' she said quickly.

'Oh yes. Two teeth and lots of lovely red hair, just like you.'

Immy laughed. 'Just like her mother, you mean,' she corrected.

'That too,' James conceded. 'So when are we going to start?'

Once she realised what he meant, Immy began to laugh. 'Let's get the wedding over first! Everything in its right order—'

'Yes, but when is that going to be, Immy? I'm impatient to make an honest woman of you.'

He was half-teasing, and Immy felt herself blush. Not since that one clandestine weekend in London had they had the chance to renew the bliss – or the guilt – of being lovers. So long ago now . . .

'James, you know my feelings about marrying in wartime,' she said haltingly. 'I know you think I'm being ridiculously superstitious, but I'd much prefer to wait until we can have a proper wedding without worrying that duty will part us again at any minute. And we both know it's far from over yet.'

'And I'm twiddling my thumbs thinking how much happier I'd be if I had a wife to come home to. You're not superstitious about being left a widow, are you, darling?' he said lightly, but she didn't miss the edge in his voice now.

'Of course not! I just want everything to be right for us, James.'

'Well, I never thought your sister would be braver than you.'

Her heart skipped a beat. What had begun as one of their usual loving telephone calls was degenerating quickly, and she didn't quite know how it had happened, nor how to stop it.

'*Daisy*, do you mean?' she said, remembering how he had always laughed at her madcap ideas.

'No. I mean Elsie. She was willing to take a chance and marry Joe, even though he might have been sent to Timbuktu, wasn't she?'

'James, don't let's quarrel, please,' she pleaded.

'We're not quarrelling, we're discussing,' he said, and she could almost hear his father's lawyer's voice. And then it softened. 'Immy, you know I'd marry you tomorrow if you'd say the word, but once this war is over, I promise you the biggest and most extravagant wedding that money can buy.'

'Does this mean we're engaged then?' she said, even though she was finding it hard not to let the tears overflow.

'I thought we already were.'

Even though there was no ring on her finger, no outward sign that they belonged to one another, and it wasn't her place to suggest that they made it more formal. She knew very well they didn't need an outward show to know that they intended spending the rest of their lives together. All the same . . .

She must have been silent for too long, because he spoke again.

'Immy, let's at least make it official the next time we get leave together. What do you say? Do you fancy raiding the London jewellers to choose an engagement ring?'

'Well, what do you think I'd say? I say yes, of course!' she said, her heart leaping with happiness now.

And unwilling to admit, even to herself, that there *was* a

secret worry in her mind about marrying in wartime, when both of them were in the services. She didn't worry about herself, but James's job was such a dangerous one, despite his dismissal of all the tank training sessions they had to undergo. The very vehicles were cumbersome and dangerous, and once they really went into action, who knew what may happen? According to Aunt Rose's letter, Daisy had apparently been talking to a group of soldiers who were going to the North African desert – which was the ideal place for tank warfare – if you could call any kind of warfare ideal.

Immy wouldn't go so far as to say she had any kind of premonition about James, but she did have the idealistic notion that as long as he had their wedding to come home to, something wonderful to look forward to, then he would be safe. She had never told James such a thing, of course, nor said it to anyone, but she stubbornly refused to change her mind about it.

But then she thought about buying an engagement ring, and the happiness bubbled over again, replacing the anxious thoughts. And she couldn't resist telling Captain Beckett, who was now a friend as well as a fatherly figure and her superior officer.

'Am I being silly in wanting to wait until after the war, Sir?'

'Of course not. I think you're a very sensible young woman.'

'Oh Lord, that's what my aunt used to say about me, and it always sounded so deadly dull,' she said with a groan.

He laughed. 'Nobody could ever call you dull, Imogen. So when is your young man's next leave going to be? We'll have to see what we can do for you. Another weekend in London, is it?'

She blushed furiously now, and turned away from him.

'My dear girl, love wasn't invented yesterday, you know,' he said gently. 'We were all young once, and being parted is one of the hellish things about war. My advice, for what it's worth, is to make the most of every moment.'

'Thank you, Sir,' she gasped, and left his office quickly, her face fiery.

It was one thing for her and James to enjoy each other in ways that were private and intimate. It was quite another for people to be aware of it. She didn't want that. Couldn't bear it.

But then her wayward thoughts calmed down. What did he really know, anyway? What did anyone know about what went on behind closed doors? Anyone could surmise, but nobody really *knew*, unless you were foolish enough to tell them, and she would never do that, and neither would James.

But she called Elsie that evening, just to hear about James's visit.

'He's such a love, isn't he, Immy?' Elsie said enthusiastically. 'He'll make a lovely father one of these days, too. He played with Faith for ages, and he kept saying how like our family she was. What he really meant, of course, was that he was thinking of the time when you and he have a baby just like her. All in good time, of course!' she added with a laugh.

'Oh, of course!' Immy laughed back, but after they had spoken for ten minutes, and she had learned all about how marvellous Faith was, and how she was definitely going to end up with a Yorkshire accent, she almost wished she hadn't called her at all. It seemed as if everyone was edging her towards marriage – all except Captain Beckett. And she didn't want it. Well, she *did*, more than anything, but not until the time was right. And that wasn't now.

She wrote frequently to Daisy, and after her sister had been at Flayton Camp for six weeks, she guessed the new posts would be imminent.

Dear Daisy,
So what's happening to you? Have they put you in the

130

kitchens scrubbing pans, or stuck you behind a desk handing out weekend passes to any devious private who tries to charm you into being sorry for him by saying he has a sick wife at home? You want to watch out for them, Daisy! Some of them will chance their arms when they see a pretty face who doesn't know the ropes yet.

How's your Canadian fellow, by the way? Have you heard from him lately? James is bored silly with his tank training exercises – but I think that may change soon, and I'm not saying anything more about that. Elsie's enjoying life on the farm despite not having seen Joe for weeks now. I heard from Helen the other week, who's now taking a catering course. Knowing her, she'll probably end up being a lady chef to royalty.

I hope you've got a nice set of girls where you are, darling, and aren't finding it all too much of a strain from what you expected. Write to me soon and tell me all. Well, nearly all, anyway.

Your loving sister,

Imogen.

Immy's letters were all the same, and although Daisy wrote back quite often, she never said much about what was happening at Flayton Camp. Immy would know all about basic training anyway. They were Jills of all trades while the army decided what to do with them, and several months after first donning a uniform, Daisy felt herself to be a seasoned recruit if nothing else, and she was laughing when she put Immy's latest letter into her locker.

'Boyfriend?' Molly asked, knowing how avidly Daisy waited for letters from Glenn.

'Sister. And she thinks I'm the scatty one. She can't seem to keep her mind on one thing at a time. But she's chirpy enough, considering she does nothing more interesting that driving her middle-aged Captain around here, there and everywhere. He's in Intelligence or something.'

'Lucky her.'

'Yes, but you wouldn't want to do that, would you, Molly? I know you're mad about car engines, but just driving and waiting around all day seems pretty dull to me. Anyway, it looks as if you're going to get your wish to train as a proper mechanic, doesn't it?'

'Fingers crossed,' Molly said, suiting the action to the words. 'So what was so funny then?'

'Oh, Immy thinks I'm either scrubbing out kitchens or sitting behind a desk warding off the cheeky devils trying to get an extra bit of leave.'

'Which you have been. But you mean you haven't told her about the rest?'

'I haven't told any of them yet,' Daisy said. 'I'm keeping it strictly to myself until I know for certain what's going to happen.'

'When are these people coming down to audition you?'

'In a couple of weeks' time, as far as I know. It's a bit vague, to be honest,' Daisy said, feeling as though her heart was about to turn cartwheels at the thought. 'I can't believe that Naomi wants to audition as well, though. That was a turn-up, wasn't it?'

Molly grinned. 'Not really. You could hardly imagine her getting her hands dirty at anything, could you?'

Daisy paused. 'That's not what you think of me, is it?'

''Course not, silly. I think you've got plenty of guts if you want to know. I couldn't face standing in front of hundreds of leering squaddies and singing my heart out. I'd be frightened to death.'

Daisy laughed. 'And it would help if you weren't tone-deaf, of course.'

'I know,' Molly said cheerfully. 'But what exactly is Naomi hoping to do?'

'Have you heard her sing?'

'Good Lord, you mean she's going to be in competition?'

'No. We're thinking of forming a duo,' Daisy said. 'It's

132

something I once thought about, and Naomi has quite a good voice, deeper than mine, so we complement one another. At the next dance, she's going to ask the compère if we can do a turn. A sort of try-out before the big event.'

It had seemed like a good idea at the time, but Daisy was wishing now that she felt as confident as she sounded. The monthly dance at the local Forces Club was hardly the same as entertaining a group of war-toughened troops. It wasn't the same as singing to a captive audience of staff and patients in Weston General either. But if an attack of nerves was going to assail her every time she thought about it, she wasn't going to be much use to anyone. On the other hand, Naomi said everyone had nerves before making a speech or going on the stage. If they didn't, they'd get overconfident and wouldn't give their best. It was the nervous adrenaline beforehand that made you give a good performance. So Naomi said.

What Naomi didn't tell her until much later was that there would be several people at the Forces Club that evening who were not just regulars from the nearby camps. People who were rather important as far as they were concerned. Naomi was one of those types who seemed to gather information without even trying.

It came from her autocratic air of authority, and the fact that her father was a brigadier, they had discovered later. If they'd known that in the beginning, Molly said dryly, they'd have been too scared to speak to her at all. But although she might be posher than most in their barracks, she was also what the nobs called 'a thoroughly nice gel'.

'So, who are these people?' Daisy demanded, as they got ready to leave for the Club the following Saturday. 'Not royalty, are they? You're not telling me the King and Queen are dropping in on us, are you?'

The thought was so unlikely that the first wild shot of nerves fizzled out a little. Besides, they had rehearsed their number a dozen times already, but the nerves still persisted to twist her stomach. More than she had expected.

Naomi gave her low-pitched laugh. Even *that* was posh, according to Molly.

'Daisy, you are funny,' she said. 'Of course it's not the King and Queen. But these people might just be the sort to persuade the powers that be that we're serious about our duo act, and that we've got what it takes, as they say.'

'Talent scouts?' Daisy almost squeaked, her mind still on the Hollywood movie they had seen recently, where an unknown girl working in a diner, whatever that was, had been discovered and thrust into stardom overnight.

'No dear,' Naomi said kindly. 'It's someone who worked in a nightclub in London before it got bombed, and has been entertaining the troops in various parts of the country. My father knows her people, and he mentioned us to her, and since she's in the area, she'll be at the club tonight with some friends.'

'Oh Lord, now you've *really* scared me,' Daisy groaned, her nerves jumping anew. 'It's not Vera Lynn, is it?'

'It's Penny Wood. *Miss* Penny Wood actually.'

Daisy and Molly both looked blank, and Naomi shrugged.

'Oh well, darlings, I was forgetting that you come from the sticks, so you probably won't have heard of her. She was the resident singer in the Flamingo Club in London until earlier this year when the club was bombed and flattened. My parents and I went there a few times to listen to her. I don't think she's been in the ATS for very long, but she's joined ENSA now, so she can give us a few tips, and she'll be able to assess whether or not we're any good. And we *are* good, aren't we, Daisy?'

'Oh yes,' Daisy said, her stomach turning to water. It was even worse than she feared. A professional coming to assess them.

Oh Lord, the whole thing was beginning to assume far greater proportions than she had imagined. She wasn't sure she was ready for this. Wasn't really sure that she would ever be, or that she truly wanted it after all. She was in such a blue funk that she realised she was shivering, and that her lipstick was in danger of sliding all over her face as she tried to apply it.

She blinked, and her image in the mirror blurred for a moment, and then she seemed to hear her mother's gentle voice, telling her that she could do anything she wanted to do. She was five years old and about to recite a Christmas poem for the family and neighbours they had invited into the house at Vicarage Street for the festivities, and the words wouldn't come out. Aunt Rose was frowning at her and Uncle Bert was pulling silly faces behind her back to make Daisy smile.

And in the end, she did it; of course she did. Because she didn't want to let her mother down. And she wouldn't let her down now. Frances would expect her to go out on that stage with her head held high and a smile on her lips. Frances had always said that the show must go on, no matter how you were feeling inside.

'Thanks, Mum,' she said silently.

'So are we ready to show Miss Penny Wood what we're made of?' Naomi was demanding. 'She won't eat you, Daisy!'

Daisy straightened her shoulders. 'I never thought she would. Besides, anything she can do, we can do, too, can't we?'

'Attagirl,' Naomi said, movie-style.

At that moment, buoyed on by Naomi, she was prepared to say that of course she could do anything Miss Penny Wood could do. She was curious to see her now. And so was everyone else. Once word got around the camps the Forces Club was packed out, and the singer was practically mobbed the minute she appeared. The applause was deafening. All that, and she hadn't even opened her mouth yet. Daisy might not have heard of her, but it was obvious that plenty of other people had.

'She's a stunner, isn't she?' Molly bawled in Daisy's ear

to make herself heard as the excitement ran around the hall in waves.

'She certainly is,' Daisy said with a gulp.

Naomi had also discovered that Miss Penny Wood was her stage name, and in reality it was the impossibly Cornish name of Wenna Pengelly, which would hardly stop anybody's heart. Daisy thought the name would hardly matter, since she had glorious black hair and the most vivid blue eyes Daisy had ever seen. She was exquisitely beautiful, and she had a stage presence that Daisy could only compare to her mother's. The kind that Daisy didn't have. Could never have . . .

It was inevitable that Miss Penny Wood would be persuaded to sing. It seemed faintly ridiculous to Daisy that everyone, herself included, always used her full title, never just Penny Wood. Despite the fact that she normally wore a uniform like the rest of them here, it gave her status.

And once she stood on the stage and the applause died down for her to begin her song, Daisy knew it was well deserved. The voice was husky, plaintive, making every man think of his sweetheart, and making every girl long to have those emotional words said to her. She sang four songs before the audience let her go, and then she said laughingly that she needed a break, or her friends would think she was just here to give a performance.

The roars of approval cheered her on, but the compère stopped it in mid-flow, saying he was sure they would honour Miss Penny Wood's need to be with her friends. Besides which, they had a little home-grown talent of their own to follow after a couple more dances.

'God *no*!' Daisy said vehemently, hearing a few whistles and cat-calls at that announcement. 'Not after that. Naomi, I just can't.'

'I think you're right,' Naomi said. 'How can we follow that?'

Daisy drew in her breath. 'I'd like to have a word with her

though. You said she was Cornish, and I know Cornwall well, so it might be a point of contact.'

The girls at her table looked at her as if she was a prize idiot, and she knew it was the flimsiest of reasons to approach the singer. She wasn't quite sure why she wanted to do it, anyway, and her mother always said it was very bad form to intrude on an entertainer's privacy. But if she didn't do it now, she never would. Besides, there was always the possibility that Miss PW might have heard of her mother. Daisy swallowed her nerves and zig-zagged her way across the crowded hall until she reached Miss Penny Wood's table.

One of her male companions looked up with a small frown.

'Miss Penny Wood is not giving interviews this evening,' he said at once.

Daisy ignored him. 'I'm really sorry to intrude. But I had to tell you how much I enjoyed your singing, and I wondered if you'd heard of Frances Caldwell.'

The words tumbled out, unprepared, stupid, childish, sycophantic. The minute she'd said them Daisy cringed at her own clumsiness, and wished she could melt away into the crowd. It wouldn't be difficult to let it swallow her up.

'Frances Caldwell?' the man who had spoken before looked at her sharply. 'She's a bit passé now, isn't she? But wonderful in her time, of course.'

'She was my mother,' Daisy said, choked.

Miss Penny Wood still looked a little mystified, and why not? Frances's heyday would have been well before her time.

'You look a little unwell. Why don't you join us for a drink?' Daisy heard her say in that soft Cornish voice. 'And tell us what you're doing here. Are you in the services?'

Before Daisy could answer, the music had stopped, and the compère was announcing their very own camp duo was about to give them a song. It made them sound like the worst kind of amateurs, and the cheers that accompanied his words were raucous. She felt her head swim, and would have got out of there in a minute, if Naomi hadn't appeared at her side and dragged her away, spluttering a little, and hissing at her to get up on that stage with her and do what they had rehearsed.

Like the Red Sea, the crowds parted to make way for them, and slow hand-clapping and whistles followed them on to the stage. And if she didn't want to look completely infantile, Daisy knew she would have to go through with it.

Eleven

'It was a disaster, an absolute bloody disaster!' Daisy stormed over the phone.

Elsie was the only one she could bear to confide in. Elsie wasn't involved in the services, and she was far enough away so that Daisy didn't have to see her face and witness her complete humiliation.

'Darling, I'm sure it wasn't that bad.'

'Yes it was,' she raged. 'From the minute we stood on the stage and Naomi sneezed into the microphone, they all started to laugh, assuming we were supposed to be a comic act. She has an allergy that she gets every summer, which she conveniently forgot to mention, and every few bars she gave this enormous honking sneeze and every time she did it, everyone cheered. Oh, we were a sensation if you like Laurel and Hardy!'

'How awful for you, Daisy.'

'You're not laughing as well, are you?'

'Of course not. But what about you? Didn't you manage to carry on alone?'

'I just went to pieces. My voice cracked and squeaked, when it came out at all, which only added to the so-called comic turn. There was a professional singer in the audience who I was hoping to impress, and what she thought of me I have no idea. When we'd got through the ordeal, she had gone. She probably couldn't stand it any more than I could.'

'Daisy, I'm so sorry, but please don't let one little setback put you off. I'm sure Mother had problems to start with.'

139

Daisy went grimly on. 'Mother was a star, and I'm not. This Miss Penny Wood is a star as well. She had what Mother always called stage presence. The audience went quiet the moment the band started playing her music. They just adored her. When Naomi and I got up there, you could still hear the buzz of chatter and the clink of glasses, and when we began, well, you know what happened then.'

'Perhaps it was a mistake to try to be a duo, darling,' Elsie ventured, hearing how shrill and tense her sister's voice was becoming, and nervous of saying the wrong thing. Her confidence may have taken a severe battering, but she still had the artistic temperament.

'It was a mistake, full stop. I don't ever want to put myself through that kind of humiliation again.'

'You don't mean you're giving up the whole idea? But it's something you've wanted for so long. You can't give up now.'

'Well, thank you for the vote of confidence,' Daisy said bitterly. 'But you know me. Always changing my mind. First wanting to be a singer, then a nurse, and anything else that came along and took my fancy. There always has to be one in every family, doesn't there?'

Elsie was more alarmed by this self-condemnation than she let on. It was so un-Daisy-like. 'Daisy, why don't you come up here when you get some leave? Come and see Faith and spend some time with us. It's so relaxing on the farm, and it may be just what you need. Aren't you supposed to get a few days' leave at the end of your training?' she added vaguely.

'I'll think about it. Thank you anyway, Elsie.'

'And darling, don't do anything rash, please.'

'Rash? Me? I thought you knew that's exactly what I'm known for! It was a mistake to think I could do this at all. I know it now. Once and for all. I could never follow in Mother's footsteps, and I should have known it all along.'

'Daisy, I simply don't know what else to say,' Elsie said after a small pause. 'I'm so sorry, I really am.'

'So am I. Anyway, now that I know my place, I've put in a request to be sent to a military hospital, so I can do what I'm good at. That is, if they don't think the new nurse will give all the patients heart attacks by her comic antics!'

She just couldn't say any more. She almost slammed down the phone and went back to the barracks to throw herself on her bed and tell herself what a fool she had been. It wouldn't have been so bad if she hadn't told everyone at home that she and Naomi were going to make their debut that evening at the Forces Club, and so far she hadn't been able to report to any of them, except Elsie, what an abysmal failure it had been.

And almost the worst of it was that she and Naomi were no longer speaking. It was childish and pathetic, but neither of them could bear to look at the other one, and Naomi's continuing honking sneezes still rocked the barracks. Her Harley Street man called it rhinitis, otherwise known as hay fever, she kept gasping apologetically. It happened every year. Whatever it was, it was still a humiliating reminder to Daisy, and hilarious to the rest of them.

They were all due for forty-eight hour passes in a few days, by which time they would know where they were being sent. Molly was almost sure she would go to Southampton to the large military vehicles depot, and Daisy didn't care where she went, providing she could pick up where she had left off and merge into the nursing background. She was ashamed of her perpetual indecision, but once and for all, she knew she was definitely not 'going to be a star'.

And strangely now, whenever she got into a real state of jitters, wondering just how shallow a person she really was, it wasn't the thought of her mother that crept into her mind. It was Lucy. It was that day at the annual gymkhana at the Luckwell farm, when Lucy had so wanted to win the coveted rosette and her horse had stumbled and fallen on her, winding her and giving her a badly sprained ankle. It could have been so much worse and it had been Daisy Caldwell who had come to the rescue, knowing just what to do until the doctor arrived, calming her and keeping her still, and receiving praise for her quickness and common sense, and knowing at that moment that she wanted to be a nurse.

'Look out, Daisy,' Molly suddenly whispered. They were getting dressed for their last camp dance before being sent their separate ways. Orders hadn't come through yet, but they expected them on Monday morning. Daisy had refused to go to this dance at first, until Molly said she was just being stupid and she should show her face and make the most of it. And nobody would remember the last time, anyway . . .

At Molly's warning voice, Daisy's head jerked around from fastening her suspenders to her stockings. Coming purposefully down the barracks towards her was Naomi. She was dressed to kill as usual, blonde hair immaculately stiff with sugar water to keep every wave in place, and a silk dress that certainly hadn't come from a market stall. She held out a manicured hand to Daisy.

'I've come to say I'm sorry,' she said, her voice thicker than usual due to the persistent hay fever, but still managing to sound upper class. 'It was an appalling thing to happen, Daisy, but I'd like to call a truce. How about it? Friends?'

Daisy capitulated at once. It just wasn't worth it. She stretched out her hand to shake Naomi's. At the same instant Naomi snatched hers back, clapping it over her face as one of her head-rocking sneezes belted out.

'I'm so sorry,' she gasped, her eyes streaming, and threatening to ruin the perfectly-applied make-up. 'But it's not catching, honestly.'

Daisy's shoulders were shaking as well now, but mercifully with laughter as she saw the funny side, and then they were hugging one another and laughing together, and Molly was heaving a sigh of relief.

'Thank God. Now can we all go to the dance?' she said mildly.

There was a palpable sense of relaxation in the barracks,

and there was even a small round of applause when Daisy and Naomi appeared together at the Forces Club. But if anyone thought there was going to be a repeat performance they were sadly mistaken. Even so, it had been the right thing to do to come back again. It was like falling off a horse. The best thing you could do to conquer your fear was to get right back up on it again. Lucy had discovered that, eventually.

It was odd how her name and her image kept turning up in Daisy's mind again. Comforting, too. As if she was a kind of guardian angel watching over her. And Lucy would have loved all this. The laughter, the friendships, the excitement of dancing with young men you hadn't been properly introduced to, but all within the bounds of comradeship. It was all very proper really, but in ways unheard of before war had thrown them together.

Daisy had just about recovered from being whirled around in the arms of someone called Bob, protesting that she had to sit down with Molly to give her feet a rest. Gallantly, Private Bob went off to buy them both a glass of lemonade.

'Keen, isn't he?' Molly said with grin. 'You'll have to watch out for him, Daisy. He'll be expecting a goodnight kiss at the barrack gate tonight.'

But Daisy was no longer listening. Some latecomers were arriving at the Club, and the compère tapped the microphone, prior to making an announcement.

'Ladies and gentlemen, boys and girls, let's give a warm welcome to some of our heroic boys in blue who are joining us this evening.'

There were cheers at the arrival of the airmen, as well as a few good-natured jeers of 'glamour boys', and Daisy's heart began to beat in double-quick time. The crowd was partially obscuring her view, but she thought . . . she was almost certain . . . and then her blisters were forgotten as her feet skimmed across the floor, where she was caught up in Glenn's arms.

'What are you doing here?' she gasped. 'I can't believe it's really you!'

'It had better be,' came his teasing voice, 'or these folks will think you're a fast woman in the habit of embracing strange men!'

Daisy was dimly aware that there were more cheers going on around them now from those who had witnessed the unexpected sight of Private Daisy Caldwell throwing herself into the arms of an air force officer. Moreover, an officer who seemingly had no intention of letting her go for a good few moments.

'We realised we were in striking distance of your camp, so we hijacked a vehicle and came in a bunch. I knew you came to these monthly bashes, and we figured they wouldn't throw the lot of us out, and my God, was it worth it, just to see you,' he said, his voice deepening.

'And you!' Daisy said breathlessly, still wondering if she was dreaming. She had so nearly stayed away this evening in a fit of petulance. And if she had . . . it didn't bear thinking about. Instead, she was here in Glenn's arms, floating around the room as the band played a haunting waltz tune, and even the distant sound of guns and the wail of an air-raid siren couldn't spoil these moments.

'Some poor devils are getting it tonight,' Glenn murmured in her ear. 'Thank God it wasn't our turn to intercept them. I'd much rather be here.'

'Oh, I'm so glad you're here too. I've missed you, Glenn.'

'That's the best news I've had in a long time,' he said softly. 'I've missed you like hell, too, but I don't feel like spending the next coupla' hours sharing you with all these other people. Is there anywhere we can go to be on our own?'

Daisy shivered, partly from excitement and partly from nerves. She so wanted to be alone with him, too. It was so long since they had been together, and each time they met it was like the first time. Each time, she wanted him more.

'We could go outside for a walk,' she said, knowing how feeble it sounded. 'It's a warm night –'

'And the stars are out. OK, let's go. Nobody will miss us in all this crowd.'

Daisy rather doubted that. Her own mess-mates were taking great interest in the tall, good-looking officer with the Canadian accent who seemed to have swept her off her feet. Then she forgot all about them and hugged Glenn's arm.

'So, let's go,' she repeated huskily.

They slipped out of the hall to the usual chorus of 'Close that door' because of blackout regulations, and seconds later they were outside in the balmy summer air, the dance tunes muted behind them, the night closing around them, creating their own special world.

She was warm in his arms as they moved away from the club, thinking that these must be some of the most romantic moments in her life. Wanting to hold them for ever . . . like the moments in a movie, when the hero comes back unexpectedly from the war and the sweethearts recapture their love with waves crashing on the shore, the crescendo of music filling the air . . .

As they moved away, they became rudely aware that the thundering noises in the air had nothing to do with music, nor the rapid beat of their hearts.

'God, just listen to that,' Glenn muttered, as the roar of the ack-ack guns made the earth shake beneath their feet. 'It's a bad one tonight and no mistake. Looks like it's over Portsmouth.'

The searchlights were beginning to criss-cross in the distance now, and the angry buzz of enemy aircraft was unmistakable. As the earth shook still more an orange glow began to appear to the west, evidence that the German bombs were finding their targets.

'Do you wish you were up there?' Daisy murmured, wondering if the thrill of war that all men seemed to feel was taking him momentarily away from her. Jealously she wanted to keep him to herself.

'Not right now,' Glenn said, his arms tightening around her, 'Right now, all I want to think about is you.'

She shivered again, and he asked if she was cold.

'No. Just a bit scared. Which I know I shouldn't be.'

'Everybody gets scared. We wouldn't be human if we didn't. My mother used to say the trick is to look ahead. Whatever today brings, however scared you are, all you can do is your best. But tomorrow is another day. Another chance.'

'I like the sound of your mother.'

'I hope you will like her. She's looking forward to meeting you.'

Daisy's heart gave a gigantic leap. 'You've told her about me?'

'Why wouldn't I tell her about the girl I'm going to marry?'

She gave a small scream as the sound of the bombardment to the south almost deafened them, crackling like thunder in the still air.

Almost drowning out the sound of Glenn's words. Almost.

'Let's get out of here,' he said, catching hold of her hand.

They ran towards the parked vehicles, and he bundled her inside the one he and his buddies had arrived in. It didn't shut out the noise, it just gave them some small feeling of security and privacy.

'Will they close down the club for the night if this goes on much longer?' he asked, as she nestled in his arms.

'No. The band always plays on to the bitter end. They just play louder and louder, and nobody leaves unless they're ordered to do so.'

'That's the British for you,' he said, a smile in his voice.

'Are you making fun of us?' Daisy said twisting in his arms, and thinking how deliciously decadent this all seemed, and how outraged Aunt Rose would be if she could see them now. Or maybe not.

'Absolutely not. I just think how brave you all are.'

'We're not brave. Just stubborn. As Mr Churchill said, we'll fight them in the air and on the beaches, and we'll never give in.'

'Amen to that,' Glenn said, and she realised how serious they had become in seconds. How almost tearfully serious on her part.

'So are you going to marry me when all this is over?' he said.

She drew in her breath, completely taken off balance. It was hardly the time or place, shut up in the stuffy atmosphere of a military vehicle, and hardly the most romantic of settings, with guns blazing in the distance, the roar of enemy aircraft overhead, and the sky periodically lit up by bomb blasts. But to Daisy it was still the most romantic moment of her life.

'Yes, please,' she whispered.

His kiss was very sweet on her lips as she wrapped her arms around him and felt his heart beating in complete unison with her own.

And then the perfect moment was brutally broken as the door of the vehicle was ripped open, and Glenn's colleagues were bursting inside.

'Sorry mate,' one of them said harshly. 'We've been recalled. You'll have to get your little gal out of here p.d.q.'

Daisy gasped, but the engine was already revving up, and the driver was yelling that he'd drop her as near to the club as possible, but she'd have to make her own way back inside. There was no time for finesse, and she could feel the energy in them all, wanting to get back to base, wanting to be up in their flying machines and do what they had been trained for.

And all she could do was sit tight, clinging on to Glenn's hand until she was unceremoniously tipped out and sent on her way.

'I'll be in touch as soon as I can,' he called out, seconds before the vehicle was swallowed up in the night, and she was left reeling, wondering if it had happened at all. Had he really proposed, and had she really accepted?

The noise of heavy artillery reminded her that she had better get inside, and she slipped into the hall, blinking in the contrast between dark and light, stumbling through the cavorting dancers until she found Molly.

'There you are! Bob's been trailing around with a glass of lemonade for you for ages, but I think he's given up on you and given it to some other girl. I don't know what happened a little while ago, but all the boys in blue suddenly made a bolt for the door and left as if all the demons in Hades were after them.'

Daisy looked dumbly at her friend, finding it very hard to bring herself back to the reality of the dance that was still going on. Music was still playing, couples were still dancing, relentlessly determined to have a good time while they could, and Molly was still chattering. Until she looked at Daisy sharply.

'What's up? What's happened? He didn't do – Daisy, you *are* all right, aren't you? You know what I mean.'

Daisy's mouth was so dry she could hardly answer until she grabbed Molly's glass of lemonade and took a long drink without asking. Then she gave a shaky, disbelieving laugh.

'What he *did*, if you mean Glenn – my darling Glenn – was ask me to marry him. And I said yes!'

'Cripes, Daisy! How exciting!' Molly squealed.

They both flinched as the noise of the battle to the south shook the Forces Club for a few minutes, but the band still doggedly played on, and the dancers kept dancing. Above it, they could hear the whine of retaliating aircraft, and Daisy knew that in a very short while, Glenn would be among them.

But she wouldn't think of it. She simply would not think of it.

'Let's tell the girls,' Molly said excitedly. 'They'll all want to celebrate before we part company. It'll be a great way to go, Daisy!'

'Well, I suppose it's all right to tell them, even though it's not official yet. But I'm not going to tell any of my family.'

Molly stared at her. 'Good Lord, why ever not?'

'Call it superstitious, if you like, but I'm not telling any of them until Glenn and I can tell them together. It wouldn't be right, otherwise. Sort of lop-sided.'

'Not even these sisters you keep writing to and telephoning?'

'Not even them,' Daisy said firmly.

'We're privileged then,' Molly said, clearly not understanding, but knowing that glint in Daisy's eyes when she saw it. They all knew it by now, especially Naomi Tyler-Smythe. Which reminded her.

'Anyway, I've got news for you,' she said, raising her voice again as the shattering noise outside continued. 'If we can't get home on our forty-eight, we're invited to spend it with Naomi's folks in the country. What do you think about that? Do say yes. It'll be fun to see how the other half lives.'

Of course Daisy had intended going home. But she wasn't sure she really wanted to just yet. Not until she knew what post she was going to be offered, and if it was in nursing as she had now requested, then not until she could speak calmly about her change of decision. Even telling a blatant lie, saying she had to go where she was sent, right now she didn't think she could be convincing enough to do that.

'Are you sure Naomi included me?'

'She *especially* included you, idiot. I think it's a kind of peace offering.'

Out of the corner of her eye, Daisy could see Naomi weaving her way towards them.

'Was that your lovely Canadian?' she asked her by way of greeting.

'It was, and he asked me to marry him, and you're one of the first to know,' Daisy said, and at her delighted exclamation, they both knew the truce was well and truly in place.

'Has Molly asked you about coming to my place for our forty-eight? Do say you will, Daisy, and we'll have a little celebration for you.'

'I'd love it, and thank you,' Daisy said, smiling. 'My sister keeps asking me to visit her in Yorkshire but this will be much more fun.'

'It will. We'll be the three musketeers – or something,' Molly said vaguely.

'More like the three *caballeros*,' Naomi said, airing her Spanish.

After her storming conversation with Elsie, Daisy felt she had to write to tell her of her proposed visit to Hertfordshire to Naomi's home for their leave.

'It's not that I don't want to go home, nor to come and see you and Faith, who I'm quite sure is adorable by now, but a forty-eight hour pass is so short that it takes most of my time travelling. Anyway, I'm dying to see this wonderful home of Naomi's. She makes it sound little short of a royal palace. What a lark. Molly and I are sure she's exaggerating, and that it'll be a small cottage in the country or something. Then again, her father *is* a brigadier – unless that's all a fantasy as well. I'll keep you posted, Elsie.

'And by the way, I'm quite over my last little problem, and Naomi and I are firm friends again now. She couldn't help having an allergy, could she? And she hasn't been able to see "my man in Harley Street" for some treatment recently. That's what she calls him. She's a scream, isn't she?

'I've kept the most important news of all until last. Glenn turned up at one of our Camp dances. It was such a thrill to see him so unexpectedly, but as usual the Jerry bombers came over and ruined the evening by sending the whole lot of them back to their base. It was lovely seeing him for an hour or so though.'

And that was all she was going to say about it.

Molly and Daisy got the postings they wanted. After their forty-eight hour leave Molly was going to the motor vehicle division at Southampton as a motor mechanic maintenance worker, and Daisy was being sent to a military hospital in Sussex. It would be considerably nearer to Glenn's base, she thought with a glow of pleasure. They would be able to see one another more often at last.

As for Naomi . . .

'Well, I'm not sure what to make of this,' she said, frowning ever so slightly, and ever mindful of her perfect forehead. 'I know I've taken the courses here, but I didn't think I had any real aptitude for clerical work, especially in a hospital, and I'm sure it's not a good idea with my rhinitis –'

'Of course it is, providing you don't sneeze over all the patients, and think of all those lovely doctors on hand to give you treatment whenever you need it. Anyway, it's clearing up now, isn't it? It's only a summer thing, and summer's pretty well over now,' Daisy said encouragingly.

Naomi was still uneasy. 'You're right. But I'm just no good around ill people. Never have been.'

'You'd be surprised what you can do when you have to,' Daisy told her, feeling rather like Matron with a new recruit. 'But in any case, you'll be in a little office dealing with patients' records, not mopping up sick.'

Naomi visibly paled, and Daisy wished she hadn't been so sharp. It wasn't her fault she'd been brought up hardly having to lift a finger to do anything.

'What did you expect to be doing after you'd joined up?' she asked.

'I don't know. I rather thought something with horses, perhaps,' Naomi said vaguely. 'I know how to deal with them—'

Molly hooted. 'You should have applied for the Land Army then, though I can't see much difference in all that farming muck and working on a hospital ward with all that blood and guts. It's all shit, isn't it?'

Molly liked to shock her, and she was clearly tiring of all this class-conscious nonsense. And Daisy could see their friendship whittling away by the minute, and the forty-eight hour leave vanishing before it had even begun. She spoke decisively, linking her arm through Naomi's and giving it a comforting squeeze.

'Naomi, you'll be fine, honestly. And at least we're going to the same hospital. That's a bonus, isn't it? It'll be fun.'

She crossed her fingers, knowing that no hospital job was ever fun, but she would be in the thick of it on the wards, not Naomi.

'And you can always ask for a transfer if it gets too much for you,' Molly said, her sarcasm lost on Naomi as her face brightened.

'I can, can't I? I'm sure Daddy could pull a few strings if I asked him. Well, that makes me feel better about it, so let's get our things together and be on our way. I shan't be sorry to see the back of this beastly barracks.'

Molly's raised eyebrows said there was really no hope for her, but Daisy ignored her and got on with her packing.

This afternoon they were setting off for Hertfordshire and Naomi's stately pile. The civvies could come out, and they could forget all about the war for a blissful forty-eight hours and feel human again. And *that* was a bonus, if you like.

Twelve

The focal point of every family's day was gathering around the wireless set to listen to the calm and measured tones of Bruce Belfrage announcing the nine o'clock news. All hopes were pinned on the Americans entering the war, but although they were declared allies, while still avowing their neutrality, so far their involvement had relied on their ships escorting British vessels in the German U-boat-infested waters of the Atlantic.

The young boys were not allowed to stay up long enough to hear the nine o'clock bulletins, but Vanessa was, and she had lately begun taking more notice of the news, each girl in her class making a diary account for posterity, as their English mistress called it.

At one time, Vanessa had avoided listening to the news as much as possible. If she didn't hear what was happening, then it wasn't happening. But now the trauma of her own experience in the blitz was fading from her mind because Weston seemed so safe compared with London.

She was bright enough to know that it wasn't really safe, of course. They got their share of raids, and the town had suffered casualties from the bombing. But it was nothing like the carnage that was happening in the major cities such as London and Bristol and Coventry and Plymouth. Contrary to the way many other people felt, Vanessa felt safe for the first time in her life. Safe, secure, and blinkered, and well-integrated into her life at the County School.

'These news announcers never tell you half of it, anyway,'

Bert scowled, on his high horse as usual as they were preparing to listen to the latest bulletin. 'It's all glossed over to make us feel better, and it's the same with the newspapers, too. They're forbidden to print half of what goes on, and the bloody lot treat us like infants. Don't they think we've got a right to know the truth?'

'Hush, Bert,' Rose told him sharply as he fiddled with the controls to get a better signal. 'Don't get so heated about it, and I don't want you waking up Teddy and Harry either.'

'Pipe down a minute, will you, woman?' Bert snapped, as the wireless continued to crackle and whistle. He knew very well he should have got the battery re-charged before now, and that she was about to tell him so.

It didn't help his temper, which was fraying more and more as the weeks went by, and his nightly stints with the ARP watch were taking their toll. Bert was a man who needed his sleep, and he just wasn't getting as much as he needed. As for sleeping in the day-time, he considered that for old men and invalids, and he was neither, thank you very much. He conceded to a couple of cat-naps and that was all. But it was all having an adverse effect on his normal easygoing nature, and the rest of the household had to like it or lump it.

In the end he gave up trying to hear the news that evening, almost ready to put his fist through the black bakelite wireless set. It was mocking him, he raged, sitting there as proud as Punch with its shiny surface nearly polished to death by Rose's diligent hands and at the thought, he wondered if he was going mad. They said lack of sleep could do that to a person.

'Oh well, it looks as if we'll have to wait until tomorrow to hear what went on today,' Rose remarked calmly. 'Never mind. No news is – well, no news, so who's for a cup of cocoa before we all have an early night?'

'I'll make it, shall I?' Vanessa said, jumping up at once.

Rose watched her go appreciatively.

'That girl's turning into a much nicer person than when

she came here the first time, when we had all that trouble with her.'

'And I suppose you're preening yourself on your part in that, are you?' Bert said, still not ready to be pacified over not being able to hear the news broadcast on his own wireless set. 'You mark my words – they say a leopard never changes its spots, and I wouldn't get too complacent if I were you.'

'Oh, you're such an old grouch these days,' Rose exclaimed. 'I don't know what's got into you sometimes. Vanessa's being perfectly pleasant, she's trying hard at school, and all you can do is complain.'

'Well, I'm not fooled by her. Kids have no respect for their elders these days, and it's probably all a sham,' Bert snapped. 'It won't last, but it's not her I'm complaining about. It's this bloody war that's getting on my nerves.'

Fed up with his language, Rose managed to bite back the sharp retort that he wasn't the only one on that score, and put her arms around him instead.

'I know, love, it's getting on my nerves, too, but don't take it out on the rest of us. We all have to get through it as best we can, don't we?'

Vanessa came back from the kitchen at that moment to ask if either of them wanted a biscuit with their cocoa, and grinned at the pair of them. Her voice was brash and breezy, and loaded with her old East End cheek.

'Well, don't you two look like sloppy love-birds! Shall I go out and come in again when you've finished with all the kissy-kissy stuff?'

Bert's face went an angry red, and Rose sighed, knowing he couldn't tolerate that kind of chit-chat the way he once could. And wishing Vanessa hadn't chosen that moment to revert to her old ways.

'You see what I mean?' he snapped. 'I don't want any bloody cocoa. What I need is a pint, so I'm going to the pub to hear the news, and I shall stay there until I go on watch. I'll see you sometime in the morning.'

He gave Rose a quick peck on the cheek and strode out to the hall for his overcoat, slinging his gas mask and his ARP warden's hard hat over his shoulder before slamming the door and going out into the September evening.

'Well, what's got into him?' Vanessa said, dumping the tray on the table and glaring at nothing in particular. 'Was it something I said?'

Rose sighed. These upsets with Bert were becoming more and more frequent. In the past, they had always enjoyed their little spats which were like a breath of life to them. Within the family they were famous for them, and the bickering had always ended amicably, but not any more. She didn't quite know how to handle these aggressive moods. She could handle Vanessa, though.

'Vanessa, do you know what the word precocious means?' she asked mildly. 'If not, why don't you look it up in the dictionary?'

The pub was full of the usual locals. There was less beer than gossip, but it was a men's meeting-place for a chat, for a game of darts or skittles or dominoes, and a few hours away from the wife, according to some.

Bert had never felt the need to get away from Rose in that way, but he put up with the initial chaffing of his contemporaries, knowing he had got there with only minutes to spare before the news came on, and he knew they would all be silent then as they crowded around the communal wireless set.

Germany was still marching into Russia and winning ground all the time, and there was more than a hint that British and Russian counter-attacks were making ground from the middle-east countries.

'That'll be Iran and Saudi,' one knowledgeable local said. 'They'll be sending in the tanks next, you see if they don't. Good desert weapons, tanks. Hot as hell inside though, by all accounts – and even hotter in Saudi.'

'Sending our troops to the desert won't do any good,' grunted another. 'We're not suited to them hot conditions this time, any more'n we were in the last.'

'Where's your loyalty, man?' Bert put in testily. 'If the Jerries can stand the heat, I'm bloody sure our boys can.'

'You ain't got kids, have you, Bert?' he was asked.

'What in tarnation's that got to do with anything?' he rounded on the man. 'I've got nieces in the forces, and a nephew who drowned at Dunkirk, so don't go lording it over me, Dan Willcocks.'

'Oh ah, I was forgetting your brother-in-law's boy. No offence, man.'

'None taken,' Bert said grimly, simply because it was the obligatory reply. He bloody well did take offence, though. He might not have a son to send to war like many of them here did, but he knew the heartache of it through Baz, and the fury of it through his brother-in-law's shop being blown to smithereens.

He knew the stress and frustration of Rose wanting to fill their house with evacuee children, half of them not wanting to be there in the first place, and one of them running back to London at the first chance she got, and now this new one who never said a word. Unnerving, it was. Bloody unnerving.

Though he had to agree with Rose that Vanessa had calmed down a lot since she'd come back to them with her tail between her legs and a willingness to learn at the fancy school she was at now. He admitted, too, that he'd been out of order earlier on that evening. He couldn't do anything about that tonight, but he'd make it up to them both tomorrow.

He agreed to a game of darts with Dan Willcocks before he had to report for duty. The truth was, although he was feeling so bloody tired these days, doing something positive to help the war effort at least made him feel that he wasn't on the scrap heap yet. In the first lot he had been as fired up and ready for action as any of the young bucks doing their duty now.

It was why he'd had every sympathy for young Baz, needing to get away from the stifling job of shop assistant and into a man's world. Even though that need had finally killed him, at least he'd gone down fighting . . .

'Are you playing or not, Bert?' he heard Dan yell at him. 'You've been standing there with that arrow in your hand for a good five minutes now. Is it glued to your hand, or summat?'

He blinked, throwing the dart indiscriminately towards the board, and hearing his mates cheer derisively as it fell right outside the wire.

Hopeless was the word for it all right. But he just wasn't in the mood, and he knew it. And there was still an hour to go before he had to report for duty. The darts game was nearly over, and he was throwing it away. He'd be due to stand a round of drinks before he was done, and he didn't really care. It was just as Rosie had said. He was turning into an old grouch.

'Never mind, Bert, old chap,' one of the others called out. 'Maybe you'll do better at dominoes.'

He scowled. Dominoes was for old men, too. The irony was that he usually won, so that must say something. By the time he left the pub, he was slightly swaying, and had never felt less like standing around in the cold and damp, straining his eyes for the sight and sound of enemy aircraft and wishing himself nicely tucked up in his own bed.

But there was a job to do, and he had four hours of sleepless night to do it, along with his fellow volunteers. Their patrol base was out on Birnbeck Pier, with a good vantage point of the Bristol Channel and the Welsh coast. Though who would want to blow Wales to Kingdom Come, Bert couldn't think, wanting to have no truck with the Welshies as a breed, but for no particular reason, he admitted. Except that on Sunday nights when the pubs in Wales were dry, they frequently got droves of the buggers coming across on the steamer to fill the Weston and Clevedon pubs. And that was reason enough in his opinion.

But this was a particularly dark and unproductive night. With the heavy cloud cover there was no likelihood of air raids tonight, no sense of impending doom, he thought, using one of Vanessa's fancy phrases since she'd taken to reading poetry. He grinned, having to agree with Rose that she wasn't turning into such a bad kid after all now, and that he should probably show it more.

And at last his four-hour watch was over and another gang could take over. He walked back the length of the pier with his mates, none of them saying much, each feeling the need to get home and into the warmth and safety of their own four walls around them. He could hear the weathered planks creaking beneath his feet, and the suck of the water ebbing and flowing far below the old iron supports.

Bert always liked the sound of it. It was eternal, the sea. More powerful than puny humans. Poor young Baz discovered that. He pulled himself together, realising he was going farther and farther down the maudlin road lately. Baz was gone, but there were others who needed him. There was Rose, and Teddy, and the vaccy kids. A man had to be the strong one.

He said goodbye to the others and struck out towards home. The early hours of the morning were still pitch black, and dawn was still a long way off. It was silent now, with no enemy bastards threatening the peace of the town he knew and loved. It was almost surreal, with no street lights to guide him, because of blackout regulations, and no glimmer of light showing behind dark curtains at this hour. If there had been, it would have been his duty to knock on a door and remind them that they could be alerting enemy aircraft. According to the stern regulations, even a cigarette lighter could be a signal to a keen-eyed pilot, crazy and far-fetched though it seemed to Bert. But rules were rules, and you had to obey them.

You didn't even need to look both ways crossing a road in

the darkest hours. It was unlikely there would be any traffic about, and if there was, you could have heard a pin drop, so you'd certainly hear the sound of an car's engine. Right now there was nothing, and after his earlier bouts of misery, if not aggression, Bert felt a extraordinary sense of peace creeping over him as he neared the home that he and Rose had so lovingly created.

He didn't even see the lamp-post looming up in front of him. He didn't have time to side-step, nor even to cry out. He simply walked straight into it, hitting the front of his head with an almighty bang that winded him instantly. His vision was suddenly filled with a kaleidoscope of red and orange stars for a few seconds, and then he crashed like a rock to the ground.

Rose usually slept reasonably well. By now it had been decided that they would all sleep in their own beds until or unless the siren went, and then they would decamp (Vanessa's word) to the safety of the cellar where the emergency beds were made up. The boys had changed their minds about the creepiness of it all, and almost relished being woken from their beds and trooped downstairs to the dungeon below, until Vanessa had put that particular word on it.

She really was a bit of a madam, Rose had thought, with rough affection as she settled herself down to sleep that night, while hoping Bert wasn't having too bad a time of it. She didn't begrudge him his times at the pub with his mates before his watch. It was what men did. Gave them a chance to let off steam against their womenfolk amongst other things, according to some.

Rose smiled into the darkness. That didn't do any harm either, providing they didn't give away any of their private business, and she was pretty sure Bert would never do that. They had a strong marriage, for all their bickering, and they both compared that to no more than ripples on a pond. It made no difference to the real fabric of their lives and the love they shared, even if they weren't in the habit of talking about it. They didn't need to, anyway. It simply existed, as solid as the Rock of Gibraltar.

At first, she didn't know what woke her. When Bert got in from his shift, he usually managed to undress and climb into bed silently, considering he was such a large man. But it wasn't Bert sliding in beside her. It was something else.

And then her heart jolted. There was a noise downstairs. Someone was stumbling about, blundering into things, knocking things over. She heard the sound of glass breaking, and a muttered voice cursing. And she knew it wasn't one of the children's voices.

Rose swallowed her initial fears, mindful she was an adult, and that there were three children in the house, and that she was responsible for them. And absolutely determined that no clumsy or inept burglar was going to wreck her home, or steal any of the things that she and Bert cherished.

She slid out of bed, pulling her dressing-gown around her. No burglar was going to catch Rose Painter looking less than dignified either – or as dignified as she could be in a candlewick dressing-gown and slippers, with her hair a tortuous porcupine of metal curlers. None of it mattered. She grabbed a heavy vase from the bedroom window-sill, and with her heart beating horribly fast, she opened the door and crept down the stairs in the darkness.

The buggers always use the element of surprise, Bert always said of the Jerry bombers. And Rose was going to do just that, in a domestic way.

Once in the sitting room, she fumbled for the electric light switch and flipped it on. It was impossible not to blink in the sudden change from dark to light, and it took a few seconds for her to register what she was seeing.

The same could be said for the person swaying in front of her, clinging to an armchair as if it was a lifeline, as if he would surely fall without its support.

'*Bert!*' Rose almost screamed in a mixture of relief and

rage. 'You nearly frightened me to death. What on earth do you mean by creeping about like that and falling over things? Are you drunk?'

'Shut up, woman, and let me sit down,' she heard him slur.

As he fell heavily into the armchair, Rose looked at him properly then, and felt a second shock. One that sent a huge tremor of fear through her.

'Bert, what's happened to you?' she said shrilly. 'You look terrible.'

'It's nothing to make a fuss about,' he muttered. 'I just need to get to my bed with a couple of aspirins and I'll be all right when I've had some sleep.'

'But what's *happened*, you old fool? I can see that something has. You look positively grey, and you've got a lump like an egg on your forehead.'

He touched it carefully, not prepared to admit to her how badly it throbbed, nor intending to say how he had come by it. Walking into a lamp-post in the blackout, for God's sake . . . it was hardly the stuff of heroes!

'I had a bit of an accident, that's all,' he went on, still muttering, still not prepared to admit what a bloody old fool he felt. They might laugh about it in the morning, but not now. Not yet.

'I can see that. Sit there while I fetch some witch hazel.'

'Oh, don't fuss me, woman. Just let me get to bed.'

'*Sit!*' Rose ordered, as if she was speaking to George.

Actually, she found herself thinking when she went off to the medicine box, what a fat lot of good George was as a house dog, sleeping the sleep of the just in his basket, snuffling and dreaming, and oblivious to the fact that somebody had entered the house in the early hours. But then, of course, he would know Bert. He knew Bert was now in the habit of returning at unearthly hours.

All this thinking was to keep her heart from jumping, and thinking just *how* ghastly Bert looked. Knowing how he always strode along in his usual eagerness to get home after an ARP watch, he must have had a terrific bang on the head. It was a wonder it hadn't knocked him out. Or maybe it had, and he wasn't telling.

She hurried back to the sitting room with the bottle of witch hazel and a pad of cotton wool. He was leaning back in the chair now, his eyes closed, looking completely exhausted. The ugly lump on his forehead seemed to be swelling by the minute, and Rose felt a new surge of alarm. It should be looked at by a doctor, but she guessed what his reaction would be if she suggested calling him out, particularly at this hour. Lot of nonsense, woman!

Just as though Jerry's victims were always injured nice and tidily in the middle of the day. To her mind, Bert was just as much one of Jerry's victims as anyone hurt in a bombing raid. Viciously, she attributed it to Hitler that they had to have blackout regulations at all. And middle-aged men like Bert, who had done his duty in the first war, shouldn't be out patrolling the streets at all hours.

'What are you doing, woman?' he slurred again, as vague as if he'd forgotten already, as she knelt down beside him.

'I told you, I'm going to put this pad of witch hazel on that lump,' she said sharply. 'I don't like the look of it at all.'

'I don't exactly like the bloody feel of it either,' he grumbled, with a tiny spark of his usual spirit.

He winced as he felt the coldness of the witch hazel pad on his forehead. It probably wouldn't do any good. A stiff drink of brandy might be more to the point. Good for shock – although if he mentioned it, Rose would probably put on her pious voice and insist that hot sweet tea was just as good.

His thoughts were wandering, and what he needed more than anything was a good night's sleep. That, and some aspirin to try to deaden the appalling pain in his head. By the time Rose had brought them, and a glass of water to take them with, he was more than ready to stagger upstairs to bed.

'I'll be as right as rain in the morning,' he told her, once she had helped him out of his clothes and tucked him in as tightly as a bloody trussed chicken.

But he wasn't all right in the morning. Rose knew it as soon as she opened her eyes after a fitful couple of hours sleep beside him.

In the morning, Bert Painter was dead.

It's a funny thing about death. Well, not funny, Rose amended distractedly, but odd. When you were expecting someone to die from a long illness it was inevitable and easier to accept. When you had seen someone go out to his usual nightly ARP duties, put him to bed with a sore head, and then woken up to find him stiff and cold beside you, it takes every bit of reason from your mind.

It turns you into a screaming madwoman. It takes away every semblance of sense that you ever had, shamefully turning your bowels to water, your legs to putty. It destroys your dignity, your self-respect . . .

Rose found herself furiously shaking the man she had loved for thirty years, pinching him, pummelling him, screaming at him to wake up at once and stop being a bloody old fool . . . to stop pretending . . .

She wasn't even aware that she was screaming until she heard the three childrens' footsteps running into the bedroom, the sound of the dog barking madly downstairs, and the rattle of the milkman's cart somewhere down the street, all cutting into her consciousness.

'What are you doing, Aunt Rose?' she heard Vanessa shriek. 'What's the matter with Uncle Bert?'

'Is he dead?' Teddy howled.

Harry stood behind him, white-faced, hiding behind Teddy, not wanting to look or to know, but unable to move away.

Rose pulled herself together with an enormous effort. All of these children had already seen enough death in horrific circumstances: Teddy seeing his mother fall into the Clifton gorge and learning how his brother had drowned in France;

Vanessa and Harry both having had their families wiped out in air raids.

'Uncle Bert's been taken ill,' Rose gasped, when she could get her shattered thoughts together. 'Go and telephone the doctor, please, Vanessa, and you boys go and get yourselves washed and dressed and then go down to the parlour. Vanessa will get you some breakfast before you go to school.'

She looked at the girl wordlessly.

But she knew. Of course she knew. Vanessa had probably been streetwise before she had been six years old, and now she was a surprisingly mature fourteen, and Rose had never needed her more.

She saw the girl nod, and then she shooed the boys out of the bedroom and went to do Rose's bidding. Knowing that the doctor was needed, not to make Bert well again, but to confirm that he had died.

And then Rose was alone with Bert. She trembled as she looked at his face, the craggy, beloved face of the man who had shared her life for all those years. The man with whom she had fought and loved with equal passion, and who had thought the world of her. She smoothed his greying hair back from the swollen forehead, seeing how very angry and discoloured it was now, and with the memory of her old first-aid training coming to the fore, she knew there must have been some massive internal bleeding. A haemorrhage that had taken him away from her.

She bent and kissed his blue lips very gently. When she spoke, her voice was no more than a whisper, more full of pain than it had ever been before.

'Oh Bert, my love, I always loved you, and I always will.'

Thirteen

R ose couldn't rid her head of macabre thoughts. Once the doctor had been and confirmed that Bert was indeed dead – as if she didn't know that – she wanted to keep him here until the day he was buried. Here in the bed they had shared. Here, where his bulky warmth had comforted her for all those years.

As the marriage service said – for better or worse, in sickness and in health. And what about in death? He was still hers – to have and to hold.

The doctor insisted gently that they would have to take Bert to the hospital to determine the cause of death. It was necessary. And then he should go to the hospital Chapel of Rest until the arrangements could be made – which would also be a good thing since there were young children in the house, he had added delicately. All tidy and clinical. Disposing of Bert.

So, when she had been forced to agree to it all, and the hospital people had come and taken Bert away, she looked at the bed where he had lain. Empty now, but with the indentation of his body still there; the dent where his head had been; the smell of him; the nearness and the dearness of him.

Fiercely possessive now, she wanted to keep those sheets on the bed for ever; to lie on them; to wrap herself in them; to absorb whatever was left of Bert into herself. She had always been so strong – the acknowledged steely one, the acerbic one in the family. And now she felt as if everything in her was dissolving. She hardly realised she had collapsed on to the bed, almost in supplication, until she heard Vanessa's scared young voice.

'I've made you some tea, Aunt Rose. Shall I help you strip the bed and get the sheets and pillow cases into the wash boiler?'

'Why aren't you at school?' Rose mumbled into the pillow. Bert's pillow, full of the hair grease he plastered on his head. She could almost taste it, no longer finding it annoying because it was difficult to remove in the wash, but part of who he was.

'I've taken the day off. I've sent the boys and I'm staying here with you. I thought I should. There are things to do. People to tell.'

Her voice faltered and fell away, and Rose slowly sat up, her hair tangled, her eyes wild with tears and pain. Vanessa was dry-eyed, her eyes huge in her heart-shaped face, but she could tell the girl was suffering, too. They all were. Bert had been the heart and soul of this home, and now he was gone. Now she had no one. He was her family. None of these children were hers. She had no family . . . no one. She was suddenly shaking from head to toe. Without warning, Vanessa rushed across the room and wrapped her arms around Rose's trembling body. Seeing the disintegration of this stalwart woman, she quickly became passionate and tearful herself.

'Oh, Aunt Rose, we loved him, too. We may not always have shown it, and I know I was sometimes a terrible bleedin' trial to him, but we did love him, me and Teddy and Harry. And all the others.'

'Others?' Rose said vaguely. And then, for the first time since she had woken to find Bert cold beside her, the world around her that had narrowed to encompass only grief, was forced to widen.

'Yes. Of course. I must let my brother know – and the girls – they'll be so upset. Oh, my poor Daisy . . .'

She didn't know why she especially mentioned Daisy,

except that she and Bert had always had a special empathy for one another.

'You see? You're not on your own,' Vanessa said, just as if she could read her thoughts, and still acting far beyond her years. But of course, she had seen it all before, Rose remembered. 'They'll all want to come and be with you, so what do you want to do first? Change the sheets or telephone people?'

Rose gave her the glimmer of a smile. Who was the adult here?

'You're a proper little Hitler on the QT, aren't you, Vanessa?'

She bit her lips hard, wishing she hadn't said quite those words, in the circumstances. She took a shuddering breath, knowing she couldn't talk to anybody yet, because once she put it into words, the nightmare would come true.

'We'll both do the sheets, and then you can give me moral support while I make the telephone calls.'

What she meant, and they both knew it, was in case the words choked her and Vanessa needed to take over. It was still unbelievable, unreal. Bert had gone out last night, grumbling and scratchy, just being Bert, but she had been quite confident that he'd be his old self by the morning. Instead of that, he was dead.

'Righty-ho, sheets first, phone later,' said the girl. 'But first of all, drink this bleedin' tea before it goes cold. Tea don't grow on trees, you know.'

Quentin and Mary said they would come down to Weston that same afternoon and that Rose wasn't to worry about a thing, of all the daft things to say, Rose thought, with a small spark of normality. By then, she had recovered a tiny bit of her composure, only retiring to her bedroom now and then to weep in private, and then to reappear with her chin moderately high. They had contacted Immy without too much trouble, and she said she would be able to get down tomorrow.

Elsie just blubbered into the phone and said that she and Faith would be on the next train, no matter how much Rose protested that it was far too long a journey for her with a young baby. The vicar had come and gone, telling Rose to call on him whenever she needed the church's comfort, whatever the hour.

Aware of all the activity, several neighbours had called in to offer their sympathy, and Rose's old friend Mrs Luckwell from the farm had arrived, sharing Vanessa's endless cups of tea, until Rose thought she would be awash with them.

'Now there's only Daisy,' Vanessa said.

As yet, they hadn't been able to contact Daisy. All the telephone lines to Flayton Camp seemed to be permanently engaged, but since there had been some heavy air raids in the vicinity on the previous night, it wasn't surprising.

Almost in surprise, Rose had registered Mrs Luckwell's comments about it. The war and everything about it was very far from her mind.

'Perhaps she's already on her way home to surprise you,' Vanessa suggested. 'She was going to get some leave soon, wasn't she? That'll be it, I bet. She'll turn up when we least expect it.'

'I hope she doesn't,' Rose said distractedly. 'The last thing I want is for Daisy to burst in here to discover what's happened without being pre-warned.'

Seeing her new distress, Mrs Luckwell took charge and did the only practical thing she could think of, which was to offer to take the two boys to the farm for as long as Rose felt it necessary. They would think of it as a small holiday with her own evacuee children, so if Rose wanted to pack a few things for them now, she would meet them from school that afternoon.

Rose couldn't think of anything so mundane as packing clothes, so Vanessa disappeared upstairs to sort out the clothes and toys and comics.

'You've got a good girl there,' Mrs Luckwell remarked,

when she was out of the room. 'I never thought I'd say it, but she's turned up trumps, hasn't she?'

'Yes,' Rose said vaguely.

'A proper Caldwell girl, in fact!' the farmer's wife added, awarding her no greater compliment.

The chauffeur-driven motor car purred into the winding, tree-lined driveway, and ahead of them the Tyler-Smythe mansion was bathed in the mellow splendour of late September sunlight.

'Gosh,' Daisy said.

'Gosh and *golly* gosh,' Molly muttered.

Naomi laughed. 'Oh, come on girls, you've seen a house before!'

'This ain't a house, it's a bleedin' palace,' Molly squeaked. 'You might have warned us we were spendin' our leave with royalty.'

'We're not royalty, you goose, just people.'

'And I suppose we have to dress for dinner?' Molly went on sarcastically, which Daisy knew was to cover her nervousness.

'Not any more,' Naomi said seriously. 'Mummy decided we should dispense with all that when half the staff were called up.'

Daisy swallowed convulsively, hardly daring to look at Molly's face, and knowing this would just about put the finishing touches to her fright. The first sight of the uniformed chauffeur meeting them at the station, and tipping his cap to Naomi as if she was the queen, had been fright enough. But obviously all this magnificence was perfectly normal to Naomi – and nothing like anything either of the other two had seen.

Molly was already wishing she was somewhere else, but Daisy was looking forward to being in a normal family home again, even if was an enormous one. Anything was better than being in constant earshot of bombs and air raids. And

170

apparently, deep in the Hertfordshire countryside, they were well away from it all.

'Oh, come on, Molly, cheer up! We're going to have such fun,' Naomi was saying enthusiastically.

As they neared the house, the front door burst open and a small figure came running out. He was about six years old, and Naomi gave a mock groan at the sight of him. But when she got out of the car she swept him up in her arms.

'Hello, Squirt,' she said, with real sibling affection. 'My goodness, haven't you grown! Come and say hello to my chums.'

Until that wonderful forty-eight hour leave, they hadn't even known that Naomi had a small brother, nor an older one at boarding school who was destined for Eton and great things. They hadn't expected her mother to be such a darling, either, despite talking with a whacking great plum in her mouth, according to Molly, or that they would be living in quite such luxury for these blissful few days. They could hang up their uniforms and wear ordinary frocks again, and almost forget there was a war on at all.

It was on their last evening, after Naomi's small brother had gone protestingly to bed, and the four women were sitting in the drawing room drinking cocoa and exchanging stories, when the maid entered the room to say there was a telephone call for Miss Daisy Caldwell.

'For me?' Daisy said in surprise. 'But nobody knows I'm here!'

Molly chuckled. 'Obviously somebody has tracked you down, Daisy. It must be somebody who wants to get hold of you in a mighty hurry, so it's probably your lovely Canadian.'

Daisy felt herself go pink. She *had* told Glenn she and Molly were going to spend their leave with Naomi, but she had never expected him to call her here. It must be important. Perhaps he, too, was getting leave and was hoping to see her.

'I'm so sorry about this,' she said to Naomi's mother. 'Please excuse me.'

'My dear girl, of course.'

Daisy went out to the telephone table in the hall, her heart leaping with excitement. It had to be Glenn of course. But just in case it wasn't . . .

'Hello,' she spoke coolly into the mouthpiece. 'This is Daisy Caldwell.'

She couldn't make out the voice at the other end at first. It sounded so muffled and odd, as if someone was holding a hanky to their face. It sounded more sinister than anything else.

After her elation at thinking it might be Glenn, she thought it must be someone playing an unpleasant trick on her, and she almost slammed the receiver down again. Then the person cleared their throat very noisily.

'Daisy, I'm so sorry—'

Her head whirled. '*Elsie*?' she gasped. 'Good Lord, Elsie, is that you? What's wrong? You sound terrible. Has something happened to Joe? Or the baby?'

'It's not Joe or Faith, Daisy. And I'm in Weston—'

'What on earth are you doing there?'

'If you give me a chance, I'll tell you. I can't tell you what a terrible time we've had finding out where you are, Daisy. All the phone lines were down at that camp and when we got through, nobody seemed to know at first. Then I remembered you were visiting that posh friend of yours, but I didn't know her address. Then we thought your young man might know where you were. It wasn't easy finding him either, but thank goodness he gave us this number—'

'Elsie, just tell me what's happened,' she snapped, fearful that it had to be something dreadful, and realising that Elsie seemed to be frantically putting off the moment of actually saying whatever it was.

'It's Uncle Bert.'

She could almost hear the huge gulp in Elsie's throat then,

and her voice was full of tears, but even before she managed to say the words, Daisy knew.

When she went back to the drawing room, the others were laughing over some nonsense Naomi's mother was telling them about her youngest son, Charles, known to the family as Squirt. You had to be pretty aristocratic to be so light and casual about such a nickname, Daisy thought inconsequentially.

They all looked up as she entered the room, and their laughter faded at once. Naomi walked over to her swiftly, and put her arm around Daisy's tense shoulders.

'What is it, darling? I can see you've had a terrible shock. Your Canadian hasn't been pranged, has he?'

Daisy wondered briefly if everyone always got hold of the wrong end of the stick, or if it was something in human nature to ward off the awfulness of disaster. She had instantly thought it must be Joe or Faith that Elsie was calling about, and Naomi instantly thought it must be bad news of Glenn. Natural, really, to think it must be the one closest to someone.

'Come and sit down, my dear,' Mrs Tyler-Smythe was saying, and she realised she had been standing motionless for several minutes, just clinging to Naomi, just staring into space. 'I'll fetch you some brandy, and then you must tell us what's happened.'

'It's my uncle,' Daisy blurted out, her throat closing. 'My sister says they think he had an accident in the blackout. And now he's dead.'

She felt her legs buckle, and somehow found herself in an armchair with her head being pushed between her knees. Still unable to make her brain function properly, all she could think of was how awful it would be if she was to be sick all over the Tyler-Smythes' valuable Persian carpet.

'Drink this, Daisy,' she was told, and felt a glass being put to her lips. 'It's too late to do anything tonight, but in the morning, Grebes will drive you home.'

Grebes? The chauffeur? Driving her all that way to Weston in that posh car, and with petrol in such short supply? It was a ludicrous suggestion, but then she remembered that Brigadier Tyler-Smythe could always pull strings. Naomi had said so. It was how the rich and influential lived. Daisy felt a wild urge to laugh, which quickly transformed itself into tears.

'I'm so sorry,' she found herself sobbing in Naomi's mother's arms.

'Nonsense. You've had a shock, and it's far better to cry than to let the anguish fester inside you. I'm sure you've said that to plenty of hospital patients, haven't you, Daisy dear?'

She nodded dully. How kind people were. How unexpectedly kind, no matter what their circumstances. People had discovered that in the blitz, and she was discovering it here, in this beautiful home where anything was possible, and the fact that her daughter's friend was disrupting their precious leave was nothing compared with the consideration she was being shown.

'Were you very close to your uncle, Daisy?' she heard the voice say gently.

'He was like a second father to me. I still *have* my father, of course, and I love him dearly, but Aunt Rose and Uncle Bert offered me and my small brother a sort of refuge after my mother died, and when I started nursing at Weston General it just seemed natural for us to stay there. It's my second home.'

She realised she was babbling, and that Naomi and Molly had disappeared and left her to the care of Mrs Tyler-Smythe. It was almost bizarre that this woman, who had looked rather stern and aloof at first sight, should be so warm and understanding now.

'I'm so sorry,' Daisy whispered again.

'My dear girl, there's no need. Talk as much as you like. The girls have gone to ask Cook to make some tea, and although it sounds trite, I'm sure a cup of good strong sweet tea will help you to calm down.'

Daisy swallowed. It was terrible, but right at that moment she couldn't help a shocking sense of amusement at the absolute contrast between home and here. At home, in normal times, it would be Aunt Rose who would be bustling about making tea; here, the girls had gone to ask Cook to do it. Such a simple thing, but it so emphasised the difference between them.

'That's better,' Namoi's mother said, noticing the small lift to Daisy's mouth. 'And if you want to go on talking about your uncle, I'm a good listener.'

Daisy shook her head as the other two came back, looking at her warily. It wasn't fair to burden them all with this, even though it had apparently been a tragic accident in the blackout, and Uncle Bert couldn't help being dead. She smiled wanly at them and waited for the inevitable steaming pot of tea.

'I just want to thank you,' she said simply. 'And it's far too much trouble for you to send me home by car. I can easily catch a train.'

'I don't want to hear another word about it. It's all settled. And since you'll probably want to be home for a few days,' she added delicately, 'I'm sure Naomi will inform your new people what's happened. Everything can be taken care of, so you just concentrate on being with your family.'

And if Naomi's feelings about reporting to the military hospital for her new duties without Daisy's support were less than cheerful, it was to her credit that she stoutly supported all that her mother said.

After the tearful goodbyes from what should have been a jolly few days' leave, it wasn't an easy journey home for Daisy, but then she had never expected to be coming home to this. When the chauffeur had deposited her at the house, he tactfully refused Daisy's offer for him to come inside and take a breather before returning to Hertfordshire, much to her relief.

And once she entered the house, it was even more of a relief to see everyone there: her father and Mary; Immy, white-faced and tense; Elsie, with the baby just a year old now, a bit wobbly on her feet, and clinging to Elsie's skirt; Vanessa, whom she learned had decided to take time off school and wasn't having any arguments about it; and Aunt Rose.

Daisy went straight into her aunt's arms. She couldn't think of a single thing to say, but there was no need. They simply clung to one another mutely for a few minutes, and words were unnecessary. Then she heard Aunt Rose give a deep, determined sigh, and hold her away from her for a minute or two.

'You'll be hungry, and you'll want a cup of tea after that long journey, my love,' she said decisively.

More tea, Daisy thought in mild hysteria, and then nodded, knowing it was everyone's panacea of keeping busy, and who was she to dispute it?

Afterwards, Daisy remembered it as being like something in a movie, when the action was frozen for long minutes while the credits flashed up on the screen. And then someone spoke and broke the silence, and suddenly everyone was moving again, talking again, being busy and noisy and her father was kissing her, and Immy was hugging her. Faith started crying and Elsie scooped her up and pressed her into Daisy's arms and told her to say hello to her Auntie Daisy.

And all Daisy could think of as she looked into the baby's wide brown Caldwell eyes was how Uncle Bert would have loved all this. Maybe he *was* still loving it. Knowing Aunt Rose's belief in such things, she was quite sure Aunt Rose would be imagining him looking down on them all benevolently from some heavenly plane, and telling them not to be sad . . .

She was being remarkably brave, Daisy thought now – and if that was what belief did for you, it wasn't such a bad thing after all. She had no doubt that Mr Penfold would have been around, giving her his pious bits of comfort and she was immediately ashamed of herself for mocking him in that way. Any belief was better than no belief at all. Anything that got you through the dark days of pain and bereavement was more precious than gold. She should know that.

'Are you all right, Daisy?' she heard Immy say when she finally went upstairs to unpack her things in her old room, which Immy would share with her for a few days. 'Sorry, I know that's not a very sensible thing to ask.'

'No, it's not, and I'm not,' Daisy said with more of a grimace than a smile. 'But we have to be for Aunt Rose's sake, don't we? And where are the boys, by the way?'

'Staying at the Luckwell farm.'

'Oh.' Which of course, immediately reminded Daisy of Lucy, and the tears welled up again. She felt her sister's arms go around her.

'We have to be strong for her now, darling, the way she's always been strong for us. Right?'

Daisy nodded slowly. They had always drawn strength from each other, no matter what life had thrown at them. It was what made families strong.

'How long are you here for?' she asked Immy now. Already she realised there were things she must do herself. Naomi would put things right with the new hospital posting, but it was up to her to report in and apply for extra leave – if she could have it. Did the death of an uncle qualify for extra leave? She had no idea.

'I was due for a forty-eight anyway, and I've got it extended to a week,' Immy said steadily. Not for the world was she going to tell anyone that this was to have been the precious forty-eight she was going to spend with James, when he was going to buy her an engagement ring. Such things must wait.

'That's good. When will the – the funeral be? Do we know?'

She didn't want to talk about it. Didn't even want to say the word. It brought back the memories all too vividly, of her mother, and Baz . . .

177

'In four days' time,' Immy told her.

'I'll have to see if I can stay that long as well then,' Daisy said.

And if there was any objection, she'd bloody well stay anyway, she thought defiantly. Nobody was going to prevent her saying goodbye properly to her beloved uncle . . .

Vanessa found them weeping in one another's arms.

'A fat lot of bleedin' good you two are going to be to anybody if you're going to be blubbing all the bleedin' time,' she said fiercely, as tough and fiery as she had ever been.

They looked at her in a moment of appalled silence, and then she gave an animal cry of grief as she rushed across to them, to be enveloped in their embrace.

'I won't hear of it,' Rose told her brother firmly, when Quentin announced yet again that he and Mary were quite prepared to move in with her if she wanted them to.

The harrowing ordeal of the funeral was over, Elsie had taken Faith back to Yorkshire, and the boys had been delivered back from the Luckwell farm, subdued, but with gentle assurances that Uncle Bert was now happy and safe in heaven with Baz and all his old friends who were waiting to welcome him there. Teddy found some solace in clinging tightly to George, who was still whimpering and whining over the inexplicable loss of someone important in the house, and clearly relieved to see the children back again.

Daisy wasn't sure how much they believed the story of Uncle Bert being happy in heaven, but even Vanessa was doing her best to assure them it was so – and threatening to box their ears if they dared to doubt it in front of Aunt Rose.

Immy and Daisy were obliged to get the train out of Weston that day, after their extended compassionate leaves were up, but Quentin was still arguing with his sister about moving in, even if was only for the duration.

'Mary wouldn't mind living in Weston one little bit, and

the fire service will be glad of my services wherever I am,'
he went on.

'Now you listen to me, Quentin,' Rose said. 'I know you
mean it for the best, and I thank you both for your kindness,
but you have your own home in Bristol, and you're still
practically newly-weds, for goodness' sake. Why would you
want to move in with a household of noisy children?'

Mary blushed, and said they could hardly be called that
at their age. But all the same, Rose could see a flicker of
relief in her eyes, and she didn't blame her for that. But on
her own account, Rose needed to get back to some kind of
normality. Grief didn't end with the funeral, but it was a
means of closing a chapter. Bert would always be with her
in her heart, but there were others in her care, and life had
to continue. She was glad to have the boys back in the house,
too. There was a certain normality about it again, with Teddy
shouting at Harry, Vanessa badgering them both, and Harry
doing his usual Houdini trick of burying his head in the sofa
cushions and pretending to be invisible.

One curious thing happened, though. Harry suddenly
started talking again. He had always been able to speak,
he simply hadn't felt the need to do so unless he was
obliged to at school. It happened one evening after supper,
when George had been curled up at the foot of Bert's chair,
whining for half an hour, and generally getting on everyone's
nerves. And Harry had suddenly said what everyone knew,
and wasn't saying. His voice was hurt and angry with all the
bewilderment of a five-year-old.

'He misses Uncle Bert. I miss Uncle Bert as well. Why
did he have to go and die and go to heaven and make us all
miserable? I don't like people dying!'

'Well, neither do I, Harry,' Rose said with admirable
composure. 'But I think it must be God's plan. If some people
didn't die, there'd be no room in the world for new ones to be
born. There wouldn't be enough food to go around, or places
for them to live.' And please don't remember that you don't

actually have any place of your own to live in any more, she begged silently. But his five-year-old logic didn't take him that far. He had a logic all his own, especially having recently seen Faith for the first time, playing with her and tickling her to make her laugh.

'I expect that's why baby Faith was born then, to take somebody else's place who was dead,' he said, his face brightening.

'I expect that's right,' Rose replied.

This was clearly important for him to understand, and despite the poignancy of his words, and the way he nodded with satisfaction now, Rose couldn't help catching the look in Vanessa's eyes, and knew she was finding it hard not to laugh out loud at Harry's solemn voice.

In an instant, she felt that urge, too. Not to give the kind of rip-roaring belly-laugh that Bert sometimes did, but a companionable, sharing laugh. The kind that she and Bert used to have sometimes when they both enjoyed something the children had said. And she found she was smiling. Amazingly, she was smiling, with the extraordinary sense of having Bert's smile surrounding her.

Fourteen

B y the time Daisy reported for duty she felt as wrung out as a damp dish rag from the train journey, and nervous at being obliged to be late. The prospect of her and Naomi going to the new hospital posting together had all seemed a bit of a lark. Especially as Naomi had been the nervous one then, twittering on about how she was going to cope with things she didn't understand, and knowing she would have to spell medical terms she had never heard of before, when she was useless at spelling anyway, and all the rest of her nonsensical complaints.

And Daisy had been 'oh, so – confident' in her long-time nursing role. But it was all different now. Little more than a week ago, her confidence had been paramount and now it was shattered. Little more than a week ago her adored Uncle Bert had still been alive, even larger than life, as they said, yet once again her family had been plunged into mourning. It had definitely unnerved her. First her mother, then Lucy, then Cal, then Baz, and now Uncle Bert. There was no security in anything any more, and she had felt as if she was simply lurching from one day to the next until she had got on the train.

It was something of a relief to leave it all behind, even though she felt so sorry for Aunt Rose, who was being an absolute brick. The boys were all right, boisterously thankful for one another's company, but not having the maturity to really know why. As for Vanessa, that girl was a bit of a dark horse, Daisy thought, not too sure how much she cared for Aunt Rose relying on her quite so much, and practically taking the place of a proper niece.

And who was being a dog in the manger *now*, she thought shame-facedly. They should all be grateful that Vanessa had turned up trumps in the end.

It had been hard to receive Glenn's phone call at home and have to explain to him what all the anxiety had been about, but she had managed it out of earshot of everyone else, and it had been comforting to hear his sympathetic voice saying how much he hoped they could get together again soon.

But there was a limit to how much sympathy anyone could take, even from those you loved the best, and once she had reported to Matron, the formality and regime of familiar hospital surroundings was almost like a breath of fresh air. Which was a contradiction in itself, considering the antiseptic and other unmentionable smells that permeated the corridors and wards.

But finally she was unpacking her belongings in the cupboard of a room the two friends had asked to share, and Naomi was virtually creeping around her, not knowing what to say because her uncle had died. And it was all too much.

'For pity's sake, Naomi, stop treating me like the best china,' Daisy said in exasperation. 'You'll have to get used to people dying when you work in a hospital, especially a military one. And if they don't actually die, they often have ghastly injuries, and you won't be able to avoid them, so you'd better learn to cope with that, even if you do spend most of your time behind an office door!'

The minute the tirade ended, Daisy clapped her hand over her mouth, shocked tears starting to her eyes.

'Oh Lord, Naomi, I'm sorry. I didn't mean that. I'm not usually so spiteful.'

'You are sometimes, darling' Naomi said conversationally. 'You have a pretty sharp tongue on you, but I forgive you, anyway.'

Daisy grimaced. 'Thank you. I think I must be getting more

like my Aunt Rose than I realised. She always says what she thinks, and no nonsense about it, but we always love her, anyway.'

'There you are then,' Naomi said, which they both knew was her way of saying it didn't matter. Then she softened the prickly tempo of their conversation by giving Daisy a quick hug.

'I do know how you must be feeling, Daisy darling, so any time you need someone to act as your whipping-boy, I'm your girl – if you see what I mean.'

Daisy smiled properly now. Anyone less like a boy she couldn't imagine. Even in her smart uniform there was no denying Naomi's femininity. She was tall and willowy and striking; her blonde hair and baby-blue eyes making her a target for many a soldier's roving eye as well as the medics, and it didn't take many weeks for Daisy to realise that a certain young doctor had discovered her, too.

By then they had settled into their new routines and life was too busy and demanding for her to be able to dwell on personal sorrows for very long. And in Naomi's case, personal matters were definitely looking up.

'He's asked me out,' she announced one evening, without even bothering to say his name, since they both knew who she meant. 'Should I go, do you think?'

'Should a duck swim?' Daisy said dryly. 'He's very nice, so why not? Even if you haven't been formally introduced,' she added, trying to keep a poker face.

'Oh, those things don't seem to matter quite so much these days, do they?' Naomi said quite seriously, confirming that Naomi had already come a long way from her pampered upbringing.

Between themselves they called him Doctor Den. His full title was Doctor Dennis Stevens. He lived in London and he had been to Oxford University before medical school. His father was a judge, and he had an impeccable background. Just the sort of husband the Tyler-Smythes would approve of for their daughter, Daisy found herself thinking comically, her romantic heart racing away with her.

'We're going to the cinema, and then out for dinner,' Naomi confided next, once the date had been confirmed.

'Gosh, that didn't take long, did it?'

'No sense in hanging around, darling. There is a war on you know.'

Though quite how the two things added up to Naomi being totally infatuated with Doctor Dennis Stevens, Daisy didn't quite know. It became obvious that she was, though – too soon and too fast – and on her first leave in the middle of November she invited him home. And Daisy went back to Somerset.

She arranged to spend the first night of her leave at her old home and find out from her father how her aunt was coping. She said so little in her letters, but that was Aunt Rose, stoical to the last.

The minute Daisy stepped off the train in Bristol, she was appalled at the scenes of devastation all around. Air raids weren't a nightly occurrence here now, and were more intermittent as Hitler found other targets to bomb throughout the country. It didn't help the nerves though, wondering which city he was to favour with his evil messages of hell, and if it was going to be their turn tonight . . .

What it did mean, was that the city resembled the aftermath of an earthquake. Places that Daisy knew and loved from her childhood were reduced to little more than empty, dust-filled shells and a legion of people seemed to be working to tidy it all up, as her father called it, sending yet more choking grey dust into the air. It was as if all the heart and soul had been ripped out of the buildings. Centuries-old churches, famous facades that had helped to fashion the city's history, established shops, and whole streets of ordinary houses – the homes that had once been cherished by those who had lived and loved in them.

Daisy's throat was thick as she hurried away from the station towards Vicarage Street. It was a miracle that anyone ever survived in such hell, and if they did, that they had enough strength to carry on. Several people that she knew called out to her and asked how she was getting on. How could they be so cheerful, going about their lives as best they could? She wanted to keep her head down, not seeing anyone, feeling suddenly as if she had turned her back on the city that was home, deserting it, even though she knew she was doing a worthwhile job. It was a stupid and unnecessary feeling, but it was very real at that moment.

'Daisy, for heaven's sake, what are you doing here? You nearly walked right into me!' she heard a laughing voice say. A voice that reminded her vaguely of Naomi's, but only because it was rather more educated that the voices of the other people who had spoken to her that day.

'Cripes, Helen, I didn't recognise you!' she said, as her head jerked up. She gaped at the vision in army uniform in front of her. Helen Church. Immy's friend, and the sister of James, Immy's young man, her spinning thoughts registered.

'I'm not surprised, you seemed to be miles away, but it's good to see you, Daisy, and I was so sorry to hear about your uncle. Immy wrote and told me, of course. Look, I presume you're on your way home, but why don't we go and have some tea first, my treat? It's such ages since I've seen any of you Caldwell girls, and you must tell me how that delicious baby of Elsie's is coming along.'

Daisy was laughing by the time she paused for breath.

'Oh Helen, you really do me good, and I'd love a cup of tea after that frightful train journey. Daddy doesn't know what time I'm coming, anyway, and I was feeling a bit down in the dumps, if you must know, seeing all of this.' She spread her arms out to encompass the scenes around them.

Helen linked arms with her, giving Daisy's a squeeze.

'It's pretty beastly, isn't it? But James says we musn't let the buggers get us down.'

'Why, Helen Church, I've never heard you swear before.'

Helen laughed. 'Oh, I think we all do things nowadays that we never did before. I don't often descend to gutter talk, but now and then it's the only way to let off steam, isn't it?'

Daisy couldn't help agreeing She had never really got to know Helen before. She was Immy's friend, not hers, and she had always been slightly in awe of her, living in a big house in Clifton and with a lawyer father and a mother who was into 'good works' and charity affairs. But all their horizons had shifted and broadened, and just as she had warmed to the constant company of Naomi, Daisy found herself liking Helen more and more. It was true that war created strange bedfellows, and some of the class snobbishness had gone out of the window, and probably all the better for it.

They settled down in a nearby tea-room, ordered tea and scones, and smiled at one another in sudden awkwardness. Then they both spoke at once.

'I really was sorry to hear about your uncle, Daisy.'

'Immy tells me you're in catering, of all things, Helen.'

They both laughed. 'This is odd, isn't it?' Helen said lightly. 'We both know so much about one another and yet we've never really talked before, have we?'

'That's because I was always considered the young and flighty one in the family, not sensible like my sisters, and never knowing what I wanted to do,' Daisy said frankly.

'And now you do?'

'I just want this war to end!'

'Well, we all want that, don't we? But I'd say you've made a pretty good job of growing up, Daisy. I know Immy's proud of you.'

'Good Lord, is she?' Daisy said, starting to laugh, but Helen was serious.

'Oh, I know all about your working on the hospital ships and going back and forth to Dunkirk. That took some guts, and you're not thought of as the little Caldwell girl any longer.'

Daisy felt her face flush, feeling better than she had in ages. And this nice girl had made that happen.

'I'm so glad I ran into you, Helen – almost literally!'

'I'm glad, too. So tell me if there's a young man on the horizon yet. It's not all blood and gore, is it?'

Several elderly ladies at the next table tut-tutted at such language, and they chuckled over their tea and scones as Daisy related the unexpected encounter with Glenn at the dance, and how magical it had been to see him there.

'You're very lucky, Daisy,' Helen said softly. 'I always seem to meet the wrong kind of men, so hold on to him, darling. I expect you'll marry him and go to live in Canada after the war then, and live happily ever after.'

'I expect I will,' Daisy said smiling, remembering to touch wood as she said it.

She felt far more cheerful by the time she went home to Vicarage Street, where Mary and her father greeted her warmly. This was their home now, Daisy remembered, and since Mary was obviously making her father happy, she harboured no resentment. But she changed her mind about staying overnight.

'I really do want to get to Weston before dark, and you know what the trains are like these days,' she told them both.

They said they did, even though they rarely travelled on trains nowadays.

'We thought you were staying the night, Daisy,' Mary said.

'I know, but I'm rather anxious about Aunt Rose, and I'm sure you understand. I also want to visit Lucy's mother, and pop into Weston General to say hello to everyone, especially Alice Godfrey, and a leave goes so quickly, it's hard to fit everything in.'

'All right, darling,' Quentin said, laughing. 'We do know

what a busy life you lead, and we won't try to tie you to the bedpost!'

She gave him a hug, thinking how much younger and sprucer he looked since his marriage, despite the demands of his fireman's job, which couldn't be pleasant to say the least. But Mary was definitely good for him.

And going back to Weston wasn't as traumatic as she might have feared. Superficially, at least, Rose seemed more or less her normal self, and Vanessa was getting the boys organised in the mornings in a way Daisy would never have believed.

'I had to do it for our kids back home,' she said, almost defensively. 'Half the time me Mum never knew what day it was, so if I didn't get 'em up and out for school, they'd never have got clean socks or anything to eat.'

Having come from an organised household herself, Daisy hardly knew what to say to that, and seeing it, Vanessa smirked.

'You don't really know how the other half lives, do yer, Daisy gel?' she said, reverting to her old accent.

'Oh, I'm learning, believe me,' she answered lightly.

'So how's yer love life?' the girl asked next.

'*What?*' Daisy asked, startled.

'Got yer there, didn't I? When that Canadian feller of yours phoned about yer that time, I told 'im if he ever got tired of yer, I'd be happy to do the business.'

'*Vanessa*, you didn't!' Daisy raged.

'No, 'course I didn't. But you shoulda seen your face!' she chortled.

She hadn't changed all that much, Daisy thought furiously. Not deep down, however much of an asset she was to Aunt Rose now – and she had to admit she was that all right. Practically taking Daisy's place.

'You're not jealous of her, are you, Daisy?' Alice Godfrey said, as they took an afternoon walk along the sands the next day.

Though it wasn't so much a stroll as a battle to keep

upright as the sea-front wind buffeted them, blowing whorls of sand up into their faces, stinging their cheeks and eyes. The advertising posters on Weston railway station called it bracing. Privately, they each thought they must be mad to be here on such a blustery day, but it was as much of a ritual as cleaning your teeth every morning, and a chance of getting away from everyone else.

'Jealous!' Daisy echoed.

Alice had asked the same question of her once before, and she had firmly denounced the idea then. But she was older now, maybe not wiser, but older anyway. 'Well, perhaps I am, just a bit. I always felt Aunt Rose sort of relied on me as much as I relied on her, and now it seems I'm not really needed.'

Alice hugged her arm. 'Don't be so daft. Nobody could ever take your place. Vanessa's here at a time when she needs somebody now, so you should be glad about that. When you're back for good, everything will be the same as before.'

'And that's a *really* daft thing to say, isn't it? When this war is over, nothing and nobody will be the same as before, least of all me.'

'That's the most profound thing I've ever heard you say, Daisy.'

'Oh really? Well, if you think that, I must have said some awful rubbish in the past then!'

But they were arguing good-naturedly, and it was a good feeling. They even found themselves laughing as an extra strong gust of wind nearly knocked them off their feet and made them cling to one another.

'We must be quite mad,' Daisy gasped. 'Let's go back, before we're blown to bits. Summer's really gone, isn't it? And autumn too.'

'Oh Lord, the way you talk, it'll soon be Christmas! And talking of that, are you going to organise your singing group in your new hospital?'

Daisy shook her head decisively. 'Definitely not. I suppose the nurses will sing some carols for the patients, unless we get an outside group to do it, but I'm not organising anything!'

Alice's look said she'd believe that when she saw it.

Anyway, Christmas was a long way off, and Daisy didn't want to think about it. When you had lost someone, anniversaries like birthdays and Christmas were always the worst times. In fact, she thought Christmas was the *very* worst, because the whole world was supposedly having such a jolly time, when in these dark days, half of them were grieving for someone they loved.

After her leave, she returned to the hospital feeling lighter than when she had left it. She hadn't realised how anxious she had been at the thought of facing Aunt Rose again. But she should have known. Aunt Rose was a survivor.

In any case, there was little time to think about anything else but the new influx of patients. There was a continual and successful bombardment of German cities by the RAF now, which the newspapers and wireless announcers were quick to report and praise, but which inevitably meant far more casualties than were ever reported officially. Only the dreaded telegrams arriving at homes all over the country and the crowded hospital wards gave evidence to that.

'I'm glad to see you back, Daisy,' Naomi told her, more flustered than usual. 'How was your leave?'

'Fine. Far less stressful than the last time, of course, except that we heard that my sister Elsie's husband has been pretty ill. He refused to let anyone tell her, but he's probably going to get his discharge, and Elsie won't mind that if it means having him home for good. So, how was yours with the lovely Doctor Den? Did your mother approve of him?' she asked with a grin.

She went decidedly pink. 'Of course. My father was home for the weekend, too, and he and Dennis got along like a house on fire. In fact I hardly saw him, but we're going to put that right on our next leave. Dennis knows some people who spend most of their time abroad and let out their house to their friends.'

Daisy stared at her, open-mouthed. 'Good Lord, Naomi, do you mean what I think you mean?'

'Oh, Daisy, don't be so naive,' she said crossly, going even pinker. 'Of course I mean what you think I mean. We're very fond of each other, so why not?'

She didn't say they were in love, and to Daisy, that was the all-important reason for intimacy. Maybe she *was* naive, but it was the way she had been brought up. And she was darned sure it was the way Naomi had been brought up, too. Unless things were different for the rich and sophisticated, but she knew she was probably being very short-sighted. Things were different for any two people who were passionate about one another.

If Glenn should ask her to go away with him for a clandestine weekend, she wasn't at all sure that she would have the strength to say no. She adored him, but she hoped he wouldn't ask so she wouldn't have to make that choice. But the very thought of the dangers Naomi could be inviting unsettled her for the next couple of days and nights. Naomi was refusing to discuss it any more, calling Daisy a suburban stick-in-the-mud. It caused a coolness between them that hadn't been there since the night of the dance and Naomi's disastrous attack of hay fever.

But there were far more important things to do than worry over petty squabbles, as Jerry's retaliating air raids on the south coast were stepped up. The minute they heard the sound of sirens wailing overhead, personal matters were swept out of mind as the hospital braced itself for more wounded. Throughout one particularly heavy night when the hospital itself shook, they were kept frantically busy into the early hours of the morning. By daylight, the wards and corridors were almost at bursting point with ambulances arriving every few minutes.

A great many of the casualties were burns victims, and as it was known that Daisy had worked in a burns unit at a Bristol hospital, she had immediately been despatched to the burns ward where the worst cases were sent.

'You're bloody young to be doing this, aren't you?' croaked a man in a tattered pilot's uniform, his head swathed in blood-soaked bandages, his bare chest blackened and raw with the flesh burned away and bones exposed.

'About as young as you are to be doing this,' Daisy answered him as steadily as she could, considering how her heart was beating so nauseatingly, thinking that this might have been Glenn. It had certainly been Cal, and there had been no recovery for him, nor even any gentle hands carefully removing the bandages and trying not to disturb the tender, ravaged skin.

She heard the pilot give a distorted laugh, through lips that were swollen to pulp. He tried to joke, but his voice was slurred and laboured, and she guessed he had already been given a hefty dose of pain-killing drugs in the ambulance.

'My choice, angel, but you should be home knitting socks.'

'I'll take that as a compliment, shall I?' she said lightly, noting his one good eye, and the way the other one, although completely closed, was bulging now as if there was far too much pressure building up behind it. It didn't look good.

She suddenly realised that Naomi was hovering behind her, a sheaf of papers in her hands, staring down at this shell of a man.

'What are you doing here?' Daisy snapped, praying that she wouldn't faint and present them with another casualty.

'I'm instructed to take down their particulars,' she said in a white voice.

The stricken pilot gave a strangled guffaw. 'That's one way of sayin' it. You can take down my partic'lars any time, girl—'

He gave a sudden bubbling gasp, and the next minute there

was an enormous gush of blood spurting out from every orifice on his face; his nose, mouth and ears; and out of his closed eye, forcing it open like a gargoyle. Daisy clamped her fist over the eye and yelled for some help as Naomi staggered back, her tidy uniform sprayed with bright, frothing blood.

She was still reeling at the speed of it all, being unceremoniously pushed aside by the medical team who responded to Daisy's shout. Suddenly the entire area around the man's bed was in a state of weirdly efficient chaos. There was no time for the niceties of curtains to be pulled around the bed. There was no time for anything . . . and after a few minutes, it was obvious there was no time left for the pilot at all. The doctor covered his face with the top of the bloodied bed sheet and yelled for a trolley to take him out.

Daisy found Naomi shocked and crying in the sluice room, trying in vain to scrub the blood stains from her uniform jacket. 'That doctor was so callous,' she wept. 'It was just as if he couldn't wait to get rid of that poor man and get the bed ready for the next patient.'

'That's exactly how it was,' Daisy told her brutally. 'They're either alive or dead, Naomi. We can help those who are still alive, but the rest of them have to make way for the next man. Don't worry, he'll be attended to all in good time.'

Naomi looked at her speechlessly. 'How can you be so hard? I didn't even have the chance to record his name!'

Daisy swallowed. 'I'm hard because I have to be. If I wasn't, I'd fall apart like you, and a fat lot of use I'd be as a nurse if I wept over every patient who was brought in, wouldn't I? It doesn't mean I don't *care*, and it doesn't mean that doctor doesn't care, either, if that's what you're thinking.'

But in a blinding moment she knew exactly what Naomi was thinking. She was imagining her Doctor Den behaving in the same callous way as the burns unit doctor had.

Poor Naomi, thought Daisy, having all the romance of it

knocked out of her in a single moment. Though privately she thought it was a good thing, since Doctor Den was known as a bit of a Romeo among the nurses, and Naomi would only end up getting hurt.

'We all *care*, Naomi,' she went on. 'But we have to do our job, too, and the next man to be admitted will be in desperate need of a bed, and that poor devil back there simply doesn't need it any more.'

Naomi turned and went out of the sluice room without another word, and Daisy knew she would need some time to herself to come to terms with it all.

She had never been trained to be on the wards. Military hospital wards weren't the gentle places portrayed in Hollywood movies. Naomi wasn't trained to be at war, if it came to that, any more than Daisy was. They weren't soldiers or sailors or airmen, they were just women, and although that poor pilot's words had been a bit of a slight, she probably *should* be at home knitting socks. Just being a woman, as she was born to be.

It was a *bugger*, that's what it was, Daisy thought with savage passion. A real *bugger* of a state to be in for all of them. She immediately said sorry to God for swearing, but sometimes it was the only way, it really was, she told Him.

Fifteen

Elsie didn't how to deal with this new Joe who had come home to her and Faith. When the war began he had been one of the first to volunteer, and she had been so proud of him even though she missed him so badly, especially when she was expecting Faith. He had fought on the battlefields of France and come home from Dunkirk in real danger of losing his foot from a badly infected wound. Eventually he had been pronounced fit enough to rejoin his regiment, but she hadn't been aware that the injury, and several other undetected ones at the time, had continued to flare up with the ever-present threat of gangrene.

There were bouts in hospital when he was delirious and near-insensible, but he had put it in writing that on no account was his wife to be informed, nor told how serious his condition was, which accounted for the fact that she had heard so little from him in these past months. But, finally, it was decided that Joe Preston should be honourably discharged, and although Elsie was immensely glad to have him home, she should have known how bitter he would be.

It wasn't helped by the jeering of his objectionable cousin Robert, on the day the family from York came to visit them. Joe's father and uncle had gone out to the farmyard, and the women were making tea and gossiping in the kitchen, leaving the younger ones to themselves. It wasn't the best of encounters.

'So they booted you out at last, cuz,' Robert hooted.

'Couldn't stand the pace after all, eh? I always said it was no more than a flash in the pan.'

'If that's what you call it, it was a flash that lasted two years! At least I did my bit for as long as I was able, instead of inventing all kinds of imaginary ills to keep out of the army, like some folk,' Joe snapped back.

Robert's handsome face went an angry red. 'I invented nothing. You can't deny a doctor's certificate that says you were unfit for war service due to a childhood ailment.'

'I daresay you can't, when you've got the doctor in your pocket.'

Elsie was shocked at the way these two were behaving at what was meant to be a pleasant family afternoon. Faith was quickly absorbing the atmosphere and starting to be fretful. Finally, she scooped her up and took her into the kitchen where the two older Preston women were still busy with the tea-making and preparing scones and jam. They looked up enquiringly when Elsie flounced in, unused to seeing her so ruffled.

'Do those two argue about everything?' she burst out.

Joe's mother laughed. 'Bless you, that's what cousins do. Mebbe you don't have any, Elsie love, but I'll bet you and your sisters have arguments from time to time. 'Tis no more than friendly family rivalry.'

'Aye, you must be proper saints if you don't ever argue,' Robert's mother said with a laugh that matched her sister-in-law's.

Elsie stared at them. They were both buxom, homely women, looking as much like rosy-cheeked siblings as their husbands were brothers. She didn't want to spoil the pleasure of their afternoon if they considered it was no more than friendly family rivalry between Joe and Robert, and maybe this was the way they had always behaved. But she knew how sensitive Joe had become to such remarks since being discharged. Robert would have meant it in jest – probably – and she gave him the benefit of the doubt. Joe wouldn't

196

have taken it that way though, and she knew he would be brooding on it until the time they were alone – and taking troubles to bed with them had been something they vowed never to do.

But that was then, and this was now. She would never wish for Joe to be away from her, especially fighting and in danger, but if doing his duty as a soldier meant having him whole in spirit again, instead of festering inside the way he was now, then she would rather spend the rest of the war alone. She knew he wasn't sleeping well, and that he lay awake for long hours in the darkness, staring up at the ceiling. She knew it, because she lay sleepless beside him.

She would hear the tormented sound of his breathing that seemed to go on for hours. And when he finally did get a few hours' sleep, it was always uneasy, interspersed with muttering and sometimes outright shouting. And the worst of it was, he was ashamed for her to know it. When she reached out for him in their old loving way, he inevitably pushed her away and turned his back on her, leaving her frustrated, confused and afraid. He was no longer her gentle, darling Joe, but a stranger who shared her bed, but gave her little of his love. She had no doubt the love was still there, but somehow it had become submerged in the pain of all he had been through, and there seemed to be no way that Elsie could reach it.

It was impossible for his parents not to be aware of it, too. For weeks they virtually tip-toed around him, giving him all the time he needed to re-adjust to family life. The war hardly touched them here, except in the regular reports they heard on the wireless and in the newspapers, and Elsie knew his mother was in the habit of hiding them from Joe in case the reports upset him. Hetty was treating him as a child, when in her heart Elsie knew it was all wrong.

Problems had to be faced – and Joe wasn't facing them. His mother simply hoped that Joe would find the peace and restoration he needed in his old home, while his father continually urged him to take over the running of the farm so that he and Hetty could retire gracefully – if it was possible for two lumbering old fogies like them to be graceful about anything, he always added with a chuckle .

And it was during one of these mild-mannered discussions that Joe's temper finally erupted.

'For God's sake, Dad, give it a rest, will you!' he blazed. 'I'm sick and tired of hearing about the wonders of the bloody farm.'

Thomas Preston's face darkened with anger, and his wife gasped. Elsie bit her lip, not daring to interfere, because this was between Joe and his father. But she had never heard him swear in the house before, and she cuddled Faith to her as the baby started to whimper.

'Now just hold on, lad,' Thomas Preston snapped. 'We all know you've had a rough time of it, but there's no point in getting on your high horse with your mother and me. And we don't need no blaspheming in this house neither.'

'You know nothing about the time I've had,' Joe raged, as if he hadn't even heard the rest of it. 'You know nothing about the sights I've seen, and the friends who have died in agony right there beside me. You know nothing about what it's like to go to war, because you stuck to your bloody farming in the last one as well, so don't tell me you know what it's like.'

'Somebody has to stick to farming, as you call it, you ungrateful pup,' his father shouted now, puce in the face. 'People still need food to eat, even in wartime, and there's those that can grow the crops and produce the meat and those that can't, so don't you dare sneer at your background, my lad.'

'We're only trying to help, Joe love,' his mother protested faintly. She went to him, putting her hand on his arm.

'I don't need anybody's help, damn you all, and will you please stop treating me like a child!' he yelled, pushing her away.

Elsie stood by, appalled, as the scene continued. She had

never known Joe to raise his voice to anyone before, least of all these two, who, for all their anger now looked completely bewildered. This was clearly not their Joe, any more than he was hers. He was a stranger, a battle-scarred stranger. But suddenly she felt fury rise up inside her, as acid as bile.

What right did he have to speak of such things, when he was still here, still able to walk, albeit not as well as before; still able to talk and see and *be* . . . when others were not.

'How *dare* you,' she said in a shrill, trembling voice.

They all stopped to look at her. She had put Faith down, and the baby was now clinging to her skirt. Elsie's hands were clenched at her sides, her whole body stiff with anger, her eyes glittering with pain as she faced her husband.

'Elsie, keep out of this,' he snapped.

'I will not keep out of it. Nor will I stand meekly by and listen to you feeling so sorry for yourself. Do you think you were the only serviceman ever to come home wounded? There were others who didn't come home at *all*. My brother was only sixteen when he was horribly drowned. He didn't even have to go to war at all. He was just a boy . . .' Her voice cracked, but she wouldn't be stopped now. 'My sister Daisy has seen as many horrific things as you have, day after day, in fact. She's little more than a child, too, and you come home whining and complaining, when you should just thank God that you're able to come home at all to a family that loves you.'

'Elsie, please—' he broke in again.

She ignored him, while the two older Prestons stood in embarrassed silence, until Hetty picked Faith up and pressed her to her ample bosom.

'You've had your say, and now I'm having mine,' Elsie went on passionately. 'You may not think so, Joe, but I was just so thankful to have you home, it wouldn't matter to me if you had one leg or none at all. You're here and you're whole, and that's all that matters, and you had an honourable discharge. You did your duty, and the army recognised that. You can get on with your life now, knowing that nobody can ever dispute that you did your best, not even that stupid cousin of yours. My Baz never stood a chance to face the future, and neither did Daisy's young man, Cal. They died for their country, but you – *you*, with everything to live for now – all you can do is whine and bleat and feel sorry for yourself. You make me ashamed to be your wife.'

She turned on her heel and ran out of the room and up the stairs to their bedroom. She threw herself on the bed, tears blinding her eyes, and hardly able to believe she had said such things to Joe – her brave, darling Joe.

Moments later she heard the front door of the farmhouse bang shut, and then Hetty tapped timidly on her door and put her head inside it, still with Faith clutched tightly to her.

'He's gone out, love. He'll be needing time to think, I daresay. Do you feel like having a cup of tea?'

Elsie sat up, swallowing hard. 'Oh, Mother Hetty, whatever must you think of me?' she whispered. 'I don't think I have ever lost my temper like that in my life before.'

'I think you said what had to be said,' Hetty said calmly. 'Being cruel to be kind is sometimes the only way, lass.'

'But I was cruel, wasn't I? And you know I'm not really ashamed to be Joe's wife. I could never be that!' she said, as the tears welled up again.

'Then 'tis not me you should be saying it to, is it? He'll be gone up top.'

'Up top?' Elsie said vaguely, then realising that it must be the rocky outcrop on the moors above the farm where Joe used to love to scramble as a boy, surveying the farm and the sheep dotted about the hillside, frozen by distance, like the miniatures in a child's picture-book. His world.

''Twas always his favourite thinking place,' she was told, 'and if I know our Joe he'll need to be doing a deal of thinking now.'

She looked at Elsie steadily, and Elsie slid off the bed,

already reaching for a coat and scarf, because the Yorkshire moors were cold in November, and she had no idea how long she might need to be with Joe, trying to piece together the remnants of this dreadful day.

'You'll take care of Faith?' she asked Hetty.

'You don't need to fret yourself over that. The little lass will be quite safe wi' me and her grandpa.'

Elsie paused just long enough to drop a kiss on Faith's head, and to squeeze Hetty's arm. And then she left the warmth of the farmhouse and went out into the biting wind of the November day. It blew through these dales every bit as fiercely as it did along Weston seafront, she thought inconsequentially.

Fervently, she wished she was there now. She wished she could turn back the clock, and for everything to be as it used to be. No war, no pain or tragedies to touch their lives, but that was the child in her thinking, because the clock could never be turned back, and nothing could ever be the same as it used to be. If it was, her mother would still be alive, and Baz, and Daisy's friend Lucy, and Cal . . . and oh dear Lord, Uncle Bert, too . . . horrified, Elsie realised she hadn't even given her dear Uncle Bert a single thought in all this turmoil.

She paused for breath as she toiled up the steep slopes that gave way from the coarse grassy dales to the rockier rise leading to the moors. She could imagine how Joe had loved it – and how he must still love it if he could ignore his pain to climb all this way. But she knew this was his refuge, his escape, as necessary to him as a means of security as Faith's favourite blanket was to her. And she was apprehensive of approaching him to break into his special space. What if he rejected her, as she had so recently rejected him?

She couldn't see him yet, and then she caught sight of a movement high above her. A bird soared into the sky, disturbed by the human activity, and her eyes followed its course into the greyness above, and then went back

to its starting-point, near the outcrop of rocks where Joe
sat, his knees drawn up to his chest, his body hunched
and beaten. He wasn't looking her way, and she felt an
immense pity for him. He had always been so strong, so
vital, and she could only guess at how humiliating it must
be for him to be sent home like a wounded animal. She
wasn't the only one to reject him. The army had done
that, too.

But oh God, how she wished she had a tenth of Daisy's
nursing training now. Daisy was two years younger than
herself, the prettiest one, the frivolous one, but so much
more skilled in dealing with human suffering than she was.
She didn't have the skills, she thought in sudden panic, but
she did have love. So much love for this man who needed
her now, whether he accepted it or not, and who was going
to face up to it sooner or later.

'Joe,' she said softly. She actually thought she had called
out his name, but her voice was carried on the wind, and she
was sure he couldn't have heard it. But some sixth sense must
have told her she was near, because he lifted his head and
looked down at her from his vantage point.

'What the hell are you doing here?' he almost snarled.
'Don't you know it's dangerous? You could fall and hurt
yourself, and then we'd have two cripples in the family
instead of one. A fine husband I've turned out to be, haven't
I?'

Her anger flared again for a moment and then subsided
just as quickly. She climbed a little higher until she was well
within earshot, and then she shook her head and folded her
arms defiantly, rocking just slightly on her feet in order to
keep her balance in the blustery wind.

'Oh no you don't, Joe Preston. You might be sorry for
yourself, but you're not going to make me feel sorry for
marrying you. And since you think it's dangerous for me to
climb up to your precious place, why don't you come down
and help me? Or are you going to shut me out of that too,

the way you're determined to shut me and your parents out of everything else?'

When he didn't answer or move, she thought for a minute she had gone too far. But if he rejected her now . . . she couldn't bear the thought of it. Then very slowly he got to his feet, and now she felt a different kind of fear. He had been injured after all, and there was an ongoing weakness in his leg. What if he fell, and she had goaded him into it?

'Joe, no don't. Wait there, and I'll come to you.'

'Stay where you are,' he said, his voice still angry. 'What kind of foolish woman climbs these fells without knowing them intimately, and without even wearing suitable footwear?'

She looked down at her feet. She had remembered her coat and scarf, but in her haste to get out of the farmhouse, she was still wearing house shoes, and she realised how the stony ground was starting to hurt her feet. Such things were so trivial she could easily discard them in the circumstances, but without warning, she swayed a little, and in seconds, it seemed, Joe was beside her, and pulling her roughly into his arms.

'I never knew I'd married a madwoman. This wind's really getting up now, and I thought you were the sensible one of the family.'

'Only in marrying you – and I'm beginning to have my doubts about that,' she said sharply, simply because she was so relieved that he was holding her, even if it was none too gently. And she meant it as no more than a joke, a tease, but she realised he wasn't taking it that way.

'We'd best go down,' he said grimly.

'Not yet,' Elsie said. 'I want to visit this wonderful place you escape to when you want to get away from the rest of the world. If you're not afraid to climb up there, neither am I.'

Her eyes challenged him, and they both knew that what she really meant was that if she wasn't afraid to climb up to his secret place, he shouldn't be afraid to take her there. If he loved her enough to share his refuge.

'The going gets rougher nearer the top,' Joe said finally by way of agreement. He held out his hand and she placed hers tightly in his.

'I can face anything as long as we're together, Joe.'

But her heart was thudding wildly by the time they reached the point where they rounded a small slope to where the rocks jutted outward, forming a small plateau, and she gratefully sat down beside Joe. Then, regardless of all else, she gasped as the majesty of the view below unfolded in front of her. The valleys stretched away, serene in their solitude, the white-painted farmhouses with their smoke curling from their chimneys resembling something out of toy-town, and if it wasn't for the sighing of the wind, the silence would be total.

'Oh, it's just magnificent,' Elsie breathed, her voice catching with an emotion she couldn't quite explain. 'I know now why you claimed this place as your own, and why you always came here when you needed to think things out. It's about as near to heaven as anyone can get.'

She turned to look at him sheepishly as the uninhibited words left her lips, and then she felt a huge shock ripple through her. His shoulders heaved uncontrollably, and great racking sobs tore apart. He sat inches away from her, not touching her, until she pulled him fiercely into her arms.

'Oh Joe darling, my darling, *darling* Joe, please don't shut me out!'

Her hands were in his hair, cupping his face, forcing kisses on his cheeks, his eyes, his mouth, rocking with him, sharing his pain, being a part of him in every way she could. It was a long while before the paroxysm stopped, and they had said nothing in all that time. But then Joe spoke raggedly, his face still pressed close to hers.

'I've been a real bastard, haven't I?'

Amazingly, Elsie felt laughter bubbling up inside her,

because it was said so naturally and so unexpectedly. 'You have, rather,' she said candidly.

He moved his face away slightly, to look deep into her eyes, and the brief sense of laughter faded because he looked so terribly serious.

'And you should hate me for it.'

'I could no more hate you than I could hate the day we met, Joe.'

'But you're ashamed to be my wife,' he reminded her.

'Only for a moment, and it's a small price to pay for being able to love you for the rest of my life. For having you *home*, Joe, for being so much luckier than other wives who have nothing to look forward to but loneliness and heartbreak.'

She held her breath, not at all sure that she was saying the right things. She had no idea what the right things were, anyway. There were no rules for times like these. No angel sitting on her shoulder, telling her what to say. There was only the feeling of overwhelming love she felt for Joe, and had always felt for him.

'As long as I have you—' he began, and she put her finger against his mouth, because there was a limit to how much emotion she could bear to express on this cold and wintry day, and she suddenly longed for the cosy warmth of the farmhouse.

'You'll always have me,' she whispered. 'So now can we please go home before I freeze?'

He smiled for the first time that day. For the first time in ages, it seemed.

'You don't know how good it sounds to hear you say that word, Elsie.'

'Which word in particular would that be?' she said.

'Home.'

She hugged his arm, feeling that any more words would be superfluous, and they began the careful descent together. And because of all the emotion and the way her legs were starting to wobble now, she had never been more thankful to reach the farm. Home. Joe was right. It had a very good sound.

'You know, I may never go up there again,' he said thoughtfully, as they walked towards the farmhouse with their arms held tightly around one another.

'Oh, I think you will,' Elsie told him. 'Every man needs to escape from his wife once in a while, but I'm glad you've come down from your mountain-top now. Your daughter has been missing you.'

She was smiling as she said it, but they both knew the significance of her words, and by the time they went indoors, Joe was smiling again, too.

Elsie usually wrote frank and chatty letters to her sisters, but there were some things that were essentially private between husband and wife, and she knew she would never betray Joe's feelings of inadequacy to anyone else. Nor did she expect an instant reversal of the demons in his head, but slowly and surely he began to pick up the threads of normal life again and to show interest in the farm. And she knew a real turning point had been reached when he asked his father irritably why he could never find the newspaper when he wanted to read it.

There was plenty of news to read about as November merged into December, and the fact that it was all going on in other parts of the world, and that Joe Preston was no longer part of it, no longer filled him with unreasonable guilt. He was as keen to know about the progress of the war as anyone else now, and listened as avidly as Uncle Bert had always done in the past. It was always Uncle Bert that Elsie remembered when she saw her new family crowding around the wireless set.

'Would you mind if I phoned my auntie sometime to see how she's getting on?' she asked Hetty a few days later, when Joe and his father had gone about their farming business.

'Bless you, lass, you can use the telephone whenever you like. This is your home now, as much as 'tis Joe's.'

But she left it until the evening, when Faith was in bed, Hetty was knitting socks for soldiers, and the menfolk were playing cards. Only now, some weeks after Uncle Bert had died, and the trauma over Joe seemed to have been lifted at last, did she feel able to speak to Aunt Rose without breaking down.

She didn't recognise the voice at the other end at first.

'This is the Painter residence. Who is this, please?'

Elsie stared at the phone. It certainly wasn't Aunt Rose's broad Somerset voice. It sounded like someone trying to put on airs, and for a few weird moments she found herself agonising over whether there had been a need for her aunt to have someone in the house to help her get over her loss.

'I'd like to speak with my aunt, please,' Elsie said cautiously. 'It's Elsie.'

'Blimey, is that really you, Elsie?' came Vanessa's more normal tones. 'Are you calling us all the way from Yorkshire?'

'Yes, I am,' Elsie said, crisp with relief now. 'Is Aunt Rose there?'

'No, she ain't. She's gone to one of her prayer meetings, and I'm looking after the brats.'

'You mean my brother Teddy and young Harry, I presume,' Elsie said, with the irritation that all of them were used to feeling with this girl.

Vanessa laughed. 'Sorry, and I didn't really mean it. They're not bad kids, and we've all been down in the cellar playing at bein' cavemen. If the siren goes, we're already down there then, see?'

'Good Lord.' Elsie was nonplussed for a moment, and then remembered why she had called in the first place.

'Well, I just wanted to know how Aunt Rose is, that's all. So how is she?' she prompted.

'All right, considerin'. She says her faith's keeps her going – hey, that's funny, ain't it? Her faith and *your* Faith. Get it?'

'I get it,' Elsie said, wondering if Vanessa's posh County

School accent was already being abandoned – or more likely kept for more important callers than Elsie Preston!

She heard a lot of muttering in the background, and then Vanessa snapped into the phone: 'Hold on, Teddy wants to talk to you.'

The next minute Elsie held the phone away from her as Teddy bawled excitedly into it at the other end.

'We're havin' a smashing game in the cellar, and Harry's got so excited he's just gone and bleedin' wet himself, so he's got to go and clean himself up before Aunt Rose comes back. When are you coming to see me?'

Elsie ignored the expletive – Vanessa's influence, no doubt – and felt a catch in her throat as she pictured her small brother now, his brown eyes dancing, hopping up and down from one leg to the other as he always did when he was happy. She was so glad he was happy, and she could hear George yapping like mad somewhere in the background, too. He'd be crazily tearing around the place, picking up the atmosphere from the children. The pictures in her mind were so vivid, it was almost as if she was there . . . She swallowed and spoke quickly. 'I don't know when I'll see you, Teddy, but you be good for Aunt Rose, you hear? Be sure to tell her I called and give her my love, and Faith sends you a big kiss. Go on back to your game now, and ask Nessa to sort Harry out.'

She forgot that the girl didn't like being called Nessa. But who cared, as long as she knew they were all happy? It took so little to make children happy, even in wartime. She was disappointed not to speak to Aunt Rose, but she knew how her prayer meetings gave her comfort, and that was all anyone could ask for these days. She replaced the phone carefully and went back to the parlour, her chin held high, and asked the men if anyone could join in this game of cards, or if it was exclusively a male preserve?

Sixteen

Everyone was starting to think about Christmas, now less than three weeks away. Immy was going to get some leave, and knew that this time she must go home. Her father would expect to see her, even though it would be the first Christmas for him and Mary as husband and wife, and she suspected they would be perfectly happy with their own company.

But Caldwell Christmases had always been family affairs, often spent at Aunt Rose's, and heaven only knew how Aunt Rose was going to face this one. It was up to all of them to try to be there and to make it as positive a time as possible without having Uncle Bert there to don his Father Christmas outfit and perform his sometimes appalling magic tricks to entertain them all. Her throat felt thick, remembering.

Daisy wasn't at all sure whether or not she would get any leave this side of 1942, which sounded ominously far in the future, but in fact, was no more than four weeks away. They had all expected the war to be over long before this, but there had been more heavy raids on the south coast towns recently, with plenty of military casualties to fill the hospitals, so army nurses were kept very busy.

News of another tragic casualty had stunned and upset Daisy and Naomi considerably. They had learned that Molly, bright, cheerful Molly, had been hit by shrapnel while dodging bullets as she used to call it in her bright and breezy way. She had been on her way back at night to her barracks from the depot where she worked. The shrapnel had struck her carotid artery and there had no one around to try to stem the wound or get her to hospital, and she had simply fallen to the ground and bled to death, alone and in the dark. It was the most appalling piece of news the girls had heard, and it hit both of them hard.

'We've still got each other,' Naomi said, her face white at the thought of how Molly must have suffered, even though Daisy assured her that she would soon have become dizzy and then unconscious.

'And we won't forget her, will we?' Daisy said, almost fiercely.

She didn't really mind not going home for Christmas anyway, because if she did, she would have been absorbed in memories of Uncle Bert, and feel obliged to tell what had happened to Molly, and it was all too much to bear. Far better to stay at the hospital and do her job and inevitably, agree to lead the carol-singers in the wards on Christmas Eve and Christmas Day. How could anyone with any decency refuse?

But then something happened which overshadowed every other thought in peoples' minds, as the horrific news that the Japanese had bombed the base at Pearl Harbour became headline news. Most people didn't even know where Pearl Harbour was, and Hawaii was simply a dot on the map in the middle of the Pacific Ocean when they bothered to find it.

'That'll be it now, then,' Naomi said with almost savage satisfaction. 'The Americans can't go on being neutral. They'll be in it any day now, you'll see.'

'You're a flipping soothsayer now, are you?' Daisy said, appalled at the growing news items of the carnage the Japanese had done to the unsuspecting American fleet anchored at Pearl Harbour.

Yet knowing guiltily, that a tiny part of her was almost grateful for this one obscene act, if it meant the Americans would put their immense force behind the cause, and help to end the war quickly.

'It doesn't need a soothsayer, darling, to know that President Roosevelt will never stand for this insult to the American people,' Naomi said coolly.

Her words were proved right. Within the next few days, America had joined the Allies in declaring war on Japan and Germany, and by the time Imogen joined the depleted family in Weston for Christmas, she was reassured to find that Aunt Rose was determined to carry on as usual and make this as good a Christmas as she could for the children in her care. And once Quentin and Mary arrived at the house and the greetings were over, all the talk was about how soon the American troops would be coming to Britain.

'They say the Yanks are ever so good-looking,' Vanessa was saying excitedly. 'I bet they'll look like bloomin' film stars, every one of 'em!'

'Don't talk rot, Vanessa,' Immy told her. 'They've probably got just as many fat and ugly ones as we have.'

Vanessa tossed her head. 'Well I bet they'll still look lovely in their uniforms.'

Teddy hooted. 'Chaps don't look lovely. *Girls* look lovely.'

Harry sniggered, and Teddy blushed tomato red. 'Teddy's got a girl-friend,' he chanted.

'I do not!' Teddy said, enraged.

'Take no notice of him, Teddy,' Immy said sympathetically. 'He's only teasing. Harry's technically right, though. You can't call chaps lovely, Vanessa.'

The girl's eyes flashed, and Immy instantly saw how quickly she was growing up. She had been precocious from the first day she had been sent here, an unwilling, bad-tempered evacuee, ready to blame the whole world, and Hitler in particular, for disrupting Vanessa Brown's life. Well, they could all blame the war on that, Immy thought feelingly . . .

But from being a moderately pretty child, Vanessa at fourteen was growing into quite a beauty. She was tall for her age, and filling out in all the right places now. Her glossy dark hair framed her heart-shaped face, with its high cheek-bones and wide brown eyes and that full – what the movie stars called *voluptuous* – mouth and Immy didn't need a crystal ball to guess that Aunt Rose could be in for quite a time with her when the Yanks came into town.

'What yer starin' at me like that for?' Vanessa said rudely. 'I ain't got two heads, have I?'

Immy grinned. Some things never changed. And then the grin faded as they all heard the sound of carol-singers outside. Quentin went to the door quickly, gave the children a few coppers and sent them on their way. By now, they had all learned that Rose could deal with many things in her usual gritty manner, but the sound of children singing carols was the one thing that tore at her heart.

She and Bert had never missed going to church on Christmas Eve for the carol service in all the years of their marriage, but this year, this poignant year when she was still grieving for Bert, it was simply beyond her to do so.

Mr Penfold had completely understood, and didn't press the fact. In fact, without his support, Rose said she didn't know what she would have done in these last traumatic weeks. The war went on, people were wounded and dying, and even the advent of the Americans into the war, and the devastation and horror of the events at Pearl Harbour that had been so graphically described in words and pictures, couldn't stop Rose's mind being centred on her own terrible loss.

The mechanics of looking after the home and children in her care were done almost by rote. Even the outrage of one of Vanessa's tasteless remarks that she thought the old vicar had designs on Rose now that she was a widow, was dismissed with the contempt it deserved.

During those first weeks after Bert died, her grief was kept strictly to herself, and nobody but the vicar knew about the half-world she was living in. She refused to see a doctor to give her something to help her sleep. How could she agree to go into semi-oblivion every night, when thousands of others had far more troubles than she did, she told him stoically? While all the time, she was weeping inside, and the only thing that had finally brought her back to reality was to find young Harry crying uncontrollably one day, clutching George as if he would squeeze the life out of him.

Automatically, Rose extricated the dog from his grasp, pulled the boy towards her, and hugged him. If he had wet the bed, she would cope with it. If he had torn his clothes, she would mend them. If he had been bullied at school, she would demand that the boys be punished. She would champion him in every way she could, the way she did all her children. Her 'on-loan' children, she corrected, remembering Bert's constant admonition.

'Come on now, Harry, whatever it is, it can't be as bad as all that.'

He continued to snuffle loudly for a few minutes, his small body shaking, and then the words all tumbled out at once, shrill and frightened.

'I don't want Uncle Bert to be in the ground where the worms can get him. I don't want him to get all mouldy and eaten up, nor my mum and dad neither. I want them all back!' he finished with a howl.

Rose felt a huge shock at his words. 'Has somebody been saying these things to you, Harry?' she said as steadily as she could, and knowing that they must have done, or why would be having these nightmare thoughts?

He gulped, and then rushed on. 'Some boys at school said it. They said Uncle Bert would be all mangled up by now, and soon there'd only be a skeleton left in the ground. And if the bombs fell on the churchyard all the graves would burst open, and there'd be skeletons everywhere.'

My God . . . Rose swallowed painfully. Children could be so cruel – so innocent and so cruel. 'Harry, sweetheart, nothing like that is going to happen. Uncle Bert is resting safely in his box' – she just managed to avoid saying the word coffin – 'and he's not feeling any pain, because he's not really there any more.'

Harry glowered at her. 'Yes he is. The men put him in the box and screwed him down, and then they dropped him in the ground and everybody cried. Vanessa told me.'

Well, thank you Vanessa, for graphically describing the burial that the young boys weren't allowed to attend. 'Harry, I'm going to take you to see Mr Penfold and we're all going to have a little talk.'

'I don't like him. He's scary,' Harry said at once.

'We're going to see him, anyway,' Rose said determinedly.

But before they did so, she telephoned him, and at her tentative suggestion, when he opened his door to them he was wearing an ordinary woollen pullover over his shirt and casual trousers, and looked more like a shopkeeper than a vicar.

And by the time they left the vicarage, Mr Penfold had explained as gently and simply as he could how the body was no more than a shell once a person was dead. Uncle Bert had lived in his body while he was on earth, but he didn't need it any more, because his soul was now with the angels in heaven.

'And my mum and dad, too?' Harry said suspiciously. 'And Fred?'

The vicar didn't blink. 'And Fred, too, of course.'

'Gosh,' Harry said, awed, but undoubtedly cheered. 'It must be a lovely place then. I didn't know goldfish went to heaven as well.'

Rose tried to keep the innocence of his remark in mind all the way home, as he bubbled excitedly beside her. The vicar had told him gravely that Fred was his name, too, but his mum and dad had always called him Freddie, and Harry had immediately changed his mind about not liking him. It made a man of the church seem less remote to a child, Rose supposed, and she wondered briefly if anyone ever called him Freddie now.

But after seeing Harry's unquestioning acceptance of all that he had been told, it did much to shake her into her own acceptance that life had to go on for those who were left, and reminded her that all these children in her care had experienced the death of their loved ones. But Rose being Rose, she had marched down to Harry's school the next day and demanded that the boys who had taunted him be reprimanded. She was back in battling form.

Except for the midnight carol service on Christmas Eve.

And there was also something that she didn't mention to any of the family until the very last minute. 'I've invited Mr Penfold for Christmas dinner,' she told them, ignoring the various gasps and howls. 'He's been a real brick to me these past weeks, and he has no family of his own, and I don't want to hear another word about it.'

'We haven't said any words at all about it yet, Rose,' Quentin said mildly.

'Well, please don't – and please treat him as an ordinary guest and not as a vicar,' she went on testily, already wondering if she had done a very reckless thing in inviting him. But this was going to be a very strange Christmas dinner, anyway, so one more guest wouldn't make too much difference.

'I think it's a very nice gesture, Aunt Rose,' Immy said softly.

'George won't like it,' Teddy said, sulking.

'Well, George will just have to lump it then, won't he?' Rose said tartly.

And in the end, the day passed off as peacefully as it could have done, considering the range of emotions in everyone's heart. But, as Rose said, Christmas was for the children, and Mr Penfold had arrived looking less like a vicar and just like an ordinary man, insisting that they all call him Freddie for the day, with a sly wink at Harry as he spoke. And George finally gave up growling at him and resigned himself to his basket while the extraordinary humans got on with playing party games and making such a fuss of each other.

* * *

215

'I wonder what the rest of them are doing right now,' Elsie said wistfully, and immediately felt embarrassed at the thought that Joe's mother might think she regretted being here. 'Oh, I didn't mean—'

''Tis all right, lass, I know what you mean. 'Twouldn't be natural if you didn't think of your folks on Christmas Day, would it? And I'm quite sure they're all thinking of you, too.'

'And when the King broadcasts his Christmas message, we'll know we're all listening to the same thing,' Joe said intuitively. 'It'll almost be as if we're together, won't it?'

The thought of it charmed Elsie. Despite all the privations of war, there was much to be thankful for, not least that Joe had found his way again.

And Christmas would always be Christmas. The succulent smell of the goose cooking in the vast farmhouse oven permeated through every room, and in the parlour there was a fir tree decorated with berries and baubles to enchant Faith.

Outside, a drift of early snow had turned the dales and moors into a sparkling fairyland, and at least this small family was alive and together again and determined to make the most of Christmas. Elsie and Joe and their baby, and the older Prestons. It didn't even matter that the York relatives were arriving for Christmas dinner. It should be a family time, and by now, Joe and Robert had made their uneasy peace, and Owen Preston had insisted on providing much of the day's fare. It was wise never to enquire how he always managed to obtain the things that other people couldn't. Contacts, he would say, touching his finger to his nose as if he belonged to some secret society.

'Black Market, more likely,' Joe's father would mutter darkly, 'and one of these days he'll be caught out.'

And if it sometimes seemed a little sad to Elsie that Owen Preston was a big, blustering man who seemed only able to

216

buy his way into people's affections, she put it down to the salesman in him.

The military hospital's Christmas entertainment was in full swing for the patients. Daisy was in fine voice, and even Naomi had agreed to join the small group of nurses going from ward to ward with their repertoire of carols. She was still attracting the eyes of Doctor Den, but was managing to quash any thoughts of resuming their brief fling with the autocratic looks that only Naomi was capable of giving.

To her great disappointment Daisy hadn't heard anything of Glenn for a couple of weeks. She had so wanted to see him sometime over Christmas, but he was either too busy on Ops, or communications had just been bad. Either way, she sang to the patients with as much gusto as she could, while wishing every moment that she and Glenn were spending this festive time together.

'I wonder what Christmas is like in Canada,' she said to Naomi, when the singing group had finally done their tour of the wards, and they were taking a welcome breather before going off duty for the evening.

'Freezing cold, I should think,' Naomi said shrewdly. 'All that snow and ice wouldn't suit me at all.'

'That's because you're a warm-weather person, and a rich one, too. All those holidays in the south of France have made you soft,' she said with a smile to let Naomi know she wasn't being overly critical. 'I've never been farther than wherever my nursing sent me.'

'Well, all that's going to change after the war, isn't it?'

'Is it?' Daisy said, not comprehending for a moment, and then feeling her heart give a somersault. 'Oh, you mean when I marry Glenn and go to Canada. Sometimes I wonder if it will ever happen,' she added slowly.

'Hey, what's this, Miss Optimist 1941? Of course it will happen. You love him, don't you – and he loves you – allegedly.'

Daisy began to laugh. 'Of course he loves me. But there are always obstacles, aren't there? They say the course of true love never runs smoothly.'

She didn't quite know why her moods kept jumping from happy to gloomy when everyone at the hospital was determined to be cheerful simply because it was Christmas; the nurses and doctors, the patients being as brave as they could be, no matter how painful their injuries. And every one of them parted from the people they loved the most.

That was it, of course. She was parted from hers, too. She imagined the rest of her family at Aunt Rose's house now, toasting absent friends, each of them with special, poignant memories, but determinedly playing the games they always did, charades and 'I spy', and telling Christmas stories around a roaring fire. She imagined her sister Elsie and Faith, so happy to have Joe home again, her own little family complete. Immy would soon be seeing James, when he went home to Bristol on leave. And Daisy had never felt so restless, so incomplete.

The following evening, because it was Boxing Day, there was a special dance in the nearby Forces Club. Everyone who was not on duty would be attending it, and when Daisy went to change out of her uniform and get ready, there was a message waiting for her. She knew it wouldn't be bad news, because nurses were only allowed to take telephone messages themselves if it was a matter of life or death, so she picked up the slip of paper pushed beneath the door of her room with her heart beating fast.

'Flying Officer Fraser will see you this evening,' she read. 'Ten o'clock, at the Forces Club.'

'My Lord, what's happened?' Naomi said, coming in at that moment to hear Daisy's shriek. 'Have you been promoted to Matron?'

'Nothing so daft, nor so unlikely! Glenn's coming to the dance tonight.'

'Is that all?' Naomi laughed, knowing how important this was. 'Well, make the most of it, Daisy, and have a lovely time.

Don't do anything I wouldn't do, though,' she added with a wink. 'You know what those Brylcreem boys are like!'

Daisy laughed back. Nothing could annoy her now. She was on cloud nine, in seventh heaven, on top of the world and in the pink, and all those crazy cliches that said exactly what you felt!

'What am I going to wear?' she said feverishly. 'Oh, I wish I had something *really* glamorous.'

'How about what you were planning to wear before you knew Glenn was going to be there?'

'I suppose I'll have to, but everything I've got seems so ordinary.'

'You can borrow one of mine, if you like,' Naomi said casually. 'If you don't think it an imposition to be seen out in borrowed clothes, that is.'

Daisy laughed. 'Oh yes, just as if it would be an imposition to be seen in an expensive cocktail dress like I've never owned before.' She stopped, her eyes widening, as Naomi went to her crammed wardrobe, and began pulling out a selection of glamorous dresses. 'Good Lord, you mean it, don't you?'

'Of course I do, darling. They're only clothes, and I can only wear one at a time. Choose whatever you like – whatever you think will make Glenn's gorgeous eyes pop out!'

While they were still getting ready another slip of paper was slipped beneath their door and a voice called out, 'It's for you, Caldwell.'

She was still smiling when she picked it up. And then the smile vanished and she gave a little cry. How could life be so bloody?

'What is it?' Naomi said quickly. In her opinion, Daisy had had enough knocks lately. Surely this couldn't be another one?

'Flying Officer Fraser sends his regrets,' she read, her voice barely audible in her disappointment. 'Unable to see you tonight after all. Duty calls. All love.'

'Oh, Daisy, I'm so sorry,' Naomi said, knowing that

219

'Duty calls' meant that Glenn would on Ops that night. Even at Christmas . . . they all knew that war didn't stop because of Christmas, but it was just cruel to dash her hopes like this.

'Well, that's it. I shan't go to the dance now,' Daisy said decisively.

'Oh yes you will, Daisy Caldwell. You'll go, and you'll cheer up some other lonely fellow far from home, and when you dance with him, you'll be thinking of Glenn and wishing him luck. *Won't* you?'

'Good Lord, I never knew you were such a slave driver,' Daisy muttered.

'Well, now you do. So are we going, or aren't we? I haven't got all dressed up for nothing, and you shouldn't waste that cocktail dress.'

Daisy looked at herself in the small cracked mirror. She did look good, she thought modestly, and Glenn would have loved her in this dress. He *did* love her, she thought, with a glow in her heart, and no matter who she was with, the way she looked now was for nobody but him. She made up her mind.

'All right, we'll go, but I'll wear something of my own. You do understand, don't you, Naomi? I'm very grateful to you for the loan, but—'

'Darling, you don't need to say any more,' said Naomi, not always as perceptive as she might be, but sensitive to everything Daisy wasn't saying right now. 'So change the dress by all means and put on a bright face instead – well, besides a dress of your own, I mean! And let's go and have a good time. It's still Christmas, after all.'

And so they merged into the crowded Forces Club, gaily decorated with Christmas tinsel now. Everyone was determined to have a good time, despite all that Jerry could throw at them. It was the mood of the moment. Daisy wasn't short of dancing partners, and when she danced, she dreamed she was dancing with Glenn. But hearing the buzz of aircraft overhead her prayers were winging towards him, far away from the soldier whisking her around the dance-floor.

'Hope those poor devils have as much luck as I'm having tonight, Miss.'

She jerked her thoughts around to the soldier's nice round face, smiling down at her so admiringly.

'What luck are you having then?'

'Why, dancing with the prettiest girl in the room, of course. It beats scrambling on to a boat at Dunkirk and nearly getting shot up into the bargain. Left me with a bit of a back problem, if you know what I mean,' he added, apologetic enough to alert her to the fact that he moved quite stiffly, despite his energetic dancing.

Whatever injuries he'd had, they obviously weren't going to stop him enjoying himself. But he said it all so casually, the way they all did . . . he certainly wasn't asking for sympathy.

'Were you at Dunkirk, then?' she said inanely, and then bit her lip, because hadn't he just told her so?

'Oh, most of us here were out there, doing our bit for King and country, but we don't talk about it much, and I'm sorry I mentioned it. It doesn't do any good to dwell on it, and you just have to get on with things, don't you, Miss?'

'Yes, you do,' she said humbly, wondering just what horrors he had seen, and forgoing the idea of telling him that she had been there, too, or at least been back and forth on the hospital ships; and her brother had also been there, and he had never come back. Oh yes, this chap was one of the lucky ones. His cheerful voice continued.

'I never did hear your name, and I can't go on calling you Miss all evening, can I? Sorry if that's a bit forward, and I'm sure you have a young man, a pretty girl like you, but just for this evening, I'm happy to be your escort, Ma'am.'

The way he said the word reminded her so much of Glenn, and her breath caught for a moment. It was so – so un-British and dashing – but these days everyone was catching on to the way other folk spoke. The world was getting smaller. And she remembered what Naomi had said, about cheering up some other lonely fellow, and she gave her dancing partner an answering smile.

'I certainly do have a young man, and right now he's probably flying one of those planes we heard a while ago, but he'd be glad to know I have such a polite escort for the evening. And the name's Daisy.'

Seventeen

James Church came home on embarkation leave in time for the new year celebrations. To his great relief, Imogen had returned to Vicarage Street after the few days with her aunt in Weston at Christmas and he was able to catch up with her there as soon as he had greeted his parents and assured them he was perfectly well. Parents were always parents, no matter what age you were, or how much of a man you were. James was very much a man, with all a man's desires and longings, and he ached to hold his sweetheart in his arms, and to show her how much he adored her.

His only regret was that Immy still refused to get married until this bloody war was over. He couldn't agree with her weird idea that there was anything noble or self-sacrificing in waiting – or that it was any kind of talisman against disaster. Her sensible sister hadn't thought that way, so why the hell Immy should do so was beyond him.

He loved her too much to force the issue, but on this leave he intended to make things official. Duties had denied them their lovely planned weekend in London, but he was determined that before their leave was ended, she would be wearing an engagement ring.

Immy threw open the front door and fell straight into James' arms, regardless of whether any of the neighbours were watching.

'Oh it's so good to see you at last,' she gasped, held so tightly to his chest she could hardly breathe. But what

223

did that matter? All that mattered was he was here and so was she.

'My lovely, lovely girl,' James said in response to this uninhibited greeting, and then: 'Do we have the house to ourselves?'

She felt her nerves tingle. But it echoed so much the need in her, to have him to herself alone, to know that sense of belonging and intimacy that could only be expressed in one way between a man and a woman who were so very much in love and had been apart too long . . .

'James!' she heard her father say from inside the house, and the sweet, seductive moment was broken. They moved reluctantly apart and Immy drew her lover inside.

'So much for dreaming,' she heard him murmur, seconds before he was greeting Quentin and Mary, agreeing that it had been a long journey home, and he would love a cup of tea.

His voice said all the conventional things, but his eyes were telling Immy how much he longed for her, as much as she longed to be alone with him. Leaves were so precious these days. You had to make the most of every moment, and all these niceties were simply the necessary – and frustrating – part of the social routine until you were able to be alone together.

'Sex, sex, sex,' Immy had heard one of the more brazen girls in her unit complain one day. 'All chaps want to do these days is get you in the hay and then they forget you!'

Well, some girls wanted that, too, if they were truly in love and intending to marry the man. And it didn't seem wrong, providing it was the right man, and he was your one and only. Immy knew that.

Mary was more observant than her husband, and after half an hour of chit-chat about the war and the joyous fact that the Americans would soon be sending troops over to join the conflict, and hopes that 1942 would see an end to it, she reminded Quentin that they were supposed to be visiting friends that evening.

'Were we?' he asked. 'But it seems rude to go out when James has just arrived to see us.'

'It isn't rude, dear,' Mary said, abandoning tact. 'Besides, I don't really think it's you and me that James has come to visit.'

Quentin finally caught on. 'Then we'll go and visit our friends, and we'll see you two later.'

'In a couple of hours,' Mary added, to be sure that they knew the older couple wouldn't be rushing back.

Ten minutes later, when the door had closed behind them, James drew Immy into his arms.

'I like your stepmother, darling! And now that we're alone at last, what do we do now?' he teased.

She looked into his eyes, loving him so much.

'What do you suggest?' she said, her voice husky.

'Nothing that will upset you, Immy my love, and I'm very aware that we are in your father's house—'

'It's also my house, and what goes on in my bedroom is my business – and yours,' she said, throwing discretion to the wind, and knowing full well that he was only hesitating because of regard for her feelings. But her feelings were so in tune with his, and she wanted him so much . . . she heard herself give a small nervous laugh as she went on, 'If it's going to inhibit you, James darling, we can always turn out the lights and pretend we're in an anonymous London hotel, where nobody knows us.'

He pressed her hand to the place where only two people who knew one another very well, and trusted one another implicitly, would not find it offensive.

'Does this feel as though I'm inhibited?' he asked. 'Because if not, my lovely Immy, I swear I shall burst if I don't do something about it – and *now*.'

He followed her upstairs, to the familiar room she had known all her life, and which she knew she would always see with new eyes after this night. This room where she had dreamed all her young dreams, and where it seemed perfectly right and fitting to her that it was the place where they would all come true.

'My sweet, funny girl,' she heard James say, with deep affection in his voice as he gazed around momentarily at some of those childhood things she had never quite been able to discard. An old ragged teddy-bear; a doll that her mother had painstakingly dressed in remnants of one of her own glittering gowns; a hazy photograph of the family at their favourite Cornish holiday beach; the parents, Quentin and Frances, and the four older children before Teddy was born: Imogen, Elsie, Daisy and Baz; the picture books Immy had cherished; the posters of her mother's stage appearances . . .

'But no longer a girl,' he heard her breathy response, and at once the images of childhood faded as he looked into her luminous eyes.

'Oh, I think I can vouch for that,' he said, his voice rough with desire now, as he drew her down on her bed and covered her face with kisses. And her heart soared to meet him, knowing this was the sweet prelude to love.

The news that Immy and James were officially engaged came as no surprise to the rest of the family, and his parents insisted on throwing a small party for them before they left Bristol.

'It's just for us and the two sets of parents,' James coaxed, when she protested that it probably wasn't right to be celebrating so blatantly in the middle of a war, and with most of the family unable to be there.

'We don't need the rest of your family,' James went on, 'and I make no apology for saying that, darling. We know it's impossible for Elsie and Daisy to be there, and although I wouldn't imply that your Aunt Rose would be the spectre at the feast, I don't imagine she would come without the rest of her brood to bolster her up. And I can cope with the ghastly Vanessa in small doses, but not for an entire social evening!'

Immy was laughing by the time he finished, holding up

her hands in mock surrender. 'All right, I give in! I know how much your mother adores arranging these things – but no fuss, please.'

And although it was regrettable that none of her siblings were there, it was very sweet to be the six of them. In any other circumstances it would have been Frances joining them for the sumptuous dinner Mrs Church had amazingly managed to provide, and that would have made everything perfect. But knowing how happy Mary was making her father now, Immy wouldn't let such a thought intrude.

Thankfully, the Luftwaffe was leaving them alone for the present, and they had almost finished the meal when there was a slight commotion at the front door. James's father answered it, and as he did so a laughing voice came soaring into the room.

'I'm sorry to be such a dunce, but I can't find my purse, so can someone please give me some change to pay off the taxi-driver?'

Immy leapt up at once, filled with delight.

'*Helen*! How wonderful!'

She came into the room, dropping her kit on the floor while her father went to pay off the taxi-driver, and hugged Immy hard.

'You didn't think I was going to let my brother and my best friend celebrate their engagement without me, did you? Especially as I consider myself instrumental in bringing the two of you together! I'm your big surprise, darling.'

'Oh Helen,' Immy said, her eyes shining. 'Short of having my own sisters here, this is the best thing that could have happened.'

'Well, don't go all droopy on me, I do have to wear this uniform a while longer yet,' Helen said, still laughing, but still hugging Immy's arm as proof of how much they thought of one another.

'So how is your war, sis?' James said casually. 'Still doling out meals for hungry servicemen?'

She pulled a face at him. 'And where would you all be without the Catering Corps! They say an army marches on its stomach – or something – and from the look of some of the first intakes it could be true. Not quite so true when you've been in it for a few months though, and got toughened up.'

'Well, that's enough war talk from all of you for tonight,' her mother said firmly. 'We're all together, and we're delighted to be celebrating Immy and James's engagement, so let's all be happy and make it a night to remember.'

'A night to remember,' Immy murmured, meeting James's eyes above the rim of her wine glass. This was the formal night of betrothal, but in their hearts she knew they would both be remembering other nights that were intimate and perfect and belonged to the two of them alone.

'Let me have a proper look at your engagement ring, Immy,' Helen said gaily, breaking the spell of those locked glances.

She held out her hand for Helen to admire the single diamond, flanked by two small sapphires. Inside the shank was the inscription James had asked for, saying: 'two hearts, one love'. Immy had thought it the most romantic thing ever, and it was far too personal to share with anyone else, even Helen.

She smiled at James again now, wishing this idyllic time could go on for ever, and knowing only too well that they were so soon to be parted again.

As if to underline her thoughts, they heard the dismal wail of the air-raid siren and the angry drone of aircraft, followed by an almost immediate bombardment, and Quentin got to his feet.

'I'm afraid the party's over, for me at least,' he said regret-fully. 'You folk should take care now, and I'll see you back at the house as soon as Jerry's finished with us for the night.'

He spoke coolly, but they all knew the risks the firefighters took and the risks they all took in not taking sensible precautions while the air raid lasted.

'We'll all go down to the basement and continue the party down there,' James's mother declared in her usual organising manner. 'Mrs Caldwell will be quite safe here with us.'

It took Immy a moment of mild shock to register who Mrs Caldwell was, until she saw her father give Mary a quick peck on the cheek. She turned away, still not quite used to it. Instead she busied herself in helping Helen and Mrs Church carry some of the remaining food down to the basement, which was even more set up for emergencies than Aunt Rose's – as was to be expected, knowing Mrs Church's organisational skills.

She felt James's hand on her shoulder as his father lit the emergency oil lamps, throwing a warm glow over the comfortably-furnished basement.

'Your father will be all right, darling. And do you realise it's the first time we've actually been caught out in a raid at home?'

'So what games are we going to play?' Helen put in.

They were all trying to be cheerful, ignoring the dull, and sometimes far from dull thuds from above as the house shook from time to time. Immy had always known what her father did, but somehow, being here, in their own beloved city, and knowing he was out there somewhere, in the midst of whatever holocaust was raining down on them, made it all so very real.

'Don't worry, Immy,' she heard Mary's steady voice say. 'I always say a little prayer when Quentin goes out, and God has never let me down yet.'

Immy wished she had that much faith. To be honest, apart from being with James, at that moment she wished she was anywhere but here. She wished she was back in Oxford – or London – or wherever she and Captain Beckett were required, doing the job she had been trained for, and not sitting here, playing inane card games or charades, and pretending that everything was all right. When it wasn't. It definitely bloody well wasn't, and her own fear was reflected

229

in Helen's eyes when her friend gave a huge shriek as a sound like an enormous crack of thunder seemed to shake the very foundations of the house.

Where were Mary's prayers now, Immy thought wildly? It might not be her father who was in trouble this night, but the rest of them seemed just as likely to perish, buried alive like rats caught in a trap . . .

'I have to get out of here,' she heard herself say in panic. 'I can't stand not knowing what's happening.'

James held her tightly. 'Darling, we all know what's happening, and none of us is going anywhere until we hear the sound of the all-clear. Stay calm. Take deep breaths and hold on to me.'

Her lips were chattering, and it was the first real attack of panic she had had. All this time, even in the London blitz she had managed to hold on to her nerve, but here, at home, with James's arms around her, she was in danger of becoming hysterical, and she knew it.

His parents were as steadfast as ever, she thought wildly, almost as though breeding would out and that was a fatuous thought if she'd ever had one. Helen didn't seem to be nearly as distraught as herself, either, and she was almost resentful about that.

She looked across at Mary, also being very calm, even though her husband was somewhere in the thick of it, trying to put out the fires that would be raging by now, and probably having to deal with far more unsavoury things than they ever dreamed of. Quentin never revealed some of the horrors that were found in bombed-out premises, but they all knew.

'I'm feeling stifled in here,' she croaked again. 'I need some fresh air, James. I can't stay here. I'm sorry.'

'Immy, don't be stupid –'

But she shook him off, needing desperately to get some air in her lungs before she burst. Even though the air might be filled with the acrid smell of smoke and burning, she had the terrified and nauseous feeling that if she stayed in this basement any longer she would never see daylight again.

Ignoring the entreaties of the others, James followed her up the stairs and through the house until she pulled open the front door and took in the night air in great gulps. In any other time and circumstance the sight that met their eyes would have been spectacular. The Clifton house was high above the city, and all around them the stately barrage balloons reared high like alien space-craft. The noise of the big guns almost deafened them, and the enemy planes were picked out like beautiful silver birds by the searchlights. Beautiful, but so deadly. And far away to the left, in the city they loved, the fierce red glow in the sky told its own tale of destruction.

Immy shook uncontrollably, feeling a sense of impotence such as she had never felt before. It was barbaric . . .

'Have you seen enough?' James's harsh voice said in her ear.

'I don't know! I feel as I should go down there and help.' Her voice became impassioned. 'My father and people like him – older men who should be at home with their families – will be digging people out of their shattered homes with their bare hands, while the rest of us dig ourselves into whatever hole we can for safety.'

'My father wouldn't thank you for referring to his basement as a hole,' James said, trying to lighten the moment.

Immy suddenly sagged against him. 'I'm being even more stupid, now, aren't I? And we're doing no good at all by standing out here and watching it all as if it was a glorified fireworks display. It's obscene. People are down there dying, and we're behaving like ghouls.'

'Then let's go back inside,' he said, becoming alarmed now. 'You're freezing, darling, and your Captain Beckett won't thank you for taking extra leave because you've caught the flu. As for doing no good – you do good every day you're on duty, so let's have no more of that nonsense.'

She swallowed, angry with herself now for giving way

as she had never done before. So many people were far
worse off than they were – even though they had lost Baz
and Uncle Bert – and she was in danger of turning into a
whining shrew.

'I'm sorry, James,' she muttered. 'But as long as I always
have you—'

He put his fingers against her lips, his arms held tightly
around her as he hurried her back towards the house.

'You'll always have me, Immy. I promise.'

The weather turned wintry in February, but at least in one
household there was a mixture of emotions. Vanessa and the
boys were excited at the thought that now that America was
one of their proper allies, American servicemen were coming
to the area, and would be allocated billets in the town.

'We have to call them GIs,' Vanessa told them grandly.

'Why?' Teddy and Harry said at once.

'Because that's what they're called,' she snapped, not
prepared to let the little squirts know that she didn't have
the faintest idea why.

Rose obviously did. 'I'm told it's short for General Issue,
but don't ask me what all that's about,' she added hastily
as Teddy's mouth opened again. 'The Americans like nick-
names and that's what they call their soldiers.'

'Will we be having any of them here?' Teddy went on
eagerly, going off on another tack.

'Of course not,' Rose said at once. 'I've got enough to do
with you three.'

And the last thing she wanted was to have the house filled
with strange, fast-talking young men, cooking and cleaning
for them, when she was only just getting used to the fact
that the house was empty without Bert. No matter how many
people you filled it with, if the one that mattered most wasn't
there, it was still empty. It was a truth you only discovered
when it happened to you.

But she had reckoned without the billeting officers who

oversaw such things, and who were now looking for suitable accommodation for the influx of GIs from the training base outside the town.

'You've always been such a tower of strength with your willingness to take in the evacuees, Mrs Painter,' they gushed. 'We were hoping very much that we could count on you to take in two American servicemen in this lovely big house. They are all such gentlemen, so clean and polite that I'm sure you would have no problems at all.'

No problems except that there was also a gullible and nubile young girl in the house, Rose thought keenly. The GIs might be all very polite and gentlemanly, but Vanessa was star-struck by now, and convinced that every one of them was as good as a talent scout in disguise. Not that she had any talent to offer, but that wouldn't deter her from making eyes at them.

But in the end Rose's objections were worn down, partly because both her brother Quentin and the vicar urged her to agree. She needed people around her – as if she didn't have enough already – and these young men were far from home, and needed a homely base to come home to.

The two who arrived, spruce and smiling one Saturday morning at the beginning of March, were only too happy to be living in a real English home, and eager to be of any help that they could. This included setting to work to dig over Bert's neglected vegetable patch in the back garden, helped by two willing small boys, and furthering Vanessa's education on the American legal system and details of their home towns, one in New York and the other in Iowa. And then there were the little extra rations the Americans always seemed to have, at which Rose didn't have the heart to object, especially when she saw the boys' eyes light up at the sight of chocolate bars that were almost non-existent in British shops by now.

Lance and Paul quickly became part of Rose's extended family. And when they were shown the photos of the glamorous girlfriends back home, Vanessa gave up all idea of flirting with them. They were too old for her, anyway, she told Teddy and Harry loftily. They were all of twenty-three years old.

The GIs listened just as avidly to the nine o'clock news reports as everyone else. The boys were always sent to bed before the news came on, but Vanessa was allowed to stay up and listen. And towards the end of April came the news of the Luftwaffe's reprisal raids on the cathedral cities of Exeter, Bath and York, destroying many ancient and historic buildings.

Rose was contemptuous as well as horrified. 'Bert would have said that the Germans know they can't compete on the scale that our boys are attacking their cities now, so they aim for our undefended ones like the cowards they are.'

Vanessa said nervously, 'Doesn't Elsie live near York?'

Before Rose could answer, the telephone rang, and it was Elsie. 'You've heard, then,' she said, her voice tight and anxious. 'I've been trying to get through to Father to let him know we're quite all right, but Daddy must be out fire-watching. Anyway, I've made up my mind, Aunt Rose. I'm bringing Faith home, just for her birthday in September, and I'm hoping that Immy and Daisy will get leave at the same time. It's time we were all together again, even for a little while.'

Her voice broke a little, daring her to object and say how foolish this idea was, and Rose guessed that she would be feeling torn between staying in Yorkshire, safe with Joe and his parents, and coming home where she was born to be with her sisters. Elsie, and all of them, had always had a rare and beautiful loyalty to one another, Rose thought, her own throat catching.

'You must do as you think best, my love, and you know there will always be a place for you here,' she said, 'and I'll pass on your message to your father.'

When she hung up the phone, her eyes were bright.

'Family stuff?' Paul, the GI from Iowa said.

Rose smiled. These Yanks had some quaint ways of speaking, but right now she couldn't have put it better herself.

'Family stuff,' she agreed.

Eighteen

As 1942 progressed, the girls at the County School for Girls – now elevated to the title of a grammar school – had other things to think about. On Sunday, June the twenty-eighth, there was a heavy air raid on Weston. Those who weren't on official duty or scuttling for safety in the shelters were treated to an awesome night-time display as the enemy planes dived through the searchlights. Barrage balloons were caught in the crossfire and ignited, and went spiralling, screaming, to the ground. Away on Berrow beach, the big guns thundered through the night as if all the demons in hell were let loose, and on Monday Vanessa came home from school in mid-morning, excitement blazing in her eyes.

'We've been bombed,' she shrieked. 'Our classrooms have been destroyed by incendiaries, and the smell's bleedin' awful! The books have all been burnt, and the gymshoes stink to high heaven, and the chemicals have exploded in the science lab. Gawd, it's an unholy mess, and everybody's sayin' the Jerries mistook the school for the aircraft factory at Oldmixon. It's a scream, innit?'

She became aware that Rose had gone white, and the next minute she was shaking the girl hard.

'You wicked girl. It's not a joke! Supposing this had happened in the daytime when all the pupils were there? You might all have been killed!'

'Well, we wouldn't have been, would be? The stupid Jerries only come at night, like bleedin' fleas crawlin' out of the woodwork.'

It was only then that the truth of what Rose had said, and the enormity of it all, really dawned on her. And the next minute the two of them were clinging to one another and she was sobbing in Rose's arms.

Many buildings were damaged or destroyed in that raid, but the chaos to the grammar school became the talk of the town, knowing how many young lives would have been lost if the raid had occurred in daylight. The news was suppressed from newspaper reporting, however, for fear that the Germans might hear of their mistake in bombing a school in a quiet little seaside town instead of an aircraft factory. Though how they would have heard, nobody quite understood.

Once it was known that the boys' adjoining side of the building would be made ready to accommodate the girls, keeping them as strictly separate as it was possible to be, there were unmitigated cheers from various quarters, not least, Vanessa Caldwell-Brown. But the segregation rules were not to be relaxed, and Vanessa frequently came home moaning that the teachers were even more vigilant on keeping the boys and girls apart than before.

'A good thing, too,' Rose remarked to Mr Penfold at one of her church meetings. 'That girl's imagination is far too lively for comfort.'

'She's young, Rose,' the vicar said soothingly, 'and I'm sure she'll come to no harm with your guidance.'

'You're very forgiving, aren't you, Freddie?'

'It's my job,' he said, more pleased than he admitted that she had finally managed to use his first name so comfortably.

Rose smiled at his artless words, knowing what a good friend he had been to her all this time, easing her out of the depths of despair after Bert's death.

That cheeky little madam, Vanessa, had even hinted that she reckoned he'd like to be more than a friend, but such an idea was almost scandalous to Rose, and she had squashed it with one of her scathing censures.

237

Anyway, there were other things to think about now that the Americans were forming such a large community in the town. Most of them were charming fellows, but there were boisterous and flamboyant ones among them too, resulting in plenty of punch-ups, as the more gleeful folk called them, especially at dances, and on Friday nights outside the pubs.

Their MPs were always on hand to break up the fights, great, beefy fellows that they were, but according to Lance and Paul, it was often the clashes between black and white GIs that were the cause of it all.

'I never saw a black man before,' Harry said in awe. 'Does it wash off?'

Teddy hooted. 'Course it don't wash off, you little twerp. Black men live in Africa where the sun's hot and it colours their skin like sunburn, see?'

'What they doing in America then?' Harry asked rebelliously, his knowledge of geography decidedly sketchy.

Teddy had no answer to that, and the two GIs started to put them right with a brief history and geography lesson of their country.

'I think that's enough for tonight,' Rose said, when their eyes drooped.

'I'm going to America one day,' Teddy declared.

'So'm I,' Vanessa put in, coming downstairs from washing her hair and catching the last of the conversation. 'I'm going to marry a GI and go to Hollywood and be a film star. I can't sing and I can't dance, but I'm sure I could act if I put my mind to it,' she said with a flounce reminiscent of Anna May Wong. Which sent them all into hysterics again.

The fights among the GIs were not all mild ones, and on occasion the MP took more decisive action, and some of the culprits ended up in Weston General with gunshot wounds. Private Iain Bailey awoke in a hospital bed with his arm and shoulder heavily bandaged to find a sweet-faced nurse leaning over him, and asked her weakly if he was in heaven.

'You are not,' Alice Godfrey said sternly. 'But you had a lucky escape. A few inches lower and that gun-shot wound could have been in your heart.'

'Instead of which, the only arrow in my heart is the one Cupid put there the minute I looked at you, honey,' he said, before he drifted off into his drug-induced dreamland again.

Alice held her tongue. She'd heard it all before, and not only from the GIs either. But how corny and ridiculous could you get! It was probably a line straight out of a Hollywood movie, and this guy . . . well, she had to admit he could easily pass for one of the movie stars saying the line to some gullible, wide-eyed girl. And she was anything but that!

But then his shoulder wound got badly infected, and he remained a patient for far longer than had been expected. And by then, Alice was revising her thoughts about him.

'I know it's crazy,' she wrote to her friend Daisy Caldwell. 'He can be as brash as any of them, yet at other times he's the most caring and sensitive chap I've ever met. He can be really sweet, and so nice to the other patients, too – and here's a laugh – he actually lives in Hollywood and has seen one or two movie-stars in the flesh, if you'll pardon the word! Well, I suppose somebody has to live there! But truly, Daisy, everybody loves him around here.'

And not only the patients, Daisy thought shrewdly. She knew it as surely as if Alice's words were written in sky-high letters. And how odd it would be, if it turned out not to be scatty, fanciful Vanessa who married a GI and went to America – but Alice, with her feet on the ground. And that was really letting her imagination run away with her, Daisy thought, resolving not to enquire too closely just how Private Iain Bailey came to get a gun-shot wound from an over-keen MP if he wasn't involved in one of the fights she was always hearing about.

It was a strange thing about war, though. You were thrown into contact with all sorts of people you would never have met in any other circumstances. Even young men from the other side of the world. It didn't apply to her own sisters, of course, because both Immy and Elsie had found the love of their lives close to home – well, Joe had actually come to Bristol and found Elsie, of course – but James had always been there for Immy, the brother of her best friend. It had just taken time for Immy to see it.

But Daisy was different. Daisy knew that her destiny lay across the sea with Glenn, and that however long it took, she would go anywhere to be with him. She wasn't afraid of going so far away from England, but she did fear for Glenn constantly, knowing of the persistent and blistering raids the RAF were making on German cities now. But she had total belief in their future. One day she *would* go to Canada with him, marry him and have his children. She gave a wry smile. If her family had ever considered her the flighty one, never knowing her own mind, they could revise that immediately. Because she knew it now.

Glenn was heavily involved in the air raids over Germany, but he contacted her whenever he could, and she was grateful and touched for that. There was no doubt in her mind that once this war was over, they were going to live happily ever after. Naomi, of course, thought she was seeing it all through rose-tinted glasses, but she didn't have Naomi's sophistication, and didn't want it. She just wanted Glenn to come back to her, safe and sound.

She still got regular letters from her sisters, especially Elsie, who clearly had more time on her hands than Immy. Not that Daisy thought any the less of her for that. Now that Joe had decided to take up farming with his father, Elsie was obviously turning into a proper farmer's wife – and by the time Faith was talking properly, she would almost certainly have a Yorkshire accent! Maybe Elsie would too!

It sent Daisy's thoughts off into other directions. By the time she had lived in Canada for a while as Glenn's wife, would she, too, be talking with a Canadian twang? She supposed she would. They would all change – except Immy, who would settle down with her gorgeous James in Bristol. It was good to know that one of the Caldwell girls would be staying where their roots were.

And if she didn't stop thinking that way, she'd be in danger of getting sloppy and making the bandages she was rolling all soggy, and that would never do. But Elsie's last letter had made an interesting suggestion, and she intended doing her utmost to get home for Faith's second birthday, and she was sure Immy would as well.

It was July before Immy was able to arrange a few days' leave at the same time as James. This time, she vowed, she was determined to let nothing stop them having that missed weekend together in London. James was due to go to the Middle East very soon, and she desperately wanted to spend this time with him before he left. The names of Rommel and El Alamein were on everyone's lips now, and although James made light of going into battle, Immy knew just how serious the position was. By now, she was privileged to some of Captain Beckett's inside information, and there was no doubt that the war was far from over.

After the hideous and premeditated assault on Pearl Harbour last December it was understandable that the Americans had their own grievances against the Japanese, while combining forces with the Allies. They were all in it together now, but the thought of an idyllic and peaceful England seemed as far away as ever.

'Come back to me, Immy,' she heard James murmur in the darkness of the night when they finally managed their weekend at a little country hotel well away from London. 'You've gone a very long way away in these last few minutes.'

'How can you say that?' she whispered back. Here in this double bed, with their bodies entwined and no more than a breath between them, they couldn't be closer. And yet she knew instantly what he meant.

'I can say it because I know the sound of your breathing, and I know when it slows and almost stops that you're thinking serious thoughts. And I don't want any of them to intrude between us.'

'No more do I,' Immy said more fiercely. 'I want to pretend that this night will go on forever, and that we never have to part again. Oh, James –'

He silenced her with a kiss. He knew her fears, and he had them, too. It was just that men never showed them in the same way, or admitted them, and he wanted nothing to spoil these precious hours, for who knew how long the memories would have to last?

He held her close to his heart, thankful to his soul that his darling girl was unafraid to give herself to him completely. Keeping themselves only to each other, they were as surely married in the sight of God as if a preacher had intoned the words. *Till death do us part*, the thought ran through his mind, to be dismissed at once. There was no place for it while they were so vital and alive and together.

In August there was cause for celebration as the news came through that there had been a successful landing at Dieppe. When the children came home from school, Rose read out selected parts of the newspaper report to her young house-guests.

'It was a daring daylight landing, carried out mostly by Canadians, with huge support by the Royal Navy and operational commands of the RAF, with squadrons of Canadian, New Zealand, Polish, Czech, Belgian, Fighting French and Norwegian squadrons providing cover for the attack. Flying Fortresses of the US Army Air Corps made a high-level raid on the enemy airfield at Abbeville—'

'Is the war over then?' Teddy asked, clearly getting bored.

'No love,' Rose told him. 'It means that our allies have been successful in bombing some of the German installations in France. It was never intended to be an invasion, but it proves that we can penetrate their defences and put a lot of their fortifications out of action. Before the troops left French soil they blew up their own tanks so the Germans couldn't use them.'

Vanessa scowled. 'And then they all went home again, so what does that prove? Why didn't they blow up all the Germans while they were at it?'

'Vanessa, that's a terrible thing to say,' Rose said at once.

'No, it's not. They killed my fam'ly, and Harry's, too, so why shouldn't they all get blown up as well?' she shouted.

The boys looked at her uncertainly, not used to seeing their brash companion red-faced and blotchy and near to tears.

Ignoring her for the moment, Rose turned to the boys. 'Would you two help me get the tea ready? We'll go and make the spam sandwiches, because I think Nessa would like to have a bit of time on her own.'

'Why?' Teddy objected, only half-drawn to the idea of making sandwiches.

'Because that's what girls do,' Rose said firmly.

Vanessa fled out of the room, furious at showing herself up, as her old Gran would have said. She'd felt as daft as Teddy, because for one moment she had felt a huge flare of hope at the news as well, thinking that the war might be almost over. And the thought that had surged into her mind was that she'd be sent back to London, even though she had no home and no family to go back to. And she so dearly wanted to stay here . . .

A little while later Rose found her sprawled out on her bed, staring at the ceiling, and as if she had seen right through her thoughts, Rose spoke casually.

'You know I'd like you to stay here after the war, don't you, Nessa? This house is much too big for one person, and I'd miss you and the boys far too much if you went away. We're a proper little family now, aren't we?'

Before she could say any more, Vanessa's arms were

around her neck in the first real embrace the girl had ever given her. Not one of fear, but of love. And Vanessa's eyes weren't the only ones that were damp.

But she had one more thing to ask, and it had obviously been on her mind ever since Elsie's decision to bring Faith home for a brief visit in September.

'Aunt Rose, do you think the girls will let me join them for their special get-together?' she said awkwardly. 'I know I'm not a real Caldwell girl, but I wouldn't be any trouble, and it would be much better than having these bleedin' irritating boys to talk to all the time!'

Rose ignored the lapse of language, seeing how important this was. Her voice was thick when she answered. 'I'm sure they wouldn't have any objection, love – providing Immy and Daisy can get leave together when Elsie comes home.'

Family tragedies could always overshadow the events of the war, and the Royal Family was not immune to it. On August the twenty-fifth a Sunderland flying-boat carrying the Duke of Kent crashed on a mountainside in Scotland. All the occupants except the rear-gunner, were killed. Poignantly, the duke's third son had been born only seven weeks previously.

There was more gloom as more results of the successful Dieppe raid became known. It was insisted that it had only been intended as a reconnaissance raid, to assess the likelihood of a future invasion, but there were great losses incurred on both sides, including eighty-two German planes being destroyed, and ninety-five allied planes. Many prisoners were taken during the raid, which dampened much of the initial optimism that this had meant a turning point in the war.

Three years, the more garrulous newspaper headlines screamed out, as August merged into September, and there was still no end in sight. For Daisy Caldwell, the news that there had been so many allied planes destroyed in the Dieppe raid meant more anxiety, until she heard from Glenn that he was safe.

'I can't say it wasn't an exhilarating experience,' he told her over the telephone. 'I'd be lying if I said that, and it's what I joined the RAF for, Daisy.'

'But not to be killed!' she said passionately.

'Well, I wasn't, was I?' he said, in answer. 'Otherwise I wouldn't be here talking to you, sweetheart. And there are risks for everyone, even for you in that hospital of yours. Hitler's not too fussy where he drops his bombs, so remember to keep your head down, darling. And with luck, I'll see you soon.'

It wasn't a satisfactory phone call, Daisy complained to Naomi. Glenn was obviously as high as a kite, the way all flyers seemed to be these days.

She ignored the unconscious irony of the thought. But it was like a drug with them, the Brylcreem boys, the 'daredevils of the air', when all she wanted was for Glenn to come home in one piece and not in pieces. She knew all about patching them up and sending them off to fight again, and she didn't want it to happen to Glenn. Not her Glenn . . .

'He'll be all right,' Naomi said with supreme confidence. 'He's got that look of luck about him, Daisy. Some have it and some don't.'

'And you do talk absolute rot at times,' Daisy retorted. 'But thank you all the same.'

'So have you got that leave you applied for?' Naomi asked casually, to take her mind off Glenn for the moment.

'Yes, and Immy's managed it, too, which is nothing short of a flipping miracle. We're all going home to see Elsie's wonder-child.'

But her smile belied her flippant words, because it would be truly wonderful to be all together again. Just as it used to be, the three of them. And one of the things she wrote adamantly to her sisters was that she and Immy should discard their uniforms and just be themselves for those blissful few days. At least, they would be blissful providing Hitler left them alone, she amended silently, but that was something you could never count on.

It was something of a reunion, all the same. Rose had hoarded some of her precious rations and made a special cake to take up to Bristol, where the girls would stay for this short break, because it was clearly the only place for the family to be. The GIs were never short of invitations, and they had somehow got hold of a big old car and offered to take the Weston brood to Bristol before they went off on their own pursuits, and they would take them back to Weston before dark.

And that Sunday, the twentieth of September, Faith's second birthday, turned out to be a lovely early autumn day, the kind when in normal times Bristol folk went for picnics on the Downs, or to the seaside for a final dip in the sea before it got too cold for even the tiniest of tip-toes and a squeal back from the surf. There were almost certainly picnickers about now, as if to defy any thought of bombs raining down on them.

That Sunday, when Faith had been admired to the utmost and even Teddy and Harry had become quite attached to this brown-eyed little charmer who could flirt, even at two years old, the Caldwell girls decided by mutual consent to take a stroll by themselves. Needing the special closeness they so sorely missed.

They happily left the others to their own devices, the adults being only too pleased to indulge Faith and spoil her while they had the chance.

For a while they walked around parts of the city, gazing at streets they had once known that were no more; at the devastation wrought by Hitler's evil bombs, and the rubble that remained. They looked at the shimmering ribbon of the river where Baz had once worked so proudly on the ferry-boat, and remembered. They passed the theatres where Frances had once enchanted Bristol audiences with her sweet voice and sensitive dancing.

And then they all linked arms, fresh and bright in their summer dresses, and made their way back towards Clifton, across the sweet-smelling grass of the Downs, each of them pretending, imagining, that these really were normal times, that there was no war and no separation from those they loved.

Without realising quite how, they finally reached the spot where, years before, their beautiful mother had wandered, almost as if she floated on a cloud to the edge of the cliffs, and plunged over the edge in a macabre dance of death.

'It's so peaceful here at this moment,' Elsie murmured. 'It's hard to believe there's a war going on, or that this lovely place once caused us all so much terrible heartache.'

Immy tightened her grip on her sister's arm. 'We said we wouldn't speak of sad things today, didn't we? And I, for one, only ever think of Mother with love.'

'Me, too,' Daisy said. 'As long as we never forget her, she'll never really die, will she? And neither will Baz.' Or Uncle Bert. Or Cal, she added silently.

Immy smiled. 'You're right, of course. And we've still got each other. We're the Caldwell girls, remember? One for all, and all for one, and all that rot!'

'Like the three musketeers,' Daisy said with a grin, wondering just how crazy they must look to anyone else, three adult women, holding hands now, and forming an unbreakable circle as if they were taking part in some ritual. Crazy, and uncaring what the rest of the world thought . . .

Then, out of the corner of her eye, Daisy saw someone coming across the Downs towards them. Vanessa looked hesitant and a little uncomfortable, as if knowing she had no right to break into this closeness, and yet unable to stay inside the house a moment longer. The day had been so happy, and all that they wanted, and yet she felt oddly lost and adrift. She didn't really belong anywhere . . . nor to anyone else like these three did . . . these lucky, lucky girls.

Just as if her thought waves came trembling on the air,

the three of them knew. They broke apart momentarily, and Immy held out her hand to Vanessa.

'Room for one more, I think,' she said softly to Elsie and Daisy. They drew the girl into their big-hearted circle, and the three musketeers became four.